In Moral Love

A Moral Love Story for an Immoral Age

Anthony Cassimeon

In Moral Love
by Anthony Cassimeon

Printed in the United States of America

Library of Congress Control Number: 2002115786
ISBN 1-591603-74-9

Xulon Press
11350 Random Hills Road
Suite 800
Fairfax, VA 22030
(703) 279-6511
XulonPress.com

To order additional copies, call 1-866-909-BOOK (2665).

Chapter One

Love Defined

I was looking for love and I found courage.

True love and courage go hand-in-hand like married lovers holding hands on the edge of an ocean overlooking an arrestingly colorful and creative sunset. God's handiwork is seen in a sunset, just as His work is seen in love and courage. God created me to love and trust Him. In finding courage, I found my destiny.

Just as real today as it was in the past, love is something I need every day - something I need to give as much as receive. Deep in my heart is a desire to express love to a woman. I can feel the power of love scintillating in my soul. With amazing emotion, I am drawn to a beautiful woman. I want to honor her with a love that takes her out of the ordinary and puts her in the realm of the extraordinary. Yet, I have discovered a courage that goes beyond courage to ask a girl out on a date. I have new knowledge of a startling courage that comes with a price few are willing to pay. God has created a courage that sustains a man's soul while doing right.

Alongside my desire is my conscience, which God designed into my being. I am acutely aware of both my desire and my conscience. From them come my passion and my morality, affecting each other in a type of "passionate morality." But I wasn't fully aware of the courage in my heart. God had to engineer the right circumstances to bring it out of me.

In the end, my courage was not my own. It was courage that God bestowed on me, as answer to prayer amid the shimmering glory of His holy presence residing in my heart. It was a courage that splits darkness and light. It was an extension of Christ's being. Through courage I learned the heart of love. I learned about moral love.

Before this point, starry-eyed romance could only go so far. The true nature of love had to be revealed. My life and the life of others were depending on it. All the stylistic, superficial image enhancements had to be stripped away to get to the core. Not even human nature could dictate the true character of love, which is a creation that wonderfully defies logic and makes life worth living.

Love is patient. Love does *not* demand its own way. Love is sincere and forgiving. Love is *not* selfish. Love is generous. Love is *not* two-faced. Just as much as we understand what love is, we also understand what love is not. Counterfeit love exists, making the discovery of true love more difficult, yet more worthwhile. The freedom of true love is at odds with the selfishness of counterfeit love.

Knowing the true nature of love – and rejecting the counterfeit love – leads one on a path straight to the truth. I was on and off this path, struggling with my own self-will. Despite the bumps and bruises, I was on my way to the truth. Nothing was going to stop me because the Lord Jesus was fully in my heart and, like a friend, fully on my side. Faith in God was my only hope.

I started with faith as an act of courage, but it would go much farther than I ever thought. Who I really am – the reality of my identity in Christ Jesus – my heart would be revealed.

In the beginning, when everything was romantic and nice with a woman, I was not courageous. Instead, I was accommodating, image-making and compromising. I was paradoxically sincere in my superficiality, afraid that my Christian faith would scare away the beautiful woman.

Love was in my sight. Comfortable love! Nonetheless, the path of love was not what I expected it to be. With true love, I received a great deal more. I was bound to have to step outside my comfort zone. This is where I needed courage and I found it with each step forward in faith.

Love is different for a Christian than it is for the world, which only knows counterfeit love because of the innate self-centeredness and bent away from God. How can a person have a bent away from God and still know true love? Unbelievers know of God, but they don't *know* God, who is love.

As the essence of life's greatest adventure, true love involves giving up "self" and then filling the emptiness with Jesus, the spiritual reality who blows the doors off of anything contrary to love.

People who have not given their lives to Christ see denying self as impossible. They want to love themselves more and cherish their desires. How can we deny who we are as people with desires? The answer is simple. We are transformed by Jesus Christ after confessing our sin and committing our lives to Him by faith.

With repentance, love gains much more power. The difference in the love experience is remarkable and it affects how marriage is treated. While the world treats marriage as a rubber stamp approval of their self-willed ways, God treats marriage as a holy union of a man and a woman who have waited their whole lives to unite with each other in God-enhanced intimacy. Unbelievers are missing God-enhanced intimacy.

The conflict strikes directly at the core of the human heart.

My story is one of moral integrity and a beautiful, dangerously seductive woman who danced for herself and around God. She taught me to dance, but I could not lead. Ultimately, I had to let the Lord do all the leading for me. My future depended on Him.

Like a dancer, the Lord was leading, but I was an imperfect follower. It is amazing that God had as much patience with me as He did. I would be dishonest to say I can live well without God's involvement in every aspect of my life. I have made mistakes, but God's grace is bigger than my mistakes. Love covers many sins, but it also reveals the truth – the dangerous, seductive truth and the courageous, committed truth.

In my deepest time of need, I looked to God. Human nature has a natural bent away from God and an unwillingness to admit sin and seek forgiveness. I have the same natural tendencies as everyone else. Yet, Christ had changed my heart and I could experience selfless love. God is the initiator. God's love for me started it all. All other love in my life grew from that point.

Opportunities – both good and bad – accompanied the flames of romantic love in my life. I had to make major decisions, which were affected by the past, were affecting the present and would affect the future. Even when everything looked uncertain and chaotic, I was relieved that God was in control.

Struggling to live a moral life in a culture that shamelessly promotes sexual immorality and exploitation, I opened the Bible, read it, as if I was soaking it into my spirit, and believed it, as amazing as that would sound to non-Christians or casual, shopping-cart "Christians." At first, I took the Bible to be a collection of holy suggestions – not commands – but I discovered that Christ's commands are for my best interest and to minimize the pain for others. Love believes all good things.

In truth, love changed my life. It was the type of love that is described in the Bible as patient and kind. In love, I became a generous giver, giving away my money, my time, my efforts and my encouragement. On the surface, I was not selfish. Love without selfishness is phenomenally awesome. But I had blind spots in my perception and my understanding. When the romance with the woman I loved was intensifying, I was leaning on my own understanding at times, delaying rather than dealing with trouble. Through my love experience with a beautiful woman, I discovered how much I need Jesus at all times. If I lean on my own understanding, I would dance outside God's will and right into foolish trouble.

Before my total surrender to the Lord God, I was doing more wrong than I thought possible. I had more faults, imperfections and limitations than I ever considered about myself, but I had a terrific ability to ignore them. The truth about me was different – much more stirring – than I had imagined about myself. The truth burst out into the open, like a twirling ballroom dancing couple, after I met the dancing sensation Olga.

This is the story about me and Olga, the Russian dancer who came to America and stole my heart. My self-revelations can only be understood in light of the effect my relationship with Olga had. I had been guarding my heart, but I let my guard down.

My mind was full of dreams and wonders. I did not see the wrong steps I was taking because my emotions were trying to rule me. In the end, the truth would extend much further than wrong steps in dancing. The truth would rock my world.

God used dancing to bring me into a new season of my life. One day, I suddenly became interested in taking ballroom dancing lessons. I thought that learning how to dance would help me socialize with women, but God had a greater purpose to test me. How would I react to the test?

How would temptation serve as a test with purpose? I needed to learn.

Ballroom dancing led me to different degrees of revelations about myself. The first revelation I had was that, as soon as I was introduced to a higher level of excellence, I discovered that I couldn't dance as well as I had previously thought. My pride had been based on faulty perception. Being exposed to a higher standard revealed how much I fell short in achieving it. During my first time dancing with Olga, I felt awkwardly like a man dancing with two left feet and with the grace of a bull.

In contrast, Olga was sensational. The precision of her dance steps and body movements was outstanding. I had never seen a person dance so expertly in person. Right from the start, I noticed that Olga had a special talent – a gift – for dancing. I credited her talent to God's precise handiwork. Her dancing ability was clearly innate ability, driven by her self-will. She had no trace of imperfection in her ballroom dancing.

When she and I first danced at the International Extravaganza Ballroom Dancing Studio, she virtually tortured me. I am not exaggerating. Indeed, I embarrassed myself thoroughly in ballroom dancing. We were doing the rumba and I lifted her arm too high when I was turning her.

"I am not a giraffe," she remarked to me, as I knocked her off balance.

"Sorry," I muttered sheepishly.

On the next attempt, I didn't raise my arm high enough, so she nearly banged into my elbow. She softly slapped the bottom of my elbow and said, "Up, up!"

Again I apologized. If we had been dancing at a social club, her criticism of my dancing style would have been harsh, but we were dancing at a dance studio where the goal was to teach students to learn the right way to dance. I learned that there is a right way to do the rumba – or the tango, the swing or any other ballroom or Latin style of dancing – but there are many wrong ways to dance.

I may have even found new ways to do the dances wrong – ways that Olga hadn't seen before. I interpreted the confused expression on her face, as well as her laughter, as a sign. The dance instructor Jerry, who was Olga's boss, was also quick to laugh at me when I messed up my dancing. I had to have a sense of humor about myself just to survive.

At the start, I was intimidated by Olga, who was light years ahead of me in dancing. I did not feel worthy to dance with her, but Jerry pushed me to dance with her. He seemed convinced that exposing me to her high level of dancing would make me a better dancer faster. Frankly, I also think he had an agenda – make me feel challenged and then sell me more lessons. I learned that the ballroom dancing business is a ravenous, profit-obsessed business that plays off of people's dreams and insecurities.

I would have given up ballroom dancing if I had not met Olga. I did feel challenged to improve my dancing. Although she intimidated me, she also fascinated me. Her talent was intriguing. At most, I thought we might become friends. At worst, I thought we would have some lessons and then we would split apart. I had no thought that she would become a romantic "love interest" for me. She was physically attractive and she wore provocative clothes, but I knew very little about her.

The secretary had told me that Olga came from Moscow, Russia and had started working at the studio only a week earlier. I assumed that she didn't speak much English. She spoke to me very little during our first dancing lesson together. Jerry did most of the talking, as he acted like a hawk overseeing us. I also learned from the secretary that Olga had been dancing since she was eight years old.

Overall, I liked Olga.

Olga came into my life at a tender time. My life had fallen

...t again. I was tired of being negative, but I had little ability to be positive. I was in search of truth, but I had not been honest enough with myself.

I was dancing with discouragement, holding onto it and trying to lead it. In reality, discouragement was leading me. I was doing its bidding. I was swinging with the shadow of hopelessness and not knowing it. I was doing the tango with despair, unaware that my spiritual shoes were untied. I had greater areas of vulnerability and weakness than I had thought. But, as I learned later, I also had greater strength than I had thought. It only took the right circumstances to bring them out. My weakness could even become a badge of honor.

It took the dancing sensation Olga to lure me to the spot of honesty with her own brand of salvation. I was compelled to think about the Christ-centered salvation in my life, but I didn't want to push it on her. Ballroom dancing was like Olga's salvation and it was completely based on performance and merit.

Right from the beginning, Olga and I were coming from different perspectives. While she wanted to conquer the ballroom dancing world, I was looking to conquer my wild heart and find the love to inspire me for the rest of my days.

I was low-key, upright and inwardly passionate. She was intense, ambitious and outwardly passionate. When I watched her dance alone in the studio, I honestly thought that she danced like a stripper. Her skirt was cut high up the left side of her body. Her skin was milky white. Her long hair was jet-black. She spun around a pole, pounding her hands against it with mounting energy. I thought her breasts were going to pop out of her low-cut, loose-fitting dress. If she was a stripper, then I was a spiritual stripper because I was tempted by her sensuality and I did not flee.

It turned out that my first perception of her, based on superficial evidence, was wrong. She was not a professional stripper in the "club" sense, but I couldn't say as much for myself on the moral level.

A passion was growing in my mind for her and the more I danced with her, the closer I felt to her. I wanted to hide my conservative, moral beliefs and open myself up to new experiences of wonderful feelings. Olga was leading me to feeling comfortable. She had an uncanny way to make her sensuality seem casual and easy-going to me. She also didn't seem to have any qualms about touching her body against mine when we danced. As a man who had gone a long time without a girlfriend, I was intrigued, yet still constrained by my Christian values. How far could we go? I thought I was ready to play with fire without getting burned.

After the first few lessons I initiated a conversation with her as I was changing my shoes. She spoke much better English than I expected. Her sense of humor also dazzled me.

I said to her, "I heard that you are from Moscow. What is Moscow like?"

"Moscow is beautiful and dangerous," she replied. After a brief hesitation, she finished her thought, "Like a woman."

I broke out laughing. "That is not the answer I was expecting."

She smiled. Then she led me out to the center of the dance floor and put me through a vigorous lesson that exhausted me. At the end of the lesson, I was ready to fall over, but she wasn't tired at all. She seemed to have boundless energy. She was younger than I was. Her youth sparkled like a star in the night sky.

Her radiance of beauty, energy and youth captivated me. With the romance of dancing and touching, my imagination got carried away. The encounters seemed to be affecting my self-image as well. I felt confident and desirable for once. I noticed Olga's quick glances at me, as well as her flirtatious smiles. As dangerous as it sounds for a Christian man to "fall" for a non-Christian, carnal-minded woman, I was falling for her. Indeed, I was falling into infatuation with my dance teacher.

I didn't know if Jerry, the middle-aged manager, noticed the attraction between Olga and me. She and I laughed a little more than the other teachers and students did. I didn't care. I was feeling great and suddenly there was potential for a romance with a dancing sensation. Did she like me? Would we have things in common? I was hopeful.

My first bold move was to get a pen engraved for Olga. The inscription said, "Moscow – beautiful and dangerous like a woman."

When I gave it to Olga, she laughed.

"Thank you so much," she said, smiling brightly.

At the same time, I noticed that Jerry and other employees of the dance studio were watching me and Olga. Their facial expressions expressed something dark that I couldn't understand.

When she and I were dancing later, Olga said to me, "The owner of the studio does not allow his teachers to date students."

I felt crestfallen until she followed up her statement.

"But I don't mind. What the owner doesn't know won't hurt him," she said, giggling.

I laughed and threw my head back, as if in triumph.

"You must have a girlfriend," she said to me.

"No, I don't."

"Well, I just accidentally wiped my lip-stick on your shirt, so it looks like you have a girlfriend."

"I don't mind," I replied.

She laughed at my remark. Her freedom to laugh with me was marvelous. I could not remember having a girl laugh so freely with me.

After she and I danced a while longer, she said to me, "Why does your face look so serious?"

I didn't know what to say. "Uhm."

Then she imitated my facial expression. Seeing her face contorted and looking dramatically serious, I broke out laughing. She could make me laugh in the blink of an eye. This ease with her was making an impression on me. Like a man who had crossed the desert without much water, I was finding her flirting to be refreshing. It was also flattering. Not considering myself a particularly handsome guy, I appreciated her attention and her interest.

Yet I was still insecure. I knew very little about her. She was more of a romantic image to me than a real person at this early stage of knowing her. I was probably the same to her. I was eager to open myself up to her, but I didn't know how. I didn't want to rush it and scare her away. I wanted to have more good times with her. Less information about her seemed to feed the inflation of the infatuation. At this point, I wasn't much interested in truth. I was more interested in romance and the fulfillment of my dreams. I was not thinking at all that my emotions could betray me.

Chapter Two

DANCE OF DAYDREAMS

I was starting to live out a fantasy. I bought new, stylish clothes and new sunglasses. I also bought new, shiny "smooth" dancing shoes. I wanted to impress Olga with my style, as well as with my progress in learning how to dance. I took a week off from work, so I could focus on dancing and living out this imagined idea of excitement.

In a relaxed way, I planned to have a lesson with her each day and then go to the party on Friday night. My emotions responded by making me feel genuinely "cool" in a way that was refreshing to me. If I was making a mistake to indulge in my fantasy to dance with an attractive girl who was young and vibrant, then I was living an irony – doing something that made me feel good, but it may not have been the best thing to do.

The first lesson was on Monday afternoon. With sunshine pouring down all around me, I stepped into the dance studio, wearing my new sunglasses. I was also wearing my new, tight, black shirt and my new shoes. My hair was carefully combed. Not a hair out of place! And I tried to focus my thoughts on being easy-going.

As soon as I came inside, I saw Olga, who stood still, staring at me. Her face looked serious. She looked at me up and down. I noticed that she was wearing more make-up than usual. She looked like a fashion model.

She said to me, "I'll be right with you, Martin."

"Okay," I replied. "I'll change into my new shoes." I showed her the shoes.

She raised her eyebrows and said, "Nice."

After I changed my shoes, she returned from the backroom. She stretched out her hand, grasped my hand and led me to the center of the room. Then she told me to get into position to dance the "swing." Because I held her right hand incorrectly, she corrected my hold. She counted, "3, 4 and-"

We started to dance, but I messed up immediately.

"I'm sorry," I said quickly. "I rocked back on the wrong foot."

"That's right," she replied, glaring at me.

"I get confused sometimes."

"That's okay. Let's try it again."

When I danced with her, I was so scared of making a mistake that I couldn't focus on anything but the steps I was making. I seemed a bit stiff, but I was trying my best to do what she instructed.

"You still look very serious," she blurted out at me. Then she imitated me, as she had done before. I laughed, as I viewed her manner as jovial.

"I can't help it," I said.

"Let's do it again."

We danced for over fifteen minutes without more than a five-second rest at any point. I was doing it. I was really learning new steps in swing and I was gaining momentum. Even more, I was having fun. Olga encouraged me to look at myself dancing in the mirror. It appealed to my vanity.

She said, "You pick up new steps quickly."

"Thank you," I replied, trying to put on a humble tone. "It just comes naturally. I am not doing anything special. I am having fun and I'm sure lots of people can do it."

"No, you'd be surprised how difficult many people find the steps you are doing."

"Really?"

"Yes."

I was flattered.

"I grew up watching famous dancers like Fred Astaire and Gene Kelly," I remarked, referring to the two pre-eminent dancers in Hollywood in the 20th century.

"Fred Astaire? Like the dance studios?"

"Yes, but I am talking about the dancer himself. Did you ever see one of his movies from the 1940s or 1950s?"

"No," she said, her tone indicating that she was losing interest in this discussion.

"I recommend them," I said. Astaire was a movie icon a long time ago and I suddenly felt the grace of dancing that he must have felt. I could have danced on clouds. I was so high.

Olga showed me another step. I fumbled through it the first few times and then I did it correctly. I watched myself do it in the mirror and I was very pleased.

"Excellent," she said.

"Can I show you something I saw two ballroom dancers do on television years ago?" I asked politely.

"Sure."

"I saw a guy pick up a girl."

"Do it!" she insisted. "Pick me up."

"Really?"

"Yes."

She turned around and left her arms loosely by her side. I put my hands under her arms and lifted her with all my strength. Without much of a problem, I lifted her close to the ceiling, stretching my arms as high as they would go.

Immediately, the manager Jerry sauntered across the room and shouted, "I love it. I love it."

As I put her down, Olga asked me, "Was I heavy for you to lift?"

"No, you are light," I replied. My saying that she was light seemed to please her.

Jerry said, "Lift her again, Martin! Olga, this time I want to you to wrap your legs back around Martin's waist."

Jerry's instruction amazed me. I was sure that it would look as if Olga and I were in a compromising position, but she and I followed his direction. With her back to me, I lifted her up and she kicked her legs back around my waist. I lowered her to the ground and then gave her another boost into the air. I would have not been able to do this with a girl off the street, but this closeness was accepted and encouraged in a dance studio. I must admit that the thought of sex crossed my mind as she and I pressed against each other, but it was a lustful thought confined to my mind and I had no plan to act on it. I sadly resisted considering what Jesus said about lustful thoughts.

After I gently put Olga down on the floor, Jerry said, "Come into the office, Martin. I want to talk to you." I didn't know what he wanted to talk about. He was the one who told Olga to wrap her legs around me, so I didn't think he would scold me. I didn't grope her or do anything unseemly. Curious, I followed him into the office. Olga was last to come into the room. She closed the door behind her.

"Have a seat, Martin," Jerry said, using a very friendly tone of voice. "Are you enjoying yourself in your dancing lessons?"

"Yes, I am."

"I hope not too much," he said, letting out a strange laugh. "You are here to learn and I am pleased with your progress. But you have a lot of work to do. I know you can do it. I have been watching you and I think you would be fabulous to be part of our showcase in November."

"Showcase? What showcase?"

I looked at Jerry intently and then I turned to look at Olga, who had a blank expression on her face.

"Now, don't get nervous, my boy!" said Jerry, raising his hands. "You have four months to get ready and, with enough lessons and practice, you will be wonderful. It is an event that you will remember for the rest of your life."

"Who will be at the showcase to watch?" I asked with trepidation.

"Everyone."

I said to Olga, "That's not what I want to hear." Then I turned back to look at Jerry.

He said, "It is understandable for you to be nervous at the start, but I have been keeping an eye on you and you pick up new steps very quickly. Just between you, me and Olga, you are one of our best young dancers, Martin."

"I don't know if I will be ready by November."

"That is why you need to sign up for more lessons."

If he was trying to mask his sales pitch to me, he wasn't trying very hard, but he was so intense about my dancing at the showcase that I agreed to pay for more lessons. I don't remember actually saying "Yes" but the next thing I know he is whipping out a contract for more lessons. If I turned down the lessons, it would mean I would stop dancing with Olga.

But I did manage to say to Jerry, "I am not a rich person who can afford an endless supply of lessons."

"You'll find a way to pay for them," he said, refusing to accept my negative attitude about the price of ballroom dancing lessons. "People usually put their money where their heart is, and you are good enough to become a professional ballroom dancer one day, Martin."

Again, I was flattered. Hearing him say that I was good enough to become a professional dancer inflated my ego. It made me feel slightly above other people. I didn't notice pride slip into me, but it was there, like an undetected virus.

When Jerry let me out of the room, Olga walked me out to the parking lot. She said that she was going to the convenient store around the block to buy a bottle of water. As soon as we exited the studio, she commented to me about what Jerry had said.

"Don't let Jerry bully you!" she said. "It is his job to sell you more lessons. You don't have to buy them if you don't want to or if you can't afford to."

"But I want to dance more with you."

"How do you feel about the showcase?"

"I am not ready now for it, but I like a challenge. If I work hard enough, maybe I could be ready to dance in front of other people. I really liked my lesson with you today."

She smiled and said, "That is nice of you to say."

"You're welcome."

"So I will see you for our next lesson tomorrow."

"That's right."

"Are you going to the dance party at the studio on Friday night?"

"Of course. I am looking forward to it," I said.

"What else are you doing this week?"

"While I am on vacation from work, I plan to sleep late and spend time outside getting a sun tan."

"I wish I could get a sun tan, but my skin is too white."

"I can get a sun tan, but I don't want to spend too much time out in the sun. I don't want to get burned."

This was the extent of the depth of our conversation at this point in our burgeoning acquaintance. It was light and airy. We were feeling each other out, figuratively speaking. We could talk to each other as friends. Her confiding in me that it was Jerry's job to sell me more lessons went far to establish a new trust between us. She trusted me enough to confide in me. I appreciated it. I was realizing that we could have a "public" conversation on the dance floor and then slip off to have a "private" conversation where we dipped slightly below the surface of superficial perception. This was a seed of confidence to plant into our relationship.

I watched Olga walk across the parking lot and I thought about how I liked her. Would she ever go out on a date with me? Could we get to know each other very well? Could she be ‘the one’? These thoughts bounced through my mind, as I tossed my dance shoes into the back seat of my car and put my sunglasses back on.

Chapter Three

RATIONALIZING MY WAY

I spent most of the next day relaxing and thinking about my interest in Olga. With my tall glass of iced tea, I sat on a lounge chair on a deck outside, soaking up the sun and listening to the radio. I imagined myself dancing along a beach with Olga. Romantic ideas were swinging through my mind. Candlelight dinner, passionate music, furtive glances – all coming together for the fulfillment of my romantic ideal. I didn't know how to make this dream come true, but I was excited at the prospect anyway. I left my mind open to any thoughts that could help me.

As I was driving to the lesson at the studio later in the day, however, troubling thoughts swept into my mind like an unexpected rainstorm. I recalled that I was a Christian and I wondered what Olga would think of it. I had grown up in a Christian family and my father took me to church for years. I basically believed the Bible, but I still had trouble accepting the pain I had to endure because of obedience to God.

I started to rationalize that my Christian faith didn't prevent me from dating Olga, or that I could use dating as a way to share Christ with Olga. Christian witnessing became a convenient reason to get to know a girl. At the moment, I wasn't attuned to the selfish motive behind it. I was more interested in having a "girlfriend."

I didn't drink alcohol excessively. Neither did I smoke nor

did I do drugs. I didn't chase women habitually. I considered myself to be an honest, open person who didn't have a secret agenda or many "skeletons" in the proverbial closet. I thought that, as soon as Olga saw my good living consistently, she would be impressed with my decisions of integrity in life.

When I arrived at the studio, I overheard Olga and Jerry arguing about whether American-style or international-style ballroom dancing was better. Olga was passionate that international-style dancing was much better.

"Nowhere else in the world do people dance American style, except in America," she claimed, taking a strong stand in her tone of voice.

"The last time I checked, we are in America," he said sarcastically.

"I want to teach international style."

"No, you won't. Not here! We teach American here. People enjoy it more."

"Only because it is easier," she asserted.

"Whatever makes people happy," he remarked. Then he walked away from her, as he noticed I was listening to their conversation.

Olga seemed to be in a bad mood. Even after she turned on the music, she walked up to me and barely looked at my face. She seemed to be going through the motions of dancing. I was surprised about her sudden change in emotion toward me. It was a stark contrast to the warm feelings she conveyed to me the previous day. We danced and I paid attention to her instruction. The 45 minutes flew by and the lesson was done before I knew it.

Looking at the clock, she said somewhat harshly, "The lesson is over."

"Okay."

"Jerry doesn't like it when I give any extra time to a student."

"I understand," I said.

"Do you want to have a lesson tomorrow?"

"I think I will take tomorrow off and then come back on Thursday."

"Okay," she replied. "Are you getting tired?"

"No, I just have some other plans tomorrow."

In reality, I didn't have anything special planned, but I didn't like her moodiness, so I wanted to take a day off and let the air clear. For a few minutes, I thought she was angry with me, but I hadn't done anything bad to her. I assumed she had other things going on in her life – things she wasn't talking to me about. I wanted to respect her privacy. I didn't blame her for being in a bad mood. God knows I have had my own bad moods. But I was living in and out of my day-dreams and I only wanted superficial thrills without taking it too far.

Olga said goodbye to me as I was changing into my regular shoes. She went into the other room, which seemed to be a sanctuary for the dance teachers. I deliberately changed my shoes slowly, so I could watch the other dance teachers and students. A red-headed dance teacher was teaching a middle-aged couple in the corner. A young woman was stretching in front of the mirror. Another couple was practicing. I lingered for five minutes.

As I stood up to leave, Jerry came forward and said, "Martin, please stick around. I want to talk to you about an outfit for the showcase. Are you in a hurry? Can you stick around?"

"Sure, I guess so," I replied. I sat down again.

A tall, skinny man in his thirties walked into the studio. He was slightly balding and his face had a sunken, depressed-looking expression. He walked toward me and sat down in a chair next to me.

"How are you doing?" I asked him in order to be friendly.

"Okay."

He didn't ask how I was doing. He seemed as if he wanted to be left alone.

Olga walked back onto the dance floor and waved at the man next to me. She approached him and said, "Are you ready for your lesson, Wren?"

"Not really," he said dourly.

"Dancing will put you into a better mood."

He looked at me and said, "I doubt it."

This guy was really depressed. After changing into his dance shoes, he followed Olga to the stereo system where she was choosing a CD to play. They stood together talking at the stereo for over ten minutes. I was wondering when they would start dancing.

Then Jerry walked up to me and said, "Sorry to keep you waiting. Follow me! I want to show you the costumes that Carlos has. Carlos is the owner, by the way."

"I don't think I have met Carlos yet."

"He only shows up at certain times. He leaves the day-to-day management of the studio to me."

"Oh."

Opening the door of a large closet, Jerry pulled out several costumes that Carlos had worn to dance competitions. Next to the closet were pictures of Carlos dancing in different competitions.

"You need a costume that will make you stand out," said Jerry. "Olga will be your partner and she will be wearing something appropriate, something provocative, but tasteful. You want to be worthy of her, don't you?"

His question struck me oddly. He wanted me to focus on the superficial, but I wanted to get to know Olga at a deeper level. I didn't dare say anything about it to Jerry, whom I didn't trust. But I was hoping to go beyond the superficial with Olga. I yearned to impress her with my honesty. While Jerry was showing me different styles of clothing, I was thinking about Olga. When I looked behind me, she was dancing with the student Wren. I knew that teaching ballroom dancing was just a job for her. I wasn't jealous that she was dancing with other men. I still didn't know exactly how old she was, but her youthfulness conveyed innocence to me.

As Jerry was finishing what he had to say to me, I noticed that Wren was returning to his chair and changing back into his regular shoes. It was odd to see a lesson end so quickly. The normal lesson lasted 45 minutes. Jerry spotted what Wren was doing.

"Why aren't you dancing, Wren?" Jerry shouted.

"I am not feeling well."

"You still have to pay for your lesson today."

"I know. I will."

He didn't seem to care that he had to pay for a lesson, even though he didn't get the full lesson. He looked tense. When Jerry led him to the front desk, I walked up to Olga.

"What was that all about?" I asked.

"He was talking to me most of the time."

"I saw you two talking next to the stereo for quite a while."

"He was telling me about his problem of not being able to find a girlfriend," she said. "I don't care about his problem. I am here to teach him how to dance. All he wants to do is talk and talk." She threw her hands in the air in exasperation. She didn't have compassion for him in his trouble.

"What exactly did he say to you?"

"He was complaining that he can't meet a girl. He is very depressed."

"I feel bad for the guy," I said.

"Don't feel bad for him! He is weird. Carlos and Jerry call him 'the Killer.'"

"Why?"

"His face looks so intense that he looks like a killer," she said.

The fact that people at the studio called Wren "the Killer"

actually bothered me. Clearly, the guy was having trouble meeting the right woman. He was depressed about it. For Carlos and Jerry to make fun of him, it was unfair and unkind. I could have told Olga that I had went through a similar struggle to find a girl to be my girlfriend. I knew what it was to be depressed because of failed romances and long periods of loneliness.

But I didn't say anything to Olga. If I was going to defeat my past, I thought that I had to ignore it as much as possible and simply live in the moment.

Olga jolted me out of my concentration when she asked, "Can you stay and help me with the group lesson?"

"How can I help?"

"I need someone to demonstrate steps with me," she said.

"Am I good enough?"

"This is a class for beginners. You are good enough."

"Okay. I'll help you."

"I appreciate it," she said to me, smiling.

It was a moment when she and I connected emotionally. She had asked for help and I was responding with support. I could sense her response to my willingness to do what she wanted.

"You're so nice," she remarked to me, as she walked toward the desk. I watched her from behind. I was becoming increasingly attracted to her.

During the group lesson a half-hour later, Olga demonstrated dance steps to the class, using me as her dance partner. I was flattered that she would choose me to dance with her in front of the group. I also had the opportunity to dance with some of the female students and I noticed Olga keeping an eye on me at certain times.

When I was dancing with a young woman, Olga twirled by me and said, "You are doing very well, Martin."

Then I could have sworn that she looked at the young lady with jealous eyes. I never confirmed it, but I liked thinking that Olga wanted me all to herself. The excitement was growing in my imagination. It all seemed thrilling and, most of all, harmless.

Yet, on the way home, I was thinking of the cold way that Olga treated Wren for his depressed state of having no girlfriend. Even though I was filled with hope for myself, I could identify with Wren and I thought that Carlos and Jerry were being much too harsh to ridicule him for being depressed. I was reminded that the world can be a cold, critical place, devoid of the genuine love that the Lord Jesus Christ has for people.

Chapter Four

Inner Struggle

On the next day, an inner struggle developed in me. On the one hand, lustful thoughts about Olga flowed into my mind. On the other hand, thoughts of the Bible's warnings about romance floated into my mind from another direction. It was as if I had the devil sitting on one shoulder and an angel sitting on the other shoulder. Wanting peace of mind, I was annoyed that this conflict started in my thought life.

I justified the fulfillment of my daydreams by saying to myself that I deserved to have some romance in my life; I had waited so long, suffering through disappointment after disappointment, which had worn me down. Not only was I looking to God, but also the world to help heal my emotional scares and overcome the disappointments. An opportunity was opening for me to get closer to Olga and I wanted to walk through the door with confidence. I was tired of being hesitant and overly cautious in dealing with a girl.

I started to miss Olga. I had regretted not scheduling a dance lesson until Thursday. I should have overlooked Olga's moodiness, I told myself. I wished that I had her e-mail address, so I could write to her, but I had to wait. To pass the time, I spent the day shopping for a gift to give to her. I bought a glass rose that I intended to give to her at the right moment.

At night, I paced in my room for two hours, jubilantly thinking and daydreaming about Olga. I was elated. Hope was riding high like a chariot on the clouds. The exhilaration was pumping. I was on the verge of getting a girlfriend. That was all that mattered at the time. I wanted to prove to the world that I could be a fantastic boyfriend – attentive, creative, patient, understanding, sharing, honest and loving. Without a doubt, I planned to be the embodiment of what many women say they want. My sincerity could have been measured in miles.

Truly, I wanted to succeed where many men have failed in life. I felt a little bit better, a bit smarter, a bit more patient than other men. I just needed the opportunity to prove it, I told myself repeatedly.

When I first decided to take ballroom dancing lessons, I had a secret hope to learn how to dance and then go to dancing parties to meet women. I had no idea that I would be falling in infatuation with the teacher. But it turned out that my dancing lessons, which weren't cheap, were my means to developing a relationship with a woman with whom I would normally be too afraid to interact.

Dancing eased the tensions and was a reason to communicate, other than dating. Yet, the seeds of flirting were being planted. Nothing too overt! Olga was subtle and careful, but she had a quick smile and a certain look in her eyes. Maybe it was my imagination, but I was quickly putting her on a pedestal.

The time for the next lesson on Thursday finally arrived. I felt like I had waited a week, even though it had been less than two days. I didn't want to lose any time. I had lost years in my dark period of loneliness. Olga was a shining light to start a new period in my life. So much was stirring in my mind.

"How was your day off yesterday?" she asked me.

"Good."

Then we danced. After I practiced the steps she taught me, she whispered to me, again confiding in me, “I would rather teach you international style of dancing, but Jerry won’t let me. Don’t tell him that I said this to you!”

“I won’t.”

“If I ever have the opportunity, I want to teach you international style,” she said. I liked listening to her voice. She had an accent, but I was getting used to it.

“What’s going on with you?”

“I practiced for three hours today,” she said, as she was changing the song on the stereo.

“That’s a lot.”

“I need to do it if I am ever going to become a world champion.”

“So that is your goal?”

“Yes,” she said.

“Will you be on TV someday?”

“Maybe.”

“Who would you dance with?”

“I dance with the owner Carlos.”

The next thought that hit my mind was that Carlos would be attracted to Olga and, subsequently, I would lose the opportunity to date her. I was slightly jealous. My insecurity flared up. Suddenly, I had an interest in learning more about Carlos. I had seen his pictures on the wall, but I wanted to know what kind of man he was. Was he a man of good character?

Then a short time later, Carlos’ wife and children came into the studio. Olga pointed them out to me. Seeing them made me relax because it meant Carlos was likely a committed family man. Also, Olga said something to me that made me think she didn’t hold him up to the highest regard.

“Carlos doesn’t like to practice,” she said. “It frustrates me. He is more interested in the business of running this studio than practicing for a major competition. He doesn’t do what I want, which is to practice at least two hours a day. He is not a great partner."

I learned that Olga had high expectations of a dance "partner." She seemed genuinely frustrated that the progress with Carlos in dancing was not coming along as fast as she wanted. I knew that I could never be her partner at a professional competition because she was far ahead of me, but I admired her and I wanted to encourage her to keep her dream of being world champion alive.

"You are a great dancer, Olga."

"I am not the best," she said. Then, after a long pause, she added the word "yet."

"Thank you for another great lesson," I said at the end of the lesson.

"You are a great student. You do what I say."

"I try."

She told me that I was her last lesson of the day. "I'll walk out with you. Will you wait for me?"

"Sure," I replied.

She changed into tight-fitting, casual clothes. While she was in the bathroom, she had applied more make-up to her face. I thought she had natural beauty, so I was not sure why she used so much make-up, but she looked pretty with it, nonetheless.

In the parking lot outside the studio, she and I had a conversation, which was a great opportunity for me to offer her the encouragement to stay committed to her dream of dancing. In a way, I was telling her what she wanted to hear, but I meant it as sincerely as I knew how. I was not just trying to get her into bed. I was trying to develop a "relationship" with her. Having learned from the past, I knew communication would be important.

"I admire you for working hard to become a world champion ballroom dancer," I told her. "I believe you will make it."

"I hope so. I also plan to get my college degree."

"That's great."

"I am in a pre-law program in college."

"Great," I said, leaning toward her.

"I want to be a lawyer," she announced proudly.

"Wow, you want to be a dancer and a lawyer. You are multi-talented."

"I can make money as a lawyer and it can pay for my dancing. Dancing is not cheap," she said. "I like to study the law and I also like to discuss politics."

"Hey, I studied political science in college. In fact, I took a couple of courses on the political system of the Soviet Union. I learned about communism."

"I have no interest in the communist system of the Soviet Union," she replied. "Communism didn't represent the desires of the people. It was just a government system. I didn't pay attention in school in Moscow when the teachers talked about communism. All us kids wanted the things of the West – the music, clothes and movies. We wanted to party."

"The Soviet Union started to break up in the late 1980s. What was it like in Russia before the break-up of the Soviet Union?"

"I don't remember. I was too young. I only cared about dancing back then. Ballroom dancing is huge in Russia. Not like here in America! In Russia, people who dance well are looked up upon. In America, there is no appreciation for the ballroom dancer."

"Yeah, I would say that ballroom dancing doesn't get anywhere near the same attention that other things get in this country. It isn't a major part of our culture. Football, baseball and other sports are major parts of our American culture."

"I have no interest in those things," said Olga.

"I wouldn't expect you to."

Changing the subject, she said, "I am excited about the ballroom dancing party tomorrow night. You and I can dance in a social setting. I want to show people what I have taught you." She was very enthusiastic.

"Sounds good," I said. "I'll see you tomorrow night at the party."

I walked her to her car and, as she opened up her car door with one hand, she pulled out her cell phone with her other hand. She flipped it open and pushed a button.

"I got this cell phone yesterday and I am still learning how to use it," she said. "I like having a cell phone and I check for messages as often as I can. Do you have a cell phone?"

"I used to have one, but I lost it."

"You should get another one."

"I don't use it that much," I said.

"Well, I plan to use my cell phone plenty."

Then, suddenly, she quickened her movement and said, "Okay. I have to go."

"See you tomorrow night," I said, as I waved and then walked to my car. I noticed that she looked at my car, which was a white sports car. I was proud to have her see my car. I wanted her to know that I drove a cool car. I was more concerned about my image than I would have expected. I had not surrendered my vanity to Jesus yet.

When I sat down in my car, I pictured Olga in my mind. I envisioned her dancing by herself in front of my car in the rain. Then I felt guilty for having this sensual thought, as if an alarm went off in my conscience. I was annoyed with my conscience. Didn't it understand that having positive, ego-boosting thoughts about a beautiful woman helped me feel better? Did my conscience want me to feel awful all the time? Enough was enough, I felt.

I had every intention to move forward and see where the relationship with Olga would go. Impressed that she wanted to become a lawyer, I was constructing an image of her in my mind as intelligent, beautiful, dedicated, talented, sincere and interesting. She was all those things, but my need for a fascinating woman inflated her qualities to a much higher stratosphere, as if she wasn't even human. And she seemed to like me! Always a plus! I didn't want to ruin it by preaching the Bible or sharing Christ with her too aggressively. I was compromising. I was carefully managing my image.

Chapter Five

EYE-OPENING PARTY

Olga looked gorgeous at the party. When I walked into the studio, I saw her dart across the room to the office. She was dressed in a fancy, black outfit and she wore high-heeled shoes. Her hair was done up in a special style. She looked perfect.

Easing my way into the party, I said hello to a few people on the edge of the dance floor. Then I looked back into the office and saw Olga talking to a curly-haired guy at a computer. I had never seen the guy before. He didn't look like Carlos, the owner, whom I had seen in the pictures on the wall. I assumed that the guy worked for Carlos. He looked like a "techie" type of person.

Powerful music started and dance couples moved onto the dance floor. Jerry walked up to me and asked me to dance with a new female student named Laurie. I reluctantly agreed. I asked Laurie to dance.

"I just started taking lessons last week and I haven't danced formerly since I was a child when I studied ballet," she said to me in a quivering voice.

"We'll take it slow," I said, as if I was an experienced dancer.

I kept my word and I tried to make the dancing easy and light for her. But, to my chagrin, Jerry surprised me in the middle of dancing with Laurie. He sauntered onto the dance floor and shouted at me in his typical overbearing manner.

"You are not leading her right," he blurted out to me. "Do it this way!"

He pushed me aside and danced with Laurie himself for the purpose of showing me how to lead her. I watched and tried to imitate the movement next to him.

"Okay," I said, not liking to be embarrassed.

"You will confuse the girl if you lead incorrectly," said Jerry, as he handed Laurie's hand back to me. Jerry was like a puppeteer when it came to his students.

I knew I had to lead, but I didn't have a good understanding of how to lead. I couldn't even identify when I was making a mistake in leading. When I thought I was leading my partner correctly, it turned out that I wasn't and I may have been confusing her without my knowing it. Jerry's shouting at me seemed like he thought I was purposefully leading poorly. That would be unfair to me. I was still learning and Jerry had no patience for me.

After the song ended, I immediately thanked Laurie for the dance and I walked off the dance floor. Waiting for Olga to come out onto the dance floor, I didn't want to get stuck dancing too long with Laurie, even though she seemed like a nice person. She drifted off into the corner, looking disappointed that she didn't dance as well as she would have liked. It is astounding how trying to live up to the high standards of ballroom dancing can make a person feel like a withering flower.

The next song had a distinctive Latin flavor. A few people shouted in excitement. Moreover, the music attracted Olga to the dance floor – finally. Wrapped up in my infatuation for her like a snail in a cocoon, I watched her strut onto the dance floor and go into the arms of a man whom I recognized as Carlos. They instantly launched into complicated dance steps and movements. They were moving so fast and energetically that I would have thought fire would spark from their dancing shoes. The Latin music was stirring and passionate. Olga was in her element. Her expertise in dancing was for all to see.

When the song ended, several people applauded for her and Carlos, who had put on a little show for the crowd. It was obvious that people envied and respected them. Olga's smile glowed with pride.

Although I was in the shadows on the side of the dance floor, I was hoping that Olga would spot me and come to me. Instead, she walked to the other corner of the dance floor. I saw the curly-haired guy standing on the side. He didn't look like a dancer to me at all. He wasn't dressed as a dancer. He stuck out like a sore thumb. Yet, Olga was heading straight to him. How strange!

The next thing that happened was not what I expected at all. Olga thrust herself into the curly-haired guy's arms. As she embraced him, he wrapped his arms around her. This virtually made my heart drop to the floor. I couldn't believe it. Olga remained in the hug with him for a long time. I observed in astonishment. My emotions responded by surging like a hurricane.

Minutes later, I was able to force myself to ask Jerry, "Who is the guy with Olga?"

"That is her boyfriend," he replied.

With all my ability, I tried to hide my disappointment. I didn't want Jerry to know that I had liked Olga and now it was all coming apart. The memory of all the other times in my past - when a girl I liked had a boyfriend - came rushing back to me in order to torture me, no less. *It has happened again. It has happened again.* This is all I could think of. The challenge was going to be to remain at the party without losing my outwardly reserved demeanor.

Hastily, I went to Laurie and asked her to dance again. I wanted to divert my attention. Not once did I look at Olga for the next three dances. I barely talked to Laurie either, but

I was patient with her missteps. She could have stepped on my feet, and I probably wouldn't have noticed. My mind was elsewhere, as if it had just entered a foggy graveyard of memories.

Eventually, Laurie told me that her shoes were hurting her and she needed to sit down. I followed her off the dance floor. At that point, Olga walked up to me.

"Are you ready to dance with me?" she asked me.

I looked at her with a serious expression and said, "I am tired right now. Maybe later!"

Her face expressed bewilderment. Then I turned my back on her. I could hear the sound of her heels on the hardwood floor when she walked away from me. In addition to being disappointed, I was angry. Perhaps the two go hand-in-hand.

"Would you please excuse me?" I said to Laurie. "I need to go to the men's room."

But I didn't go to the bathroom. I left the studio. My departure was the only thing that would alleviate the stress of my emotions. Still wearing my dance shoes, I walked outside to my car and drove off. Given my emotional upheaval, I knew that the night was not going to be easy for me.

I was going home with new emotional wounds. Because my ego was crucified long ago, I couldn't cover up the pain with macho anything. I couldn't avoid the pain by telling myself, "I can do better than her. There are lots of other women out there for me. Believe me, I am a stud." This would have missed the point. The real point was that my emotions and my imagination had worked in collusion to get me all optimistic and hopeful for a marvelous romance with the dancing sensation Olga. But it was so far distant from the truth. Olga had a boyfriend and I hadn't seen it.

I had made myself believe that she was available. I was reminded how I am incapable of seeing the secrets in people's minds or finding a woman who is available. My desire for a moral, beautiful woman of faith had been dwindled down to a woman who is "available." Even that, I couldn't get.

It was as if the devil was saying to me from my shoulder, "Uh-huh, God has left you in this lonely state again. *You see, God doesn't love you.* He demands your love, but He doesn't help you get the love you need to be satisfied in life."

Yet, despite my anger, disappointment, disgust and embarrassment, I muttered aloud, as I drove home, "This is all in Your control, God. Not my will be done, but Your will be done. I submit myself to You."

Whether God had heard my prayer or not, I wasn't sure at the time. Doubts attacked my mind like termites. Were my prayers bouncing off the ceiling of my car's roof?

As I expected, the night was difficult for me. From 12 midnight to 2 a.m., in particular, I suffered greatly in my soul. The agony brought me to tears. I had to admit that I was a failure. Seeing someone you like go off with another person can be devastating. Hope seemed to fly away like a bird at the start of winter. Having experienced my infatuation for Olga only for a few weeks, I started to feel that my winter of discontent had given way to a spring of renewal, only to return to my next winter of discontent more harshly.

At 2 a.m., I had shed all my tears and I felt empty. Finding myself at the end of my self-sufficiency, I turned to God, yet again, in prayer.

"Heavenly Father, in Jesus name, please help me get through this disappointment. I thought there was a possibility for more with Olga, but now I know there shouldn't be. She has a boyfriend, as you know. You know what their relationship is like and what they do together, as You are all-knowing, Lord Jesus. I ask You to help me stay friends with Olga. I don't want to quit dancing lessons. Olga and I had not gone out on a date, so it was not like she was two-timing me. Look, she and I are not meant to be together. I need to accept it. My heart is in agony because I cannot find the right woman to be my wife, my confidant and my friend. I need Your help to meet the deepest longing and need of my heart. I don't want to give up on love."

I paused for a moment.

When I resumed my prayer, the tears started to flow out of my eyes again. "Please forgive me, Father, for my shortsighted selfishness and self-sufficiency that gets in the way of Your working out the details of my life. Have mercy on me, Father God! Jesus is Lord. I am guilty of vanity, materialism, lust and self-centeredness. I cry out to You for Your mercy and forgiveness. I receive Your forgiveness by faith. Wash me anew by the blood of Jesus! In Jesus name. Amen."

Feeling the emptiness as an emotionally-drained person, I drifted off into an uneasy sleep. If I didn't have my faith in God, I probably would have turned to alcohol, drugs or illicit relationships to cover up my inner pain. God's grace was all I had to keep me on the straight and narrow path of good living.

Despite my stubborn ways to do things my way at times, God loved me too much to allow me to self-destruct in sin. I know that He had to break my will – without crushing my spirit – in order to bless me with a closer relationship with Him. I needed the Lord Jesus more. Turning to Jesus is a great answer to a disappointment, as I found out. God comforted me and sent peace into my soul. I had made mistakes and I had had poorly tried to control my circumstances and my relationships, but I had *faith* to which God responded.

Chapter Six

Beginning Changes

Wearily, I went to my next dance lesson with Olga. I had the whole weekend to ponder the news of Olga's boyfriend. As I often did, I used my serious-looking façade to mask a soul that was hurting. Pretending that everything was fine with me, I slipped into the lesson with Olga without missing a beat.

She asked me, "What happened to you on Friday night?"

"What do you mean?"

"You didn't dance with me."

"I was very tired and, besides, you looked great dancing with the other men," I said, trying to redirect her attention.

"I saw you and then you were gone, Martin."

"I wasn't feeling well, so I left. I am not important to this dance studio," I remarked. "No one noticed that I left."

"You're wrong. People were asking for you. Jerry was asking for you. He wanted to see you dance with me."

"He'll get over it."

Wanting to dance, I lifted my arms and prepared to dance. Throughout the lesson, Olga did not make any jokes. She must have sensed my extremely serious mood. I was in no mood for jokes. If she did make any little jokes, I probably didn't notice. Though I did the dance steps she showed me, I was thinking about her and her boyfriend. It was really affecting me.

When the lesson was over, I walked to the chair to change my shoes, almost like a robot. Being nice to Olga was not something I felt I needed to do anymore. She was the dance teacher. That was all. At some point, I had to believe what I was saying. It is a torture when you tell yourself something and then you don't quite believe it, I thought. As was usually the case, I became contemplative and analytical in a time of disappointment. Why was it happening? Why did I feel that way? What was God's plan in it all? Who can I trust? The questions mounted up like a heap of sandbags.

As I was gathering my belongings, Olga walked up to the secretary's desk and started to write in a notebook. The secretary started to speak to her about her fingernail polish. Then the secretary mentioned the boyfriend to her.

"How are things with your boyfriend we met at the party Friday night?" she asked Olga.

Waving her hand like she was swatting a fly away, she replied, "Oh, he isn't my boyfriend anymore. It wasn't very serious."

"That's too bad," said the secretary.

"I'm over it," said Olga.

Walking by her on the way to the exit, I wondered whether this information would change me back to liking her again – now that the boyfriend was out of the picture. My emotional response was extremely mellow. The thought in my mind was: "I don't care either way. She is not for me."

The fact that she would display affection on a man so openly in public and then "dump" him by Monday didn't make me feel great either. The only justification I would have given was that she didn't know him very well and they hadn't been dating very long. I didn't know the facts, so I could only conjecture.

Aggressively pushing open the door, I left the dance studio, hoping that I would meet a new girl soon. Olga was shrouded in mystery, which was too much for me.

On the way home, I heard on the radio that the singer/guitarist Jonathan Butler was coming to town in a couple of weeks. Having been a fan of his music for a few years, I was eager to want to attend the concert. But who would go with me? Truly, I wanted to turn the concert into a "date" with a woman. There was a new woman I liked at work. Maybe she would like to go to the concert with me, I wondered. Despite a sense of insecurity and fear that she would say "no" to me, I intended to ask her. So, when I arrived home, I called the ticketing agency and bought two tickets for the concert on September 19.

At the next lesson at the studio two days later, Olga told me that it was her birthday. This made me feel like a heel for not getting her a birthday card.

"Why didn't you tell me before?" I asked.

"You didn't ask," she replied.

Our dialogue loosened me up and, surprisingly, we had a good lesson that was full of laughs. Olga was making fun of the way Jerry dances. Her imitation of him was hilarious. Then, toward the end of the lesson, Jerry was showing off his new shirt and tie to everyone on the dance floor, Olga rolled her eyes in a very humorous way.

"You're like a comedian, Olga," I said.

"I can't help joking."

"I know my dancing makes you laugh," I said, poking fun at myself.

"I laugh with you, not at you," she claimed.

"That's what you say," I replied with a hint of sarcasm.

Swooping up to us, Jerry interrupted us, blaring, "Enough talking! More dancing! You must get ready for the showcase." Then he darted across the floor like a rodent.

I said to Olga, "He takes this showcase extremely serious."

"It is a big deal for the studio. It is a way to make extra money."

"I am starting to think that money is more important than

dancing at this dance studio."

"This is not a charity. Carlos and Jerry wants to make lots of money," she said. "Carlos drives an expensive car and lives in a big house."

"What a life!"

"When they see you, they see money walking into the door."

"And out of my wallet," I remarked.

"They'll do anything to make money. You know the girl Laurie you were dancing with at the party?"

"Yeah."

"Carlos and Jerry convinced her to sign a long-term contract worth thousands of dollars. They convinced her that she could be a great dancer. She is a nice person. I was talking to her earlier today. She now regrets spending all the money on dancing lessons and looks like she is about to have a nervous breakdown about it. I don't like to see Carlos and Jerry use her."

"She can't afford it?"

"They don't care. If she doesn't pay up, they'll sue her, based on the contract. Carlos has a good lawyer. Be careful when you sign any contract with a dance studio."

"I will," I said. "Thanks for the warning."

"Now we better dance before Jerry comes back and annoys me again."

"Happy birthday, Olga!"

"Thank you."

We danced.

After we finished the lesson, which was comprised of steps in rumba and foxtrot, Olga pulled me aside in the corner and asked me, "I am going to a night club tonight with some friends. Would you like to come?"

"Oh, no, I can't," I replied. "I am not ready to dance in public."

"We won't be doing ballroom dancing. We'll be social

dancing. It's different."

"I am sure you get a lot of attention from men at a night club."

"I go to a night club to dance, not to meet men," she said. "I don't like it when a man asks me to dance and I turn him down. It brings negativity into the room. I don't need it. I stay with my friends and they almost protect me. I just want to have fun."

Trying to make a humorous comment, I remarked, "Just like the old song by Cyndi Lauper, girls just want to have fun."

Olga looked at me quizzically. I don't think she was familiar with the song. She wasn't as old as I thought.

"Do you mind if I ask you how old you are, Olga?"

"I'm twenty-one years old today."

Twenty-one? I thought she was twenty-five. She had an older "air" about her.

"So you are legal," I said, unable to think of anything more clever to say.

"That's right."

"Are you going to order an alcoholic beverage?"

"Of course. But I don't drink heavy."

"That's good. I don't drink much myself," I said.

That was one thing I felt Olga and I had in common.

Then I heard clapping behind me. Turning around, I saw Jerry clapping and rushing toward the front door. A man with dark features walked into the studio. Jerry seemed ecstatic to see him.

"Agelis, it is so good to see you. How was your vacation?"

"Good," replied this man named Agelis, who seemed disinterested in Jerry's enthusiasm. Agelis looked to be in his late twenties or early thirties.

Jerry said to him, "Olga is anxiously waiting for you."

I didn't like the way Jerry phrased his words about Olga, but I couldn't do anything about it. Agelis conveyed cockiness. Jerry suddenly wanted to introduce Agelis to me.

"Agelis, I want to meet one of our top new students. This is Martin."

I shook Agelis' hand and nodded. Agelis frowned and gave a weak handshake. Then he said to Jerry, "My girlfriend is meeting me here tonight."

"That's wonderful, Agelis. I am sure she is a lovely girl."

Agelis didn't respond. To me, he was acting as if he was a movie star coming onto a set. His attitude was so thick that I felt Agelis needed a swift kick in the pants to humble him, but I kept quiet.

Acting as a master of irrelevant information, Jerry said to me, "Agelis will be dancing at the showcase, also with Olga. A little healthy competition never hurt anyone."

So that was it. Jerry wanted to pit me and Agelis against each other, so we would feel compelled to compete and become better than each other. I wondered if Jerry was aware of how easy it was to see through his scheme. I wanted to tell Jerry to jump in a lake, but I held my tongue. If I lost my patience with him, I believed that it would hand the victory over to Jerry. Yet, if I remained patient under all circumstances, then it would show the strength of my character. I considered this to be a "spiritual" challenge I was taking on myself.

Before she walked away from me, Olga slipped me a piece of paper and said, "Call me at home tonight!" I wasn't expecting this at all.

"Why?" I asked.

"I need to talk to you. I can't talk now."

"Okay."

After I changed my shoes, I saw Olga dancing with Agelis. It bothered me strangely, but I bit my lip and walked out. Olga was not my girlfriend and I was fine with it. Yet, I was starting to categorize her as a friend. On the way home, I stopped at a store and bought her a birthday card, which I planned to give to her at the next lesson. As I walked out of the store, I was practicing my waltz steps. The security guards at the store were probably laughing at me.

At 11 p.m., I mustered up the courage and I called Olga at her home. When she answered the phone, it was strange to hear her voice. It was the first time hearing it over the phone. It was sweet-sounding, yet with an edge.

"Hi, this is Martin. I hope I am not calling too late," I said as politely as I could. "You asked me to call you." I went straight to the point of why I was calling.

"It's not too late. Thanks for calling. I want to tell you that I may be leaving the dance studio."

"Why?"

"I am frustrated with Carlos and Jerry. Carlos is a lazy person and he doesn't want to dance. Jerry doesn't give me enough lessons. He gives more lessons to Marie. But they expect me to stay at the studio all day. Today they asked me to help with the paperwork. I won't do it. I am paid to teach dancing and that is why I am there. I don't want to do secretary work. That is what the secretary is for."

"Olga, have you talked to them about your concerns?"

"I have mentioned it to Jerry, but he won't listen," she said. "But tomorrow I am going to demand changes. If Jerry and Carlos don't meet my demands, then I am going to quit." She sounded serious.

"You got to do what you got to do."

"If I go to another studio, you can come take lessons from me after your contract with the International Extravaganza Dance Studio runs out. Wouldn't you like to take more lessons with me?" She asked the question with a girlish tone that charmed me.

"Yes, I have learned a lot from you and I would like us to continue dancing together."

"Good."

"Did you notice that Jerry was trying to stir up competition between me and Agelis at the studio?"

"He loves to do that," she replied. "He thinks that people who compete are more likely to buy more lessons from the studio."

"Agelis seemed to have a bit of an attitude problem."

"Oh, yes, Agelis is very confident in himself. After you left, his girlfriend showed up and he treated her like she was lucky to have him. I don't think that she is his only girlfriend."

"Really?"

"He is a good dancer and he is in good shape, but I can't stand a guy who thinks he is so great."

"Like he is God's gift to women?"

"Agelis is not great as a dancer," she quipped.

Olga judged the quality of a man by how well he could dance. This was clear.

Being humble, I said, "He is a better dancer than I am."

"But you learn faster than he does."

I accepted her compliment. Then, suddenly, Olga said that she needed to hang up the phone because she needed to take her dog outside. He was barking and scratching the door. I said goodbye and hung up.

Seconds later, the phone rang. I thought Olga was calling me back, but it was my Aunt Fiona on the line. Since I still lived at home with my parents, she called to find out if I knew where my mother was. Then she started to ask me how my life was going. I had learned in the past *not* to give her honest, detailed answers to this question.

"Things are going well."

"I have a friend whose daughter is your age. You might be interested in meeting her," she said. She seemed to enjoy trying to set me up on dates with women.

"I already have a girl in mind to ask out."

"Do I know her?"

"No."

"It's not somebody at work, is it?"

"Aunt Fiona, I can't determine exactly where I meet people."

"Getting romantically involved with a woman you work with is bad," she claimed. "It can get very messy."

"Thanks for the advice."

"When you go out on a date with a woman, whatever you do, make sure that you do not ask personal questions of the girl."

"Then how am I supposed to get to know her better?" I asked, confused.

"It will happen. Women don't like it when you ask personal questions. It sounds like you are trying to find out about their secrets and women need to keep their secrets as secrets. Don't make a woman feel uncomfortable!"

Her advice seemed superficial. I knew she meant well, but I didn't quite accept her point of view. Am I supposed to ignore that a woman has personal issues that would conflict with me and my beliefs? This was a thorny issue that I was not ready to tackle. I wish that my aunt, who was not a Christian, had said nothing about dating a woman.

"Aunt Fiona, I will let my mother know that you called," I said, trying to end the conversation.

God bless my aunt.

Chapter Seven

Finally Noticed

Rattled by my insecurities with women, I couldn't bring myself to ask the woman at work face-to-face to go to the Jonathan Butler concert with me. Thus, I resorted to leaving her a voice mail, which was both a blessing and a curse. I didn't have to expose myself to her emotional reaction, but I also didn't know when – or if – she would respond.

The whole day passed by. No response from her! Another day passed. Nothing! On the third day, I was convinced that she didn't want to go. I asked myself repeatedly, "Why doesn't she respond to me with a yes or no?" Her silence was more troubling to me than anything. Was I so putrid and insignificant that she couldn't even show me enough respect as to answer my invitation? Her lack of response made me feel awful

With just a few days before the concert, I didn't have a date. It was another disappointment. I gave myself a headache trying to think of a solution. Then I commented to myself in jest, "Maybe I should ask Olga to go with me to the concert." But I dismissed the idea almost immediately. Being a Russian dancer who liked Latin music, I presumed that she wouldn't like the R&B and smooth jazz sound of Jonathan Butler, who was born in South Africa.

Another day passed and I was getting anxious. My last

option was to ask a family member to attend with me. I wanted to wait as long as possible before asking a relative. Being a young guy, I desperately wanted to go with a young lady.

Although my mind was preoccupied with this challenge to find a date, I went to my next lesson with Olga and I gave her the birthday card I bought for her.

"Here is a belated birthday card for you," I said softly, as I handed the card to her.

Her face lit up joyously and she replied, "Thank you so much."

She opened the card in front of me and read the message inside. Then, in a totally unexpected move, she stepped toward me and kissed me on my right cheek. We were right in the middle of the dance studio. People saw us. Olga didn't seem to care.

"How was your time at the night club?" I asked her.

"It was fun. I wasn't out too late. You should have come, you know."

"I'm not really a night club kind of guy."

"By the way, do you have an e-mail address?"

"Yeah," I replied.

"I want to e-mail you the Web site addresses of a few ballroom dancing Web sites. They are interesting. Lots of good information about dancing."

"Great. I'll write down my e-mail address before I leave."

She said, "I'll give you my e-mail address as well."

"Okay."

In his typical fashion, Jerry rushed up to us and insisted that we start dancing. To make a joke, I started to dance with Olga and I purposefully fouled up my steps and my movements. Jerry nearly went crazy.

"How could you dance so terribly? How can you live with yourself with such horrendous mistakes?"

"Jerry, I was joking."

Jerry looked up at the ceiling and said, "Now he gets a sense of humor." Then he looked at me and said, "Just a few short months to the showcase. You can have a sense of humor after the showcase. For now, you must be serious. You and Olga need to learn your routine. I showed Olga the beginning of the routine today. That is what I want you both to work on in this lesson. Remember, Martin, that practice makes perfect." Then he walked away to teach another couple.

"Jerry is quite a character," I said to Olga.

"He gets on my nerves," she whispered to me, making sure that no one else heard her comment.

"Did you have your big talk with Jerry and Carlos?"

"Yes. They promised me more lessons and I don't have to do paperwork."

"So you will be staying here?"

"For now," she replied.

"It sounds like they bent to your will, Olga."

"I threatened to leave them if they didn't give me what I want." Her tone of voice was edgy.

"They must appreciate you if they are willing to compromise in order to keep you here."

"They have trouble hiring good teachers. If I leave, they would lose students." She was confident in herself as a dance teacher. "They need me."

"It is good that you are getting more students."

"That is what Carlos and Jerry said. Now they have to prove it to me."

She and I began to dance. She showed me the start of our dancing routine for the showcase. I had to move fast to keep up with her in the dancing. I was struggling to keep the timing of the music. She commented every time I slipped off the right beat.

At the end of the intense lesson, I went to the side to change my shoes. Jerry was talking to a couple, bragging about his past as a champion ballroom dancer and well-known teacher in New Orleans. I was thinking about how Jerry certainly had a high opinion of himself. Since he was heavy and almost sixty years old, he must have been talking about many years ago as a dancer, but the memory was like a fountain of youth to him.

On the way out of the studio, Olga gave me her e-mail address. I shoved the piece of paper into my pocket. Putting her out of my mind, I left. The air outside was sticky. I stopped at the convenient store for a bottle of water. I needed something refreshing.

After I went home, I continued to struggle with the desire for a woman to accompany me to the concert. Anyone? Locking myself in my room for hours, I racked my brain with different possibilities. I was even going to call a woman I hadn't seen in five years.

Around 11 p.m., I pulled out the piece of paper with Olga's e-mail address on it. "What the heck," I mumbled to myself. "I should e-mail her and thank her for the dance lessons."

Turning on my computer and logging onto my Internet connection, I e-mailed Olga, thanking her for the valuable dance lessons, as intended. Then at the end of the e-mail I mentioned that I had tickets for a music concert, but I knew she was busy teaching dance lessons on a Tuesday evening. I sent her the e-mail and didn't think much of it. She always had to teach on Tuesday evening.

When I checked my e-mail the next morning, I saw that she had responded to my e-mail. In her response, she said that she didn't have to work on the upcoming Tuesday and that she would be willing to go to the concert with me. I was amazed. The first girl I asked didn't respond at all to my voice mail, but Olga responded within 12 hours.

I had a date with Olga.

She didn't even know who the musical performer at the concert was going to be. I hadn't told her, but she had accepted the invitation anyway. What a nice thing for her to do, I thought. Relieved, I e-mailed her back, thanking her and giving her the details of where the concert was. I asked her to meet me at the concert place on her own. She lived far away from me and I wouldn't have time to pick her up after work and make it to the concert on time.

Later in the day, she responded, agreeing to meet me at the club. I was pleased. This meant that I didn't have to ask a family member to attend the concert with me. Even though the International Extravaganza Dance Studio had a strict policy forbidding a female teacher from going out on a date with a student, Olga was bending the rule for me. I took it as a compliment.

On the night before the concert, I got down on my knees beside my bed and I prayed: "Father God, I ask You to make my date with Olga tomorrow night successful. I need Your help to say the right things and do the right things. Show Your light in me to her. I know Jonathan Butler is a born-again Christian and I ask You to fill him with Your Holy Spirit, so he is shining with Your love tomorrow night. Thank You for this opportunity to have a woman accompany me to the concert. I appreciate Your mercy. My life is in Your hands. In Jesus name. Amen."

I needed God. This had nothing to do with preaching to other people or trying to force other people to believe what I believe. In the privacy of my bedroom, I humbled myself before God and asked for His help and His blessing. No one could have accused me of having an agenda to "convert" people. This was not a power trip for me.

In truth, I was aware of my spiritual poverty and my inability to do "good" without God working in me and through me. I needed His grace and mercy. Even though I hid it from the outside world, my identity as a changed Christian was never totally out of my mind at any point. I knew what Christ had done for me two thousand years ago.

It was a revealed secret that was branded on my heart.

The night of the concert arrived and I met Olga in the parking lot of the club. When I saw her get out of her car, I admired her nice appearance. I was not infatuated with her like I had been before the "boyfriend" incident, but I was still physically attracted to her. I didn't see any danger in it. I was superficial.

"You look nice tonight," I said to her.

"You have finally noticed," she said, teasing me.

"What is that supposed to mean?"

"Oh, nothing," she said coyly.

I shrugged my shoulders.

"Thank you for coming to this concert."

"You didn't tell me who we are seeing in concert."

"It is a singer and guitarist named Jonathan Butler."

"What kind of music does he play?"

"It is a combination of R&B, jazz and gospel," I replied, as we walked into the club.

"I thought you were taking me to a classical concert," she said.

Surprised, I asked, "Why? I don't even like classical music."

"I don't know, but you didn't tell me who we were seeing."

"I wouldn't take you to a classical concert without telling you first."

"Good."

Olga and I were seated minutes before the concert started. Five minutes after eight o'clock, Jonathan Butler emerged on stage with his guitar. He was smiling and looked at peace with himself. He started to fiddle the strings on the guitar and I thought he was warming up. Then, closing his eyes, he started to hum and sing out, "Lord, fill me with Your Spirit." This was reminiscent of my prayer on the previous night. I couldn't help but smile. God was listening.

And I was encouraged that Olga would see a man filled

with the Holy Spirit on stage. I was hoping that she would see that he was more peaceful and happy because of his connection to God. This was my secret hope that she would notice. Lord, help Olga to understand spiritual things, I thought.

Yet, the most remarkable facet of the concert came toward the end. Jonathan Butler asked the crowd to sing along with him on a certain song called "Do You Love Me?"

"I want the women to sing first alone and then have the men join in," he said to the crowd. The audience responded positively. "Okay, ladies, I want to you to sing the line, 'Do you love me?' "

The ladies in the audience complied and sang the line with such harmony and gentleness. It was a pleasure to listen to.

From the stage, he smiled and said, "Beautiful! Couldn't be better! Keep it going." After a brief pause, he said, "Now, men, I want you to sing the line, 'Do you love, love me, baby? Do you love, love me, baby?' Got it?"

"Got it," replied several men in unison.

"And I want you to stand up when you sing it," said Butler. "All you men, stand up. Look at your woman and sing it with your heart."

Feeling awkward about standing up, I looked at Olga, hoping that she wouldn't mind if I did stand up to sing. But she shrugged her shoulders. So I stood up and sang, as best as I could.

"Do you love, love me, baby?"

As I sang, I looked at Olga, but she avoided looking at me in my eyes. She looked down toward the floor for most of the song, but I kept singing to her. It was only our first date and I was singing, "Do you love, love me, baby" to her. Not only was it unexpected, but it was dramatic and was apparently having some sort of effect on Olga, who seemed to curl up in shyness.

After the concert ended, I said to Olga, "I had fun tonight."

"Me, too," she said. "Please don't tell Carlos or Jerry that I went out with you."

"I won't," I assured her.

We had our little secret.

Chapter Eight

SENSE OF SATISFACTION

The next ballroom dancing lesson with Olga was extremely pleasant. She was extra nice to me and she didn't say a bad word about my dancing the whole time. I felt a sense of satisfaction, not only that I was dancing well, but also that I had went on a date with Olga. Yet, I was taking it in stride. Rather than being overly excited, I would say that I was being "cool." I wasn't planning for the future. Instead, I was enjoying the moment.

In the middle of the lesson, Olga whispered to me, "Thanks again for taking me to the concert."

"I'm glad you came," I replied softly into her left ear. Then I twirled her.

"I was surprised that I actually liked the music. It wasn't the usual type of music I listen to, but there was something about it I liked."

"I'm glad," I said, thinking about how the singer started the concert praising the Lord God. "Did you get home okay?"

"Sure, I wouldn't be here if I didn't."

"I know, I know. I just mean you didn't run out of gas or get a flat tire. It was late."

"No, silly," she said, giggling.

"Would you like to hang out with me this Saturday?" I asked. The question slipped out of my mouth.

"Okay," she replied without hesitation. Her eagerness pleased me.

Then we had to dance faster steps and we couldn't talk any further. Also, Jerry was drifting in our direction and I didn't want him to overhear us. Neither did Olga, who was putting her job at stake by socializing with me.

Just before the end of the lesson, Jerry walked up to me and said, "We are having a meeting of our top dancers to talk about Ohio."

"What about Ohio?"

"There is a competition," he said. "Actually, it is the top ballroom dancing competition in the country. The best dancers go there."

"Then that disqualifies me," I said with self-effacement.

"Don't sell yourself short! In your category, you could win."

"What is my category?" I asked.

"Bronze."

Suddenly, I imagined myself covered in bronze paint. It was not a pretty sight.

Probably sensing my apprehension, Jerry said, "Attend the meeting and you'll learn all about it. We will be meeting in ten minutes."

While Jerry was talking to me, Olga walked away and disappeared into the office. Even though I was uninterested in this Ohio competition, I sat down and waited for the meeting. Laurie, with whom I danced at the party, was sitting near me. She initiated a conversation with me.

"Are you going to attend the meeting about the Ohio competition?" she asked.

"Yeah, but I don't know why he is thinking of me to go. I have not been dancing long."

"I have only taken four lessons, but Carlos and Jerry think I should go to the Ohio competition."

"How do you feel about it?"

"I am nervous about it, but there's something more."

"What's that?"

"I don't know if I can afford it."

"How much does it cost to compete at the Ohio competition?"

"I'm not sure, but I've heard from other people that is expensive," she said, lowering her head.

Then Jerry clapped his hands and announced, "We are ready. Carlos is waiting for you in the conference room." Jerry led the three of us to the room. A middle-aged woman with a terminal smile on her face was the third person.

When I walked into the room, I saw Carlos who was sitting at the head of the table like a CEO of a company. He had a serious air of business about him. Chairs had been set up at the other end of the table and Jerry pointed to the chairs. Laurie, the middle-aged woman and I sat in the three chairs, as if we were being investigated. I felt like I was going to be questioned for an offense.

After Jerry closed the door, Carlos began, "Thank you for taking the time to be here today. We have a very exciting opportunity for each of you. We believe each of you would do extremely well at the Ohio competition in November. We are planning for our studio to send a small group of dancers to compete and, hopefully, win in different categories. We will spend a week in Ohio and it is an incredible experience. You get to see dancers from all over the country. It is a great learning experience for all of you. I would love to have each of you go. When I get more details about the exact dates, I will let you know, but I wanted to take this opportunity to tell you about it and have you think about it. That's pretty much all I had to say. Do you have any questions?"

The middle-aged woman asked, "Can I buy a new outfit to wear at the competition?"

"Of course, that would be wonderful."

Laurie and I were quiet. I didn't know what to ask.

"No other questions?" asked Carlos.

Then I asked, "How much will it cost?"

Carlos was quick to respond. "I will get the details in the next few weeks and I will let you know. But I think you should go and I hope you agree with me."

"I'll think about it," I said.

Backing off, Carlos said, "That's all I can ask of you."

Then Jerry ushered us out of the room, as if Carlos' attention span was about to run out. I wanted to talk to Olga and find out the "real deal" behind this competition. When I asked her what she knew about the competition, she claimed that she didn't have any details.

"But having you do the competition, Martin, is a way for the studio to make money off you. Most of the dance studios do it this way," said Olga.

"I am already paying the studio a lot of money to take private lessons."

"The dance studio wants more of your money."

"I was talking to Laurie before the meeting and she was very concerned about whether she could afford it all."

"Some students get scared about paying so much money and they try to drop out," she said.

"I have to go, but I'll see you on Saturday. Okay?"

"Great. We'll call each other."

"Sounds good."

As soon as I left the studio, I started to have an uneasy feeling about going on a second date with Olga. I couldn't understand the feeling, but I conjectured that it had something to do with stepping forward in faith amid mystery and expectations. I didn't know what Olga expected from me. I wasn't certain that I could maintain a good conversation all evening. The lack of information about Olga's past made me fear that I wouldn't say the right things. I wanted her to like me, but I was nervous.

On the night before the second date, I prayed to God to

help me get through the date "without a major foul up." I also thought about where I would take her. When I didn't have a girlfriend, I always had ideas for taking a girl on a date. Now that I had a woman who was interested in another date with me, my mind went blank. I couldn't think of many places. The nicest place was a lounge on top of a hotel.

On Saturday, I waited most of the afternoon for Olga to call me. When she didn't call me by 5 p.m., I called her and got her voice mail. I left her a voice mail and asked her to call me. From the moment I hung up the phone, time seemed to become grudgingly slow. I waited for her to call for hours. No call! Then I convinced myself that she didn't like me anymore. What had I done wrong? It was weird how my emotions became negative and caused me to fall into a sour mood.

As I was grappling with my "down" mood, Olga called me at 8:45 p.m. I was glad that she called.

"I'm sorry to be calling you so late, Martin. I was waiting for your call."

"But I left you a voice mail at five o'clock."

"But I didn't check my voice mail until a few minutes ago. I have been home all day, except when I went to walk my dog. You must have called when I was out. Then I realized that I have had my Internet connection in the phone line for hours. When I realized it, I plugged the phone back in and checked the voice mail."

"Well, sorry we missed our opportunity to go out," I said, resigning myself to a failed attempt at a second date.

"It's not too late."

"What?"

"Let's go out together now. Do you know of a place where we can go?"

"I know a lounge at the top of a hotel."

"Great. Do you want to pick me up?"

"The place is near my house. Can you meet me at my house?"

"How about if we meet someplace near the hotel?"

"Okay."

We agreed on the location and I met her at 9:30 p.m. She parked her car and then climbed into my car. I drove us to the lounge. After parking the car in the hotel's garage, she and I went to the top and stepped into the lounge, from where a spectacular view of the city could be seen.

"This is interesting," she said to me.

The waitress seated Olga and me at a table in a circular booth, facing outward. The atmosphere was intimate. Romantic music was pumped into the room through the speakers in the ceiling.

"Do you come here often?" she asked me.

I said, "I haven't been to this place in a long time. It is better than I remember it."

"I'm thirsty," she announced, as she picked up the menu.

"Get anything you like," I said.

"Okay."

"As far as eating, this fruit and cheese platter looks good," I remarked.

"That sounds good to me."

"That was an easy decision," I said, smiling.

We ordered the food and drinks and then a sense of satisfaction settled on me. This feeling was so strong that I was completely silent for at least a minute, as I stared out the large glass windows at the city's magnificent skyline. I felt at ease. It was as if one of my daydreams had come true exactly as I would have planned – unique location, romantic music, cozy atmosphere and beautiful woman who treated me with respect and interest.

I wanted to cherish the moments.

"I'm sorry I am being quiet," I finally said to her.

"That's okay."

"I feel really good right now and a lot of it has to do with the nice way you treat me and make me feel special."

Olga blushed. She put her hand to her mouth and looked down.

"I hope I didn't say anything bad," I asked, unsure.

"No, you are being very nice to me. I am not used to it. You are a gentleman, Martin," she said.

"Thank you. I appreciate the compliment. You are one of the very few people who might value me with the qualities as a gentleman. I am not outgoing like many other people and I don't always have the most clever things to say."

"But you are being yourself and that's all a woman can ask for," she said.

The waitress delivered the food and drinks. While Olga went for the cheese, I went for the fruit. In fact, I was eating the grapes so fast that she made a comment about it.

"You really like grapes, don't you?"

"Yes, but it's mainly because I am hungry."

"Try this cheese. It's delicious."

She picked up a cracker and, using a knife, spread cheese on the cracker for me. Then she put it in my mouth. I took a bite and said, "It's very good."

"I love it."

That was really nice of her to feed me the cheese and cracker. It was also romantic, in my view. How great it was to have Olga feel comfortable enough to get close to me and be playful with me! I started to think that a bond of trust was starting to form between us. I was hoping that she sensed my respect for her. I wanted her to come to the conclusion that, since I was not trying to "jump her bones," I had a higher view of romance and dating, based on respect and integrity. This is where I saw strength within myself and I was hoping that Olga wouldn't miss it.

At 11 p.m., the soft, romantic music turned into fast, dance music.

I asked her, "Would you like to dance?"

"Sure."

This seemed like vindication for all the times girls turned me down to dance in high school and college. When I stepped onto the dance floor, I had my shoulders pumping, my hips gyrating and my arms waving. It was fun, plain and simple. I even tried to make Olga laugh with a few of my outrageous dance moves. What a time!

After three songs, we sat down. In between the second and third song, Olga told me that she was thirsty.

I responded by saying, "And I need more grapes."

She laughed.

When we sat down and each sipped our drinks, Olga brought up the fact that she was looking for a professional ballroom dancing partner. She talked about how she was contacting men on the Internet. One man was trying to coax her to move to New York and become his dance partner. Another man was trying to convince her to move to Miami, according to what she told me. She was desperate to get a dance partner who could dance at her level.

Knowing that the assumption was I couldn't live up to her expectation of dancing, I didn't bother to say, "What about me?" I listened to her and, beyond the words, I heard the aching in her soul to have a male dance partner who could work with her to get to the next level of championship.

If I hadn't been having such a wonderful time, I might have been put off by her talk of meeting other men to dance. This was our second date and she was revealing a deep emotional need she had, as well as saying that only another man – not me – could meet her need.

She seemed to separate dancing with a man and dating a man, as if an impenetrable wall existed between them, in the sense that she approached dancing as a business, not as a way to meet men.

Yet, I wasn't confident about other men's motives. Other men can be great dancers and lure Olga to them, but I would question their ulterior motives. One of the most vulnerable people in the world is a young woman who is captivated by her dream of greatness. Men can take advantage of that fairly easily.

I wondered whether Olga had the inner strength to see through men's charades and avoid being used sexually.

Then I forced myself to stop thinking these thoughts. They were too deep for a Saturday night while on a date. All I wanted at the time was fun and fulfillment of daydreams. The evening was magical to me. Romance touched my heart in a profound way. It increased my thirst for romance with a beautiful woman. I could pull off a romantic date without compromising my integrity or my sense of being a gentleman. Indeed, I was pleased.

I felt like I was floating on a cloud of exhilaration after I dropped off Olga at her car. Wanting time to think about everything that had happened and had been said with Olga, I drove around town for nearly an hour, playing romantic music in the car. I had started a new chapter of memories for my life. How would it all end up?

Chapter Nine

Unexpected Drama at the Dance Studio

Feeling very relaxed, I walked into the dance studio on Monday evening and was eager to see Olga, whom I expected to be in a good mood. Yet, as soon as I saw her, I sensed that something was wrong. Her face expressed negativity.

"What's wrong?" I asked.

"Ask Jerry," she replied sharply.

I went to Jerry and asked, "What's going on?"

"I want you to use your lesson time today to dance with another teacher. She is wonderful. Her name is Marie," said Jerry, automatically slipping into his "salesman" rhetoric.

"Why?"

"I want to broaden your knowledge of different styles of dancing. You'll like dancing with Marie."

"But I've had a good thing going with Olga. Wonder if Marie dances very different from Olga."

"Don't worry yourself, my friend," he said. "You'll still be taking lessons with Olga here and dancing with Olga at the showcase in November. Carlos and I have been discussing a program to allow our students to dance with more than one teacher. This is a new policy for all the students. That way, no one gets bored with just one teacher. It's for your benefit."

Whenever a salesman emphasizes that something is for my benefit, I distrust him. It was not difficult to distrust Jerry. He emanated a void of trustworthiness. I didn't like the decision to force me to dance with another teacher. Also, I was concerned about the impact on Olga. I didn't want to see her unhappy.

After Jerry walked away from me to go do a "snow job" on someone else, I approached Olga and said, "Jerry is making me dance with Marie. Are you okay with it?"

"If you want to do it, then do it," she replied.

"I think it will mess me up."

"Then don't do it."

"But Jerry says that it is a new policy of this dance studio. I have to follow the policy."

"Can't you see that this is Jerry's way of increasing lessons for Marie while taking lessons away from me?" She was very upset.

"But you should get lessons with Marie's students, won't you?"

Olga didn't respond, even though I knew her mind was working quickly and furiously.

I said, "I think I'll try out a couple of lessons with Marie and see how it goes. Then I can tell Jerry that I don't like dancing with Marie. Then I will be able to get out of it. If I refuse to dance with her now and insist on only dancing with you, he may get suspicious that you and I have been going out with each other."

"He doesn't know anything."

"I don't want to show you too much favor in front of him and Carlos," I said.

I was hoping that she would understand, but I don't think she did. Minutes later, after we stood in silence, Jerry directed Olga to dance with a gray-haired man and for me to dance with Marie, who was a fair-skinned, red-headed woman.

"Hi, there!" she said to me, smiling in a mechanical way.

"Hi."

"I'm Marie and I have been reviewing the file Jerry has on you. I hope you like our lesson today. I'll put the music on," she stated, as she walked to the stereo system.

Before she returned to me, I looked at Olga who was dancing the waltz with her student. They were sweeping along the edge of the room along the mirrors. Dancing with another woman was not what I had planned, but I knew that I would be talking to Olga later.

Marie showed me new dance steps. I tried my best to imitate her. She asked me to watch myself in the mirror. Overall, I thought that she was an adequate teacher who was friendly and nice. I didn't have any problem with her. Being forced to make this change, which didn't make sense to me, was the problem.

Because Marie gave me five extra minutes at the end of the lesson, I missed talking to Olga, who left. It was clear to me that she was upset. Before I could leave, Jerry insisted that I schedule another lesson with Marie later in the week. I didn't have the resolve to refuse. I was more concerned about getting out of the place, no matter what.

Deciding to call Olga on the phone, I rushed home and contacted her.

"Olga, it's Martin," I said into the phone.

"Oh, hi," she said in a hum-drum tone.

"Sorry I missed you at the dance studio. You left before my lesson was over."

"To be honest with you, I didn't feel like talking," she admitted.

"I understand."

"Do you?" she blurted out with a surprisingly sarcastic twinge.

"I didn't enjoy dancing with Marie."

"Good."

"But Jerry scheduled me for another lesson with her on Wednesday night. I couldn't say no."

"You are letting Jerry control you, Martin," she said.

"No, I'm not."

"Then you should have said no."

"It's hard to say no to Jerry. He argues with you."

"Jerry is a jerk," she said.

"I know."

"What did you think of your lesson with Marie?"

I thought for a moment before responding. "Not as good as a lesson with you, Olga."

Judging by her positive response, I gave the right answer.

"Good," she remarked. "You are *my* student."

"That's right."

"I have nothing against Marie. She is a nice person. Do you know that she has a young son?"

"No, I didn't know that she was a mother."

"Carlos likes her better because she has been with him longer. Carlos gets me so angry sometimes," said Olga.

The drama of the week was only the beginning. I had no idea what was about to happen, but I was reminded once again that change is a part of life and can hit with a thud at any time.

On Wednesday night, I went to the dance studio to take my next lesson with Marie. Olga was not working and this would be the first time dancing in the studio without Olga's presence since I first danced with her. I was trying to keep an "open mind" about dancing with Marie.

What I didn't expect was for Jerry to be so involved in this lesson with Marie. He watched us like a hawk, which I found to be disturbing. Marie and I continued to dance. As the lesson went on, Jerry interjected his opinions. This was the start of real trouble for me.

"I think you should dance together with more sensuality," said Jerry. "Marie, when you turn, lean your body into his body."

She did what Jerry told her and she rubbed up against me. This seemed to encourage Jerry to continue advising us on dancing.

"Now I want you, Martin, to bend your knees and get down and then spring up like a savage in the jungle."

"No, I can't do that," I said.

Refusing to accept my reluctance, he insisted, "Try it! Try it!"

I gave in and tried it. Even though I felt awkward doing it, Jerry complimented me on my effort. He put music on the stereo and instructed Marie and me to practice these new moves. The music was like jungle music with a primal beat.

He was clapping his hands and yelling, "Sensual dancing."

In the middle of the song, he jumped forward and told Marie to grind against me. Caught up in the music and obeying Jerry, she slightly bent over and started to grind her body against my waist, erotically. It looked as if she and I were about to have sex. Jerry was smiling broadly like a devil.

Completely outraged, I was thinking, "This woman is someone's mother."

Within seconds, I stopped dancing and walked off the dance floor in protest.

With a feigned air of innocence, Jerry asked, "What's wrong?"

"I am not going to dance those jungle moves. I am not comfortable with them," I said.

In response, Jerry mocked me. "Why? Are you religious? Is this against your religion?" He laughed like a man in the gutter. "Maybe you'll get lucky, Martin."

That was it. I was fed up with Jerry.

Then, as she stared at Jerry with a bemused look on her face, Marie made a comment that enraged me even more, "Maybe Martin will give me a gift, too."

I wondered if she knew about my gift to Olga. Was I part of the gossip of the studio? The possibility irritated me greatly. I decided that I would not take another lesson with Marie, but I didn't tell her. I just walked out of the dance studio. I could still hear Jerry's laughter ringing in my ears. And the pounding of what Jerry called the "jungle music" continued to haunt me.

Was there no respect for me? Was there no respect for Marie? Did Marie have any self-respect? Was there any respect for motherhood? Why was Marie open to trying to entice me? It was evident that Jerry was trying to test my limits. He was toying with me. I had not mentioned anything about my Christian faith to him, but he had brought up "religion" in a mocking way. He was either a perverted, "dirty" old man, or a calculating puppet master who got a thrill from stirring up people's passions. I didn't want to be part of an erotic dance ritual with a married woman for Jerry's sick enjoyment. I had to take a moral stand without compromise. Immoral society was not going to dominate me.

I was done with Jerry and the dance studio. What I soon found out was that so was Olga.

Chapter Ten

CONTROL TO PLAN

I quit my job at the dance studio," Olga informed me on the telephone. "I am sick of Jerry and Carlos. They took students away from me. I don't like the way they work. They are greedy men who act jerky to me. Do you blame me for quitting?"

"No, it sounds like you have had a bad experience with them," I replied, trying to assuage her. "Your decision comes at a great time because I have decided to leave the studio."

"Because of me?"

"It's true that I don't like the way they have treated you, but another reason is that I really didn't like the way Jerry treated me at my last lesson with Marie."

"What did he do?"

"He put jungle music on and wanted me to dance like a savage. It was ridiculous. I wouldn't do it. I think he was trying to embarrass me."

"Jerry treats everyone badly, except for the people with power he wants to impress. Carlos pays him a lot of money to manage the studio. I don't think he's worth it," she said.

"He plays mind games."

After a brief silence on the line, Olga said, "By stopping lessons at the studio, you lose the money you have already paid for lessons. Does that bother you?"

"Not that much, you know," I replied.

"Do you have time to meet me today?"

"Where?"

"I can come to your area. I want to give you a CD I made for you," she said sweetly.

"You made a CD for me?"

"Yes. I was going to give it to you at our next lesson. I want to tell you about my new plan."

"Okay."

We agreed to meet in an hour near the dance studio. We were risking the chance of being seen by Jerry or Carlos, but we didn't mind living dangerously. Olga and I were so angry at Jerry and Carlos – though for different reasons – that we would have jumped down their throats. Carlos was a good businessman, but, according to Olga, he didn't practice hard at dancing. Jerry was the consummate salesman and one of the most untrustworthy people I may have ever met.

Thinking that this might be the last time I ever see Olga in person, I stopped off at a bookstore on the way to the meeting spot. Since Olga was from Russia, I bought a book by Pushkin, a well-known Russian novelist from long ago. I wanted to give a "goodbye" gift to Olga. Knowing she liked New York, I figured that she would go off to New York and to a new college. I appreciated our time together and it was time to say goodbye.

As soon as I saw Olga a short time later, the first words out of my mouth were: "What are you going to do now?"

"I am already arranging to get a job at another studio, a better studio," she replied.

"Really? In New York?"

"No, here in town. The owner is a judge with many years experience teaching ballroom dancing. He is a much better teacher than Jerry."

"How do you know?"

"I met him earlier today and his reputation is greater than Jerry's."

"What's the guy's name?"

"Bill."

"How did you find out about him?" I asked.

"Through the Internet," she replied. "He wants to hire me. He has promised to give me many lessons, which will mean more money for me. He has also promised to teach me. He thinks I have the potential to be a national champion. Three of his former students have gone on to do very well in national competitions. He also has a girl from China teaching at his studio and she was the amateur ballroom dancing champion of China. These are the kind of people I want to associate with." She sounded excited.

"That's good for you."

"Martin, I want you to move on to this studio with me and take lessons from me there."

"How much will it cost?"

"It won't cost as much as Carlos' studio. Carlos charges too much."

"Wonder if I want to cancel my lessons early? Can I get a refund?"

"Yes, Bill handles business differently. He gives refunds."

"That's good. But I'll have to think about it," I said. I didn't want to commit. My bad experience with Jerry made me skittish. I also lost money and wasn't eager to spend more immediately.

Then I remembered that I had the book in my bag.

"I have a gift for you, Olga. It was actually going to be a goodbye gift if this was going to be the last time we see each other," I said somberly.

"Why goodbye?" She sounded concerned.

"I thought that you would be going off to New York and I wouldn't see you again."

"No, silly! I will be going to a local college. I want to stay here."

"Well, now that I might be taking lessons from you at

Bill's studio, this is not quite a goodbye anymore, but I would still like to give you this book by Pushkin."

She said, "I first read Pushkin when I was five years old."

"At five years old? You must have been very smart at a young age."

"I understood it."

"When I was a teenager, I discovered the great writers of Russia – Tolstoy, Dostoyevsky, Chekhov, Pushkin and Solzhenitzyn."

"Oh, yeah, I know all those," she said lightly.

"Have you read their work?"

"A long time ago."

She looked as if she was getting bored with the subject of the conversation, so I changed the subject. I was interested in hearing more about her plans for college.

"So, Olga, you aren't in college now, but you said you plan to get your degree in law. When do you plan to go back?"

"In January, I will start full-time classes again in the criminal justice program," she said proudly.

"Great! Are you looking forward to it?"

She grimaced and replied, "I don't look forward to waking up early in the morning. I am a night person."

"Oh, so am I."

"I also hate the cold of winter, so it will be hard."

"But you will be doing it for a worthy cause. You can't get a good job without a college degree anymore," I remarked.

"I see it as a way to get a career and make money for dancing."

"Dancing is your life, Olga."

"It is what I am best at."

"You are an awesome dancer."

"And I am finally going to teach you the international style, Martin. No more of the stupid, sloppy American style that Jerry said I had to teach you. He didn't know what he was talking about. You will like international-style ballroom dancing much better. It looks better and more elegant."

I said, "I take your word for it."

The rest of our conversation consisted of Olga's plans to get a dance partner and to prove to Carlos and Jerry that they were stupid to treat her so poorly because she will be world champion one day. Her anger was palpable like a volcano oozing lava and ready to explode in a fury.

Two days later, I talked to her on the phone and she was very excited about the prospects at Bill's studio.

"This is a great opportunity for me," she claimed. "I would like you to come and sign up for lessons as soon as possible. Bill will be impressed that I brought my own student to his studio."

"Okay."

"I want to go out this weekend," she said.

"Where do you want to go?"

"I don't know. Somewhere in town."

"Would you like to go out to dinner?"

"Yes, I would," she said quickly.

"Do you want to meet in the same place we did the time we went to the lounge?"

"No, I think you should come to my house and pick me up."

"But, Olga, you live far outside of town. I live in town."

"You are on the outskirts of town."

"But I would be driving away from town and then back to town."

Despite being a Christian, I could be petty and lazy at times.

She said, "I am surprised that you are making an issue of it."

"No, it's just that I have been affected by women's lib. I didn't think a man had to pick up a woman to go out."

"But this is a date and I would like to be picked up," she said.

"I'll need to get directions from you."

"I'll e-mail them to you."

"I'll determine which restaurant to go to," I said. The thought of asking her where to go didn't cross my mind. Since she was from Russia, I assumed I knew the town better than she did. She let me have control of the planning of this date. My identity as "the planner" was already starting to emerge at this early stage in our relationship. Olga didn't challenge my control to plan.

Chapter Eleven

Finding My Way

As promised, Olga e-mailed me her directions to her house. She was recommending that I take one highway after another. This may be an idiosyncrasy of mine, but I preferred quiet "back roads" instead of major highways when the travel time difference is minor. So I pulled out my map book and mapped out an alternative course to her house. Then early in the day, I drove along the route just to make sure I became familiar with it. Unfortunately, I got lost and had to stop at a gas station for help. I finally found Olga's house and it put me at ease about the date.

Knowing where I was going is one of the most important things for me. In this case, it applied to my travel in a car. But, now that I think about it, I like to know where I am going in every facet of my life. The question has always been: am I in control or is God leading me to where I am going?

Later in the day, on my way to Olga's house, I was thinking about God. What did He think of my dating Olga? What was His plan for me in this circumstance? What good could He bring out of it? Was God interested in healing my emotional wounds from past rejection and broken relationships?

Beyond just "believing" in God as the big Grand Pooba in the sky, I trusted in God because I believed that He is personal and interested in me. This was a radical way of thinking among my peers. I could have even been labeled as a "rebel" for my Christian faith. But I knew I would be a rebel with a cause.

Before I arrived at Olga's house, I prayed for God to give me a sense of inner peace. My nerves were somewhat acting up, but I wanted Olga to see the peace of Christ in me. I didn't want to have to preach about any religious jargon. I wanted my life to be a living testimony to the power and love of God. In truth, it all depended on God.

After I parked my car, I took a deep breath and walked up to her front door. She lived in a duplex condo, as part of a large complex. When I saw flowers in her yard, the thought of "maybe I should have brought flowers" crossed my mind, but it was too late. Next time, I told myself. I was getting optimistic that there would be a next time.

After I rang the doorbell, Olga's mother opened the door, introduced herself and said, "Olga is not ready."

"That's okay," I replied, understanding that she needed extra time. I wanted to show Olga's mother that I was patient.

"Would you like a drink?" she asked.

"Yes, do you have iced tea?"

"Yes."

Then she left the room to get me the drink. Meanwhile, I looked in the large mirror in the hallway and tried to flatten a part of my hair that was sticking up like an antenna. Then Olga's dog came down the stairs. I patted his head and said, "Nice dog! Nice dog!"

Olga's mother returned with the drink of iced tea and told me about the dog's troubles. The dog was having health problems and the family was very concerned. She said that he had gained excessive weight. Although she spoke with a thick Russian accent, I understood what she was saying about the dog.

Moments later, Olga came down the stairs, as if she was floating. She looked beautiful. She was wearing a black outfit. Her hair was perfectly styled. She had blue eye shadow along the lid of her eyes.

"Sorry that I kept you waiting," she said sweetly. "I had to put my make-up on. Something you don't have to do, Martin."

I smiled and said, "You look great."

"Thank you."

"Are you ready to go?" I asked.

"I see that you have met my beautiful dog."

"Yeah, I hope he likes me. He wasn't barking at me. That is a good sign."

"He's a good boy," she said, as she bent down and kissed him on his nose.

"Did you get him here or in Russia?"

"He came with us from Russia. I got him when he was a few weeks old. A neighbor said that I could pick a puppy from the group of many puppies. I saw a puppy that looked more gentle than the others." Then she patted her dog gently.

"How did you get him to the United States? Did he have to stay in a cage under the plane?"

"No," she replied. "He sat on the seat next to me on the plane."

"Really? Did anyone on the plane mind?"

"He was perfectly well-behaved. Not a peep out of him the whole time."

"He didn't have to go to the bathroom?"

"If he had went to the bathroom on the plane alone, then there might have been trouble. We made sure not to give him water before the trip. There was no accident. If there was, I would have been the one to clean it up."

"Good thing there was no accident."

"If the airline hadn't allowed him to come with me, I don't think I would have come to the U.S."

"How did you get permission to let him sit on the seat next to you?"

"We explained that he was sick, which he was, and he couldn't be alone under the plane for many hours," she said.

"It makes sense."

I said goodbye to her mother and escorted Olga out the front door.

"You really look beautiful," I remarked. She only smiled and held her head up high. I didn't mind making her feel good about herself. I believed that a man should make a woman feel good about herself.

Proud to welcome her into my car, I said to her, "Welcome to my sports car."

"This is a sports car?" she muttered incredulously.

"Yes," I said.

"It doesn't look like a sports car to me."

Surprised, I insisted again, "It is a sports car."

"I'm kidding," she finally had to say.

"Oh. You got me going there."

"I know," she replied with a tone of satisfaction.

As I drove off, Olga started to talk to me about the condo complex where she lived. To me, it was a nice-looking place, but she had problems with the people who lived in the complex, as well as with the stringent rules.

"The policies of this condo association are ridiculous," she began. "One of the boys down the street was told that he couldn't use his Walkman radio because it was too loud."

"Was he wearing headphones?"

"Yes, but they said it was still too loud. An old woman complained when he walked by her yard. Also, they don't allow us to keep our garage door open. Stupid rules!"

"Why did you move here?"

"The place accepted pets. We wanted to move to another condo down the street, but they didn't allow pets. Besides, my parents only had two weeks to find a place and the price for this condo was low enough for them to afford."

"Only two weeks to find a place to live?"

"Yeah."

I assumed that Olga and her family arrived in the U.S. and had to seek a place to live right away. Being a U.S. citizen, I was not able to identify with the stresses of emigrating from Russia to America. But I was looking forward to learning about what it was like for Olga. I secretly hoped that she was as analytical as I was.

She asked me, "The good thing about the condo is that we have a pool, which I like. Also, access to public transportation is good. The commuter rail is not far from here."

"How long does it take to get into town?"

"Less than a half hour."

"How are your neighbors in the condo complex?"

"Terrible!" she replied. "They annoy me so much. I wish they would move away. They make noise until three o'clock in the morning. I can't sleep. They talk so loud and they argue. Their dog is always barking and they think of nobody but themselves. Do you know what I do?"

"No, what?"

"To get back at them, I put my stereo against the screen in the window and I play loud music back at them. If they want to irritate me, then I will irritate them."

"How do they react?"

"They go inside and shut up. They hate me, but I don't care," she said with a grin.

When I arrived in town, I parked in a parking lot next to an upscale hotel. It was a convenient location for where we were going. To Olga's delight, we were going to a restaurant on the most prestigious, most well-known, most expensive street in the city. I had waited a long time to walk down this prestigious street with a beautiful woman by my side. It finally came true and I was enjoying every second of it.

The "beautiful people" were around us. When we went into the restaurant, there were more beautiful people. The women wore high-fashion clothes. Having Olga by my side made me feel confident to be side-by-side with beautiful women. I wasn't intimidated anymore because I wasn't looking to meet a woman to date. All the typical pressure was off me. I was relaxed.

All of this may sound vain, but I looked at it rather naively. All it was to me was the fulfillment of a daydream that had been burned into my imagination. I also wanted to make a statement to the world that I could interact with the beautiful people of this world. As a person who was tremendously ugly with pimples in high school, I felt that I had finally arrived at a place of social success.

In the back of my mind, I was in conflict with what the Bible instructed for me. I was starting to love the world. I didn't want to think about how the world and its passions would pass away. I was tempted to love the things in the world. It seemed that I was being accepted and it drew my attention away from doing the will of God.

Even though I was not doing anything "bad" or blatantly sinful from an external perspective, I was succumbing to the weaknesses of human nature – pride, selfishness and self-life. Nobody knew about it, except for God, who let me continue in my way of doing what I wanted to do. I prayed to God when it was to my benefit for a successful date and – as far as I knew, God was answering my prayer – but I was becoming vulnerable, as if I was removing the armor of God in order to join the world's ongoing party with its enticements.

The date with Olga was a success. I tried my best to act like a gentleman to her, conveying my sincerity to her. I opened the door when we entered. Later, with each of us holding a glass of wine, I made a toast to her success as a dancer. I complimented her throughout the evening. And I paid the bill, which was high, but it was worth it.

After I drove her home, the image of her dog sitting on the seat next to her on the airplane lingered in my mind. I thought about what it would be like to be an eighteen year-old girl who didn't speak English and was coming to America. Her dog must have provided her with much security and comfort, I told myself. The sweetness of Olga stayed in my mind like a gentle haze.

Even though she wasn't a Christian, I was growing fond of her. I said to myself, "Olga is a nice girl and she doesn't want to sin to hurt me. I can have a great relationship with her." I was idealistic and I expected life to be fair. Since I had experienced so much failure with women in the past, I believed that my relationship with Olga would "make up" for lost time. Enticed by passion, I had lost sight of God's perspective, even though I still leaned on prayer as a crutch. My Christianity was shallow at this time. I underestimated people's love for sin. And I underestimated by own vulnerability to sins that society sees as acceptable.

Someday I would have to face a crucial decision for morality or immorality. God was willing to prepare me, but I was stubborn. What mistakes would I make? The difficult thing was that the "mistakes" didn't look like mistakes when I was committing them. By His grace, God would have to rescue me more than I would have anticipated. At this point in my relationship with Olga, I was not sensitive to what God wanted to communicate to me. He was making impressions on my spirit, but I was ignoring them. All I would focus on was having what I would consider a "successful" relationship with Olga. I would have to pay a price for this success.

While God was trying to rescue me, I was setting myself up to pay a big price later. This reality crept up on me very slowly.

Chapter Twelve

Getting to Know Each Other Better

Olga was excited about introducing me to Bill's studio. She felt that she had the freedom to teach me the way she wanted to teach me, not the way Jerry wanted to teach at the previous studio. Olga had won the "control battle" with Jerry by leaving Jerry's studio. In addition, Bill filled up Olga's mind with promises of making her into a "star" in the ballroom dancing world. The thought crossed my mind that Bill might be doing a "snow job" on Olga, but I hadn't met Bill yet, so I didn't want to pre-judge him.

Since Olga asked me to arrive at 7:30 p.m. for my first lesson, I arrived fifteen minutes early. I wanted to make sure that I find the place, which was on a main street. Bill's studio was on the third floor of an old building and next to a construction site. As I opened the front door, I saw a steep set of stairs and there was a sign for Bill's studio at the top.

"This climb must be to warm up the dancers' legs," I muttered, as I walked up the stairs. I could hear music seeping through the wall.

When I opened the door, I was struck by how primitive the dance studio looked. Unlike the fine wooden floor of the previous studio, the floor was cement. The mirrors were leaning against the walls, rather than hanging on the walls.

The lighting was uneven. Two old chairs were in the corner. Not exactly the ideal ballroom dancing studio!

Looking through the small crowd of people, I saw Olga, who was dancing with a student. She was hastily pointing to the floor. Even though I was in a new environment, I felt a connection to Olga, helping me to feel comfortable.

When she finished her lesson and saw me, she darted across the room to me with excitement. She seemed genuinely glad to see me.

"Hi, Martin."

"Hi, Olga. How are you?"

"Very good. I just had a great lesson."

I looked up to see the student who was waving goodbye to Olga. For a second, I wondered whether he liked Olga. Could he be competition for me? Then the thought faded away.

"What do you think of this studio?" she asked me.

I wanted to choose my words carefully, so I said, "It's different than the other studio we had been dancing in."

"Bill says that he will be doing major renovations here very soon."

"That's good. Someone needs to hang the mirrors on the walls before they fall over," I remarked.

"I'll get a drink of water and then we'll start our lesson."

When she walked away, I looked at her and I realized that she was becoming increasingly beautiful to me. I had such good feelings for her and it had been a long time since I had felt this way about a woman because women had simply ignored me for the longest time. I knew I wasn't the best-looking guy in town, but the women treated me like I was the worst-looking. Yet, Olga treated me like I was decent. I appreciated her openness with me and I wanted to pay her back by being generous, affectionate and positive, as well as a good listener.

When she returned to the spot in front of me, she said, "You know, I like being here because I now have control. I can teach what I want. Bill doesn't interfere."

Olga loved control.

"Where is Bill? I'd like to meet him," I said.

"Oh, he's not here. He teaches ballroom dancing at a local college two nights a week."

"Business must be good for Bill," I said, based on superficial information.

"Many college students come here. He has seven teachers. Many more than what Jerry had."

I saw one of the other teachers – an attractive blond woman. I wondered if she was dating any of her students, the same way Olga was dating me. I wondered if I had met the blond woman before I met Olga. Would she have liked me? It was a private thought that crossed my mind as I followed Olga to the center of the room. Without turning my soul over to the Holy Spirit on a daily basis, the lust-laced thoughts that come natural to men were harbored in my mind. I was not guarding my thought life.

I then focused on Olga.

"I am going to teach you the international style of ballroom dancing," she told me with great anticipation.

From the very first move, it was torture for me. The way I had to straighten my leg and move my body was different than what I had been doing with American-style dancing at the other studio. Feeling incredibly awkward about this new style of dancing, I danced very poorly. Olga tried to be patient with me. She encouraged me. I knew I was doing awfully.

"Look at yourself in the mirror, Martin," she pleaded. "Learn from your mistakes!"

"It's too painful to look at myself dancing this way in the mirror," I replied, half-joking.

"Don't be ridiculous."

Somehow, I made it through the lesson. My legs were aching, but I walked off the dance floor, as opposed to being carried off on a stretcher. What came so easily in dancing to

Olga was an unnatural chore to me. I didn't think my legs and body could twist and turn the way Olga had been demanding that I do in order to comply with the rigorous standards of international-style ballroom dancing.

When she and I reached the secretary's desk, Olga asked me, "What did you think of international-style dancing?"

Desperately not wanting to disappoint her and ruin my opportunity with her on a personal level, I replied freely, "I loved it. You were right. It was much better. Thank you for introducing it to me." I said it slowly so that she wouldn't think I was patronizing her. But I wasn't being totally honest. If I had been totally honest, I would have said that international-style dancing is great *for her* and not for me. I was not sensitive to my "white lies" anymore.

"Would you like to sign up for lessons?"

"Sure," I replied. "If I don't take all the lessons, I can get my money back from Bill, right?"

"Yes, no problem."

Then I went to the secretary and asked to sign up for lessons. I signed up for a package deal worth over $1,000. I was so confident in Olga and I wanted Bill to see that she can bring a legitimate student to the studio for significant money. In a way, I felt like I was contributing to the justification to have Olga teach at Bill's studio. I wanted to help her in any way I could, even without her knowing the true reason or motivation.

After we left the studio, Olga and I walked to what I started to call "Expensive Street." We went to a café and had two cups of latte. Olga told me that she had never had a latte before. Even though it was a small thing, I liked introducing her to a new thing. I was hoping to introduce her to many things in the city, which is where I grew up.

As I was gazing into her eyes dreamily, she said to me, "I think I am closer to getting a partner to dance with at high-level competitions."

I don't know if she realized it, but her bringing up her desire for a male dance partner knocked down my romantic mood. Then I forced myself to be a patient listener, as she repeated about her desire to get a top-notch dancing partner and win a championship. I shifted my emotional gears and listened attentively, sipping my cup of latte. Being focused on Olga was a pleasure to me. Olga was sweet in her innocent dreaming, I thought.

I didn't know what her future held with a dance partner. I didn't know what my future held in a relationship with her. How would we become more than friends? Would she accept my Christian identity and faith? These questions crossed my mind, but they were too deep to bring up anytime soon with her. Rarely do people change fast or often, so I had a secret hope that Olga would accept me just the way I was.

Later in the conversation, Olga talked about her mother.

"My mother is my best friend. I trust her about everything. We have a lot of the same tastes. My mother used to be a high-level manager at an accounting company in Russia. She had many people working for her."

"Does she do accounting here in America?"

"No, she became sick and she can't work."

"What's wrong with her?" I asked.

"She gets bad headaches and becomes sick."

"That's too bad. I'll say a prayer for her when I get home tonight."

"Thank you," replied Olga, apparently accepting that I was going to say a prayer for her mother's health.

I said, "My mother works as a receptionist. She works hard. And she raised us children."

"How many brothers and sisters do you have?"

"A brother and two sisters."

"All younger?"

"Yes," I confirmed.

"Even if I didn't know, I would say that you act like a big

brother. You have the seriousness of a big brother."

"Maybe. I don't know."

"Believe me. You do," she said, making me laugh.

"What does your father do?" I asked, unaware that this would change Olga's mood.

"Not much," she replied sourly. "I don't understand my father. He is weird."

The difference in the way she talked about her father and her mother was like night and day. She didn't like her father, but she wouldn't elaborate on the reason why. I didn't pry any further about her relationship with her father.

But I said, "My father has his own ways, too. He has not always been popular in my family."

As I was telling her about my father, I realized that Olga was like my father in the sense that they committed their lives to an artistic endeavor – music for my father, dancing for Olga. Having lived through the struggles with my father in his career, I had a sense of the struggles that Olga would face someday. In a way, because I had gone through the struggles in my family over the effects of an artistic career that does not make money, I felt like I could help Olga and give her wisdom before she made mistakes. Not just any guy could give Olga the insight to live successfully in a tough career, I thought.

Because it was almost midnight by the time we left the café, I said goodbye to Olga and then rushed home to go to sleep. I had to wake up early for a meeting at work.

I walked into my bedroom and I bent down on one knee by the side of my bed and prayed, "Lord, I appreciate Your allowing me to have this special time with Olga. I like her. I ask that You shine Your light through me and give me the wisdom to make the right decisions that glorify You. My love life belongs to you, God. You know far better than I do. In Jesus name. Amen."

I was giving my love life to God, but I was keeping my

fantasy life to myself. This was a conflict.

I changed my clothes and slipped under the cover in bed. After reading a couple of verses of Scripture in the Bible for daily spiritual nourishment like food for the spirit, I shut off the light. Images from earlier in the evening were shooting across my mind like shooting stars.

Five minuets later, I realized that I had forgot to pray for the healing of Olga's mother. Wanting to do it, I prayed, "Lord God, I ask You to heal Olga's mother of her physical affliction, whatever it is. Touch her life with Your healing touch. Just as You took the stripes before going to the cross, the healing comes through the blood. Amen."

Happy, I went to sleep. Olga was an angel in my dreams. She was perfect. I was falling for her. My life was changing beyond anything I could control.

Chapter Thirteen

LOVE'S IMPACT

Love grew in my soul. I knew that it was love because it had a gentle, healing touch, meeting my need for a positive feeling that goes above any mundane circumstances. Love was touching everything in my soul, inspiring me and challenging me. Yet, it was more than just a feeling. This love was like infinity, boundless and all-encompassing. Deep inside was a sense of peace.

I was not in control of this love. That much I was certain. Unlike a man who schemes to get a girl in bed, I could not turn on and turn off this powerful love that was embracing my soul. At first, I was scared of this inner experience, as I paced back and forth in my bedroom, thinking about all the ramifications. But, slowly, I began to open myself up to the possibilities of love. Then a desire to share my heart with a woman started to grow. Like Jesus who gave His life to save humankind, I wanted to give myself completely to Olga, holding nothing back and having her know the "real me."

Filled with thoughts of Olga, my mind swept across my recent memories. The past failures seemed long gone like storms of decades ago. All I had was love and it made me want to give to another person. Selfishness seemed to disappear from me. True love was cleaning me out from the inside. The dirtiness of selfishness, odious and hindering, was disappearing, as if washed in the blood of love and peace.

Enthralled by this new uplifting state of being in love, I craved to learn more about love. Wanting to hear from the author of love, I turned to the Bible and wanted the sweet taste of God's Word to quench the need in my soul for the right words to validate the love expanding in me like a kite. I turned to 1 Corinthians 13 and read the following:

> Love is patient and kind. Love is not jealous or boastful or proud or rude. Love does not demand its own way. Love is not irritable, and it keeps no record of when it has been wronged. It is never glad about injustice but rejoices whenever the truth wins out. Love never gives up, never loses faith, is always hopeful, and endures through every circumstance. (New Living)

What a wonderful conception and description of love, I thought. Staring out the window at the bright image of the moon slipping into a gray cloud as if the cloud were drinking it up, I meditated on the Bible's description. With enthusiasm, I wanted the patience and the kindness, as well as the endurance, hope and selflessness of this true love. I wanted it more than life itself, as silly as that may sound to some people.

What is life without conceiving a better way of living, thinking and acting? Am I destined to the drudgery of the world's way of treating love like it is a fast-food composite easily disposed of when the enjoyment is over? At the time, I knew that cynics would doubt that this powerful love could even exist in a world of such selfishness and pride.

But this was a challenge for me and an opportunity to put my trust in God. I may not have been able to conjure up the glorious love described in the Bible, but I believed that God could do a special, personal work in me to bless me. There is no point for the Bible to inform us that all things are possible with God if it isn't true, I thought. My faith was soaring. Love did that to me.

Renewed by love, I could understand better how God viewed people. Just as I was so willing to give myself and give gifts to Olga, God's statements in the Bible about blessing and giving to His people finally made sense to me. It was a revelation to see something from God's perspective. It was eye-opening, but this was the power of love. I had waited a long time for it.

It's a good thing that God loves a generous giver because I started to give to Olga as much as I could. And I knew from the beginning that I would not ask for anything in return. I would not expect anything in return for me. This started the purity of love that was in my heart for Olga.

I knew that it would take time for Olga and me to get to know each other at a deeper level, but I was in no hurry. Being a Christian who understood and obeyed Jesus' commands as much as I could, I was patient when it came to romance. Sure I was attracted to Olga and I would have probably married her right away and have gone to bed with her to have incredible intimacy with her, if it was what God wanted for me. But I had the sense that I had to be patient and let God unfold His plan.

This was my perspective. Call me idealistic! But I can't deny my sincerity. Reality was my love. Like a rebel against the mediocrity of sexual promiscuity, I was ready to do battle. Spiritually, the battle was already underway. A sharp attack was just around the corner.

In my next date with Olga, I took her to a movie. In the parking lot, I surprised her by pulling a glass swan out of my pocket and giving it to her.

"Olga, a swan is a very graceful creature and you are graceful, especially when you dance. When I saw this little swan, I thought of you and I want to give it to you."

Taking the swan carefully into her hands, she smiled, looked at me and said, "This is nice. I can't believe it. I wasn't sure how you felt about me."

"You are special to me, Olga."

She blushed and replied, "You haven't known me that long."

"I think you are great."

She joked, "If you talk to my mother, she would disagree with you."

"Why do you say that?"

"My mother and I had a big argument today."

"What was it about?"

"Nothing," she replied. "Nothing important. Then an hour later, we were joking with each other. That's the kind of relationship I have with my mother."

"Does your mother joke a lot?"

"More than me."

Then she and I went into the movie theater. I was pleased at how smoothly my giving the glass swan to Olga went. Being generous was very rewarding to me. What a great feeling I had to give something to someone else! I liked to surprise Olga with a nice gift. I was already planning my next gift to her, but I didn't say a word to her about it.

However, even though I was reveling in this good feeling about giving to Olga, a thought crossed my mind like a fire-tipped dart shooting across me.

Deep in my mind, the thought was: "Olga may like you now, but she'll reject you just like all the other girls and Olga will sleep with another man, no matter how much you love her."

The thought shook me. Hiding my feeling from Olga, I became angry that such a negative thought would penetrate my mind and try to disturb me with its foolishness. This thought was against the patience, kindness and selflessness of true love. But the spiritual battle didn't end.

I saw a physically attractive blond woman strut by me. She was wearing a short skirt and tight blouse. She had shapely legs and long hair that rested on her breasts. The next thought that slammed me was: "Wouldn't you like to sleep with her, Martin?" I sighed, but I hoped that Olga didn't notice.

She was saying to me, "I don't know if I want to get popcorn with butter or without butter."

While she was debating the popcorn to herself, I was experiencing an unsettling conflict in my soul. Lust reared its ugly head and I saw it as nothing but harm to my true love. It was as if it wanted to attack my ideal with vengeance, trying to sully my thought life and feelings. It was trying to appeal to my natural, sinful nature. I was aware of my weakness.

Without the Lord Jesus, my lust for a woman would have probably run wild and led me to self-destruction. I didn't want to destroy myself with sex. Sexual promiscuity seemed like a counterfeit form of love to me.

Instead, I wanted to get married someday and enjoy sex within the bounds of holy matrimony. I wanted to be so in love with my wife that I would be shouting, "Our sex together is a great blessing." I wanted to do it God's way. Truly, I was at peace with the statement in the Bible: "Love does not demand its own way." That is how I knew I could recognize true love. It would not "demand" its own way. This was a treasure of wisdom to me.

While sitting next to Olga inside the theater, I didn't really watch the movie. I was busy thinking about God, sex, marriage, lust, beautiful women and myself. Did I want to obey Jesus? Did I want what my natural desires wanted? There was a conflict – a true, dog-down spiritual conflict in the battlefield of my mind.

The good thing was that I had an option. I didn't have to pursue my natural desire and try to get another woman in bed. With God's help, I could be the man that God wanted me to be. When this thought gripped my mind, my confidence bounced back and I gave Olga the biggest hug in the parking lot. We didn't talk much during this date, but I think my gift and my hug made an impression on her.

A kind act could say more than a whole lot of words. Nonverbal communication had an impact. Being a quiet person, I wanted my words to be meaningful. In fact, I desired for this pure love to be without any pretension or self-serving tainting. I didn't feel good enough to speak the words of love, but, when I went home, I prayed to ask the Lord to give me the words worthy of loving a woman and forgive me when I don't live up to the measure and hope of true love.

Chapter Fourteen

Bottled Up Feelings

On a Saturday night, Olga brought me to a dance party at Bill's studio and she was looking to meet a man she wanted. That may sound strange to other people, but Olga was obsessed with finding a male dance partner who could dance at her level of ballroom dancing. Should it have sparked off jealousy in me? Would it have in other people who might have said, "I don't want my girlfriend to spend so much time touching another man"?

The temptation of not only jealousy, but also insecurity crossed my mind, but I responded to them with my faith. I believed that Olga could separate out the personal relationship with me and the professional partnership with a male dancer to meet Olga's ultimate goal of being a world champion.

As Olga left me to say hello to other dancers, I stood in the corner like a statue and watched everyone. The one thing that I noticed fairly easily at the dance party was that everyone was trying to outdo or upstage each other. The men and women were dressed up in fancy clothes. There were tall men and short men, extremely, thin-looking women and healthy full-bodied women. Despite the appearances, the pride among the people in the room was as thick as a blinding fog.

Olga rushed up to me excitedly and said, "Bill told me a minute ago that he wants to introduce me to a dance partner from New York. He is supposed to be coming soon." She was extremely enthusiastic.

Not wanting to disappoint or confuse her, I said with a smile, "That's great."

"I also want you to meet Ana and Paul. Well, that isn't their real names. They are from China and they adopted American names. They were the amateur ballroom champions of China last year. They don't speak much English, but I want you to say hello to them. Paul loves Ana and gives her everything, but Ana told me that she is not sure if she loves Paul. She dates other men behind his back," said Olga.

I felt that the last thing Olga told me was more information than I needed to know, but I followed her obediently and met Ana and Paul. They shook my hand, nodded and then walked away.

Olga informed me, "They have to go get ready to dance. They are doing a showcase in front of everyone here."

"Really?"

"But they aren't getting paid for it. They are doing it for free as a favor to Bill. If I was doing a showcase with a partner, I would demand to be paid," said Olga.

"That's only fair," I commented, not knowing what else to say.

Then Olga and I drifted away from each other again. I went to the table of food and picked up some snacks. When I turned around, I saw that Olga was talking to a short man who looked like a younger version of the famous singer Phil Collins. Olga was pointing at me and shaking her head. The short guy looked at me like I was a misplaced tree.

When Olga came back to me, I asked her, "What was that all about? I saw you talking to the guy who looks like Phil Collins."

"He thought that you were my dance partner. I told him that you are not."

"Boy, that's a relief," I said with a hint of sarcasm.

Suddenly, the lights went down and then quickly back up. Bill flicked the lights to get people's attention. The crowd became quiet and moved closer to the center of the room.

He announced, "I am very proud to announce that we have two fabulous dance couples to dance for you tonight. The first pair is from China and they were the amateur champions in China. Second, we have Lisa and Lance to dance American style for you. So, without further ado, I want to introduce Ana and Paul."

Since I was standing in the back of everyone, I was the first to see Ana and Paul come out of the back and, with their heads up and their noses in the air, charge into the center of the room. Their attitude made me think that they were more actors than dancers. But, as the music started, they launched into an intense dance routine. The choreography was quite good, I thought. They definitely knew what they were doing. I knew that I would never be able to do some of the dance moves that Paul was doing.

The crowd showed their appreciation to them by erupting in loud applause after they finished. Ana and Paul ran off the dance floor and passed me on their way to the room in the back. Just before they disappeared into the room, I heard Ana say something in a very sharp and intense tone to Paul, who reacted by throwing his head back and smacking his right hand against his forehead. I didn't know what that was all about. Ana had been speaking Chinese.

Then Lisa and Lance sprang out of the room. Lisa was a cute girl in the early twenties. She was extremely thin, almost sickly. She had her brown hair pulled back very tightly and pressed down on her head. She was wearing a professional-looking costume that didn't look cheap.

Whereas Ana and Paul danced the international style of ballroom dancing, Lisa and Lance danced American style. Even though I wasn't talking to Olga much during this party because she was going around the room making contacts with people in the ballroom dancing world, I was interested in observing what was going on. I was impressed with Lisa and Lance's dancing, but they weren't as good as the pair from China.

When Lisa ran off the dance floor at the end of the routine, she ran by me and went straight into the bathroom. I thought for a second that I heard her vomiting. She slammed the door closed. Everyone was clapping and making noise, so I wasn't sure whether I heard correctly. Another girl knocked at the bathroom door and was saying, "Are you all right? Are you okay?"

A few moments later, Olga walked up to me. Her face looked extremely angry. She said to me, "You won't believe what Bill just said to me."

"What?"

"He said that, if I work hard enough, I can dance as well as Lisa someday. I know I can dance much better than Lisa *now*. Bill doesn't know what he is talking about. Bill has irritated me. I am very annoyed."

"I'm sorry to hear that."

"He is a jerk."

"I thought he was a great guy."

"He is not as smart as I thought he was," she said.

"Listen, I think I saw the dancer Lisa go into the bathroom and be sick to her stomach. I think she is really sick. Something is wrong with her."

Olga's body language indicated to me that she didn't want to concern herself with someone else at this time. She was focused on Bill's insult. But she moved away from me and went into the back.

When she returned to me a few minutes later, she said, "Lisa is okay. She says that she always vomits after a performance. It's her nerves. She gets very nervous."

"That's terrible," I said. "What torture!"

"You'd be surprised at how many problems a woman will

put up with when she really wants to dance with all her soul. It's all we live for," said Olga.

I wasn't surprised by her remark. After all, she was the dancing sensation that swept into my life. I didn't agree with a person putting herself into physical harm just to dance, but these girls were young and could bounce back, I thought.

Since Bill started to play music for general dancing, I asked Olga, "Would you like to dance?"

"Okay."

We walked onto the dance floor. Very good dancers were dancing around us. I tried not to be intimidated. Recognizing the song as having a rumba beat, I did the steps that Olga had taught me. Since I was paying most of my attention on my steps, I wasn't paying attention to leading her.

"You're not leading me right," she said, stinging me with her statement.

"I'm trying to remember the steps."

My mind seemed to be going blank. With people on the side watching me and with the music seeming faster than usual, I was getting confounded.

Olga said, "You are not keeping the time right."

"I'm sorry."

Fumbling up my dancing, I looked at the crowd and I saw a woman grimace directly at me and then roll her eyes. Everyone must have seen that I was an inexperienced dancer, surrounded by experienced dancers, I told myself.

When the song ended, I asked Olga for a second chance.

"I'll try better next song. Please don't walk away!" I pleaded.

"It's not you," she said, lowering her head. "Bill's comment to me about my getting as good as Lisa is bothering me."

"Forget about what Bill said."

She replied, "I need to call my mother. I am going to call

her on my cell phone."

She went to her purse and dug out her cell phone. Then she went into the empty bathroom and closed the door. Meanwhile, a softer song was being played.

As I grabbed a cookie off the table, I started to hear Olga shouting in Russian in the bathroom. I knew she was talking to her mother. Unable to understand the Russian language, I didn't know what she was saying, but, given her bad mood, if Bill knew what she was saying, he would have probably thrown her out of the studio. I am sure that she was raking Bill over the coals, figuratively speaking, in her conversation with her mother. She was screaming. This went on for several minutes, and I was hoping that she would end her conversation before the song ended.

Yet, she didn't.

As the song was ending, Olga seemed to be getting louder from the bathroom. Then, just as the song ended on a downbeat, Olga's shouting was heard much more clearly. Several people turned around and looked toward the bathroom. I wanted to crawl under a rug and hide, but there was no rug and I didn't want to abandon Olga, even though she was embarrassing herself.

Concerned about maintaining order, I knocked on the bathroom door. When she opened it, I said, "Your screaming can be heard out here. You may want to quiet down."

Her face was serious. She said, "I'll be out in a minute." Then she closed the door in my face. As a boyfriend, I told myself that I had to be patient and support her in her position.

When she came out a minute later, she said to me, "My mother said that I should go tell Bill to go to hell and walk out on him."

"Are you sure you want to do that?"

"No. I'll get him back another way in the future. I want to meet the partner from New York he promised me. I want to steal as much knowledge from Bill as I can and then I will leave him in the future," she admitted proudly. "I don't owe him anything."

"Is the dancer from New York here yet? I'd like to leave soon."

"I'll go check with Bill."

"Take a breath and calm down before you talk to him."

"I'll be okay," she said.

Somehow, I believed her – not that she would be perfectly okay in a forgiving way, but that she was enough of an actress to make Bill think everything was okay. Olga had a flair for acting. It was becoming part of her mystique, but I underestimated it at the time.

Olga disappeared into the crowd for nearly fifteen minutes. When she didn't return to me, I walked around the studio and I spotted her dancing with a man in the center of the room. I figured that it was good for her to be seen dancing with a man who knew how to dance at a level closer to her level. I knew that she needed her freedom and I wouldn't impose on it. If this was a test of pride, I would say that pride was not getting in the way of my wanting to pursue a relationship with Olga. I wanted to trust her and I think I gave her some of my trust before she was tested for it herself. I was quick to want to believe in her.

A half-hour later, Olga came up to me and said, "Sorry. When I went to talk to Bill, someone asked me to dance and then three other guys asked me to dance. I was so angry that I needed to dance to release my anger."

So I learned that dancing was a way for her to release her anger.

"Was one of the men the guy from New York that Bill promised you?"

"No. Bill has left the party and he didn't introduce me to any dancer from New York. I think he lied to me."

"That's awful. I could have left a half-hour ago if I knew

the guy wasn't going to be here."

"But I had fun dancing," she said, tilting her head to the side.

"Good."

I became angry, but I didn't tell Olga. Yet, when we stepped outside to leave the studio, she said, "You seem tense, Martin. Is anything wrong?"

"No," I said flatly.

"You seem angry."

"I am angry with Bill. He makes a promise to you, but then he doesn't deliver. He upsets you by making a stupid comment to you."

But I didn't tell Olga that I was also somewhat angry with her. I held it inside. Communicating my honest feelings would have probably insulted her, so I didn't say anything else. She had overreacted, I felt, and she wasn't considerate of me when she went off dancing with other men.

However, despite my irritation with Olga, when I arrived home, I sent an e-mail to Olga trying to make her feel better:

> Dear Olga,
>
> Thank you for spending time with me at the dance party. I think that Bill was wrong to say what he said. You are a great dancer and you will show the world how much of a dancing sensation you are. You can use Bill's comment to motivate yourself to prove him wrong. I wasn't totally comfortable being around so many strangers at the party, but I was glad to be with you. You are special, Olga.
>
> Martin

My "hard" feelings toward Olga faded away. I attributed the disappearance of my anger to the presence of love in my soul. Love covered the sins. No debt was held against Olga.

I only wanted to do good for her. And I wanted to prove to her that I truly cared for her. I wanted to find ways to show her my positive feelings for her.

Chapter Fifteen

Trying to Please Her

For the next month I took four ballroom dancing lessons each week with Olga. Desiring to show Olga that I could dedicate myself to ballroom dancing, I pushed myself and tried to do everything she told me. In the lessons, she was in control. Yet, I continued to have problems "leading" the way she wanted me to. Even though she tried to demonstrate it to me, I couldn't understand exactly what she wanted me to do.

In addition, I continued to have trouble keeping my dance steps on the correct beats in a song. Olga was getting slowly frustrated with me, but she would make a joke about it and we'd not talk about it any further. Joking was one of her ways to address a problem.

I liked her sense of humor and I knew that other men would be jealous if they knew how great a sense of humor that my girlfriend had. If a sense of humor is truly an important characteristic in a person to become desirable as a mate, then Olga had a quick sense of humor that always made me laugh. She told me once that I was the only person who laughed at all her jokes. I laughed so much at times that she seemed to think I was faking it, but I wasn't. Genuinely, I enjoyed her sense of humor, but I could never remember any of her jokes or funny lines to tell anyone else.

In preparation for my next date with Olga, I went to a

high-class, expensive "day spa" and purchased a gift certificate for her. Knowing that she liked to get her fingernails professionally done, I planned to give the gift certificate to her for a day of pampering, involving her fingernails. I didn't see anything wrong with a little pampering of my girlfriend. This was part of my generosity. Knowing that life is difficult for everyone, I was pleased to create an opportunity for a relaxing time that a woman would enjoy.

Since our next date was at a restaurant close to Olga's house, she agreed to meet me at the restaurant. Arriving before she did, I watched as she drove her car into the lot, parked and stepped out. She looked great. I was thinking that she had also lost some weight, although she didn't need to lose much at all.

When we walked up to me, I said, "You look beautiful." Then I kissed her on her left cheek.

"You beat me here," she remarked, smirking.

"I wanted to be right on time."

"Unlike me," she joked.

We went inside the restaurant and submitted our name to the waiting list. The front lobby was crowded. A few minutes later, when two people were called and went to their table, Olga and I sat down in the inner lobby, still waiting. I noticed that she was looking around the room like a hawk. She proceeded to whisper comments to me about other people in the lobby.

"The woman over there is not a natural blonde," she whispered. I nodded in recognition of her comment.

Then she said, "The guy over there is too fat to be with such a skinny girlfriend. He should lose some weight."

I didn't respond to her.

Then she whispered to me, "The woman over there doesn't love her boyfriend or husband she is with."

Surprised by her comment, I asked, "How do you know that?"

"She looks bored. I can read people. She doesn't look excited to be with him. They could be at the end of their relationship, if I had to predict."

"Poor guy," I whispered, feeling sorry for a guy whose girlfriend or wife is bored with him. I believed in the possibility of what Olga was saying, even if there was no proof. The need for more proof than just a bored look didn't seem to stop Olga to coming to conclusions.

A minute before our names were called to be seated in the dining room, Olga made a positive comment. "I like the boots on the girl over there," she said.

I looked across the lobby to look at the woman's boots. Then I looked at the rest of her. She was an attractive woman.

Olga elbowed me and said in a low tone, "Do you think she's pretty?"

"She's okay," I replied.

"Just teasing you," said Olga. "I want to make you feel uncomfortable."

"That's not a nice thing to do," I said. "Why do it?"

"Ah, it gives me control," she replied, smiling like the devil.

"I only want to look at you, Olga," I asserted. "You are the beautiful one."

"I am not."

"You are!" I asserted strongly.

"If you say so."

Hearing our names called, Olga and I stood up and went into the dining room to eat. We looked through the menu and ordered our food quickly. Then we had time to talk. I enjoyed these times of focused conversation face to face. Olga started off the in-depth conversation this time.

"I need to ask you for something, Martin. I need to ask you for help."

"Sure. Go ahead."

"The bank won't approve my school loan without a cosigner."

"What about your parents?" I asked.

"They don't make enough money to satisfy the bank's requirements. You don't have to do it if you don't want to, but I need to ask you if you could be the co-signer for my college loan."

Without hesitation, I replied, "Okay."

"Really?"

"Yes. I have actually been trying to think of a major way to help you and this sounds like it is it."

"You are wonderful to help me, Martin."

Her smile was radiant.

"Just let me know what papers I have to sign."

"Thank you," she said, leaning toward me and grasping my hand gently.

"And I have a surprise for you," I said, reaching into my pocket.

Her face filled up with anticipation.

"Here is a gift certificate for you to get your nails done," I said, handing her the envelope.

She looked very surprised and opened the envelope with her mouth hanging open.

"I love it," she said after looking at the certificate. "This is such a surprise."

I smiled with satisfaction. I had scored major points with this gift certificate, I felt. She was beaming. The Bible verse "God loves a generous giver" crossed my mind and I was at peace. God is a generous giver and it was an honor to act like Him, I thought.

"I hope you can enjoy it," I said.

"Don't worry! I will."

Then the waiter delivered the drinks and the salads to our table and we began to eat. Olga thought that her glass of iced tea was too sweet, so she sent it back and asked for bottled water.

Initiating a new conversation with me, Olga asked, "How

is work going, Martin?"

"Good. Busy. Always involving change," I said.

"Tell me more about what you do."

"I am involved in marketing computer equipment. I create messages about products to appeal to customers and I have to package the communication in ways that appeal to the press and to customers."

"Oh, I don't like my computer," she said, drawing the attention back to her. "It is old and slow. My mother got it for me when we first came to this country. What kind of computer do you have?"

"I have a laptop."

"I like laptops. I hope I can afford to buy one someday," she said.

Bang, that was it, I thought. A laptop computer would be my Christmas gift to Olga. I decided it then and there. I wanted to dazzle her with a Christmas gift. A laptop sounded perfect. I had some money saved up and I had no problem spending it on a new computer for Olga. I was more excited about giving her a computer than if I would have been the one receiving the computer.

I kept my intention about the Christmas gift as a secret from Olga. I was a strong believer in "surprises" at Christmas. To me, romance involved a certain element of good surprises and doing something that is beyond expectation.

"I really have to say again, Olga, that you are a beautiful woman," I stated, unable to stop myself.

I enjoyed the dinner and the rest of the time with Olga. I was thinking that we had a special "chemistry" that allowed us to be very comfortable with each other. This must have been the chemistry in a romantic relationship I had been looking for all my life, I thought. My emotions were swirling. She was so attractive to me. When I started to think about sex with her, I started to think about marriage. The question "Could she be *the one*?" popped into my mind, as

I was paying the bill and she was looking into a small mirror to check her make-up across the table from me. I did not want cheap intimacy with Olga. I was willing to go on a long path to achieve a deeply satisfying intimacy, so waiting was like proof of my sincerity.

As we stepped outside the front door, Olga offered to drive me to my car because she was parked closer to the restaurant. I accepted and went into the car.

When she drove me to my car and stopped next to it, I leaned toward her and kissed her cheek. Then I said, "Thank you for a very special time. I love you. I'll talk to you soon."

Then I jumped out of the car before she could say anything and I waved goodbye. She drove off. That was the first time I said "I love you" to her.

Chapter Sixteen

Picturesque Highlights

During the week, I spent time shopping at different computer stores in search of a good laptop computer for Olga. I compared many different models and I decided on a nice-looking laptop with a DVD player built into it. Though it cost more than $1,200, I bought the computer two weeks before Christmas and stored it in my room next to my bed.

When I saw Olga on the next weekend, her hair was much lighter in color.

"How do you like it?"

"It looks great," I said.

"I used your gift certificate at the spa to get my hair highlighted. It is not as light as I wanted it, but it is a good start. I'll get it done more the way I want it next time."

"Did the value of my gift certificate pay for the whole highlighting process?"

"No, it only paid for half," she replied. "I paid for the other half out of my pocket."

"Is it worth it?"

"Yes, they did a professional job."

Then she jumped at me, wrapped her arms around me and squeezed me tightly in a nice hug. "Thank you again for the gift certificate, so I could highlight my hair" she whispered into my ear. "I am happy."

I kissed her on her lips, which were soft and supple. I felt as if she was giving me her lips. She didn't restrain herself. She kissed me with passion. I was feeling wonderful.

After our intense kissing session, we went to the dance studio to practice our dancing. She had the key to Bill's studio. What she didn't know was that I had a camera in my bag with my dancing shoes. When we arrived at the studio, I said, "You look so beautiful, Olga, that I want to take some pictures of you."

"Here in the studio?"

"Yeah, it's private."

She joked, "You're not going to ask me to take my clothes off, are you?"

"No, not at all," I replied quickly. "God hates pornography. I just don't have any pictures of you and I would like to have a few pictures. I want to put a picture of you on my desk at work."

"Okay," she said.

While she went to the bathroom to get ready for the pictures, I moved around the studio, trying to determine good angles for taking pictures. I planned to take a few close-up shots and a few distant, full-body shots of Olga. And I wanted some "action" pictures with her in movement.

She came out and asked, "Where do you want me?"

"By the wall, please."

I started to take her picture with my small camera. She looked like a natural in front of the camera. She looked relaxed. She kept her face serious-looking. I had to ask her to smile in a couple of the pictures.

She stood by the mirror and I took her picture by pointing the camera at the mirror and capturing her reflection as well as the "real" her. I wanted to know the real Olga. Taking her picture was fun, but it still only showed the external.

Continuing to take more pictures of her, I thought about the Song of Solomon in the Bible where King Solomon talked about the passion a man has for his wife. The Bible recognizes the sensuality that God created in all people, I thought. I wanted to have a biblical marriage that would bring the power of passion to the forefront of my life.

I wasn't certain that Olga was the one I should marry or not, but I looked at her with respect and I resisted temptation, even though my passions were being enticed by the soft touch and beauty of a woman. It seemed like all I thought about was the beauty of Olga. I loved the shape of her eyes, her full lips, her shapely figure and the smoothness of her skin.

God had placed a strong desire for a woman in me. I just needed confirmation of what I should do on my path to marry the right woman. Marrying the right woman has been incredibly important to me since I was sixteen years old. While other boys were getting girls pregnant as teenagers, I didn't want to make any mistakes that would ruin my future marriage, which I had accepted as a given. I also liked children and could perceive myself as a father someday.

Olga and I hadn't talked about children at all yet. But, after we finished with the photography, I told her, "I plan to give toys to a charity to help orphan children this Christmas."

"That is very generous of you, Martin," she said, as she changed into her dancing shoes.

"I believe that getting a nice toy can make a positive difference in the life of a child. Being orphans, these kids need something to smile about."

"Don't we all need something to smile about?" she remarked.

"Yes, I agree with you. What makes me smile is –" Then I paused, as I thought deeply about it.

Olga interjected during my pause, "What makes me smile is dancing."

I nodded at her. I was hoping that she would have said that

I was the one who made her smile, but it was clear that I was second to dancing on her list of priorities. She was the dancing sensation after all, I told myself.

For the next two hours, she put me through a difficult practice session. Tired, I thought that my legs were going to fall off. But she took pride in teaching me and seemed to want to accelerate my progress. She wanted me to dance at a higher level, so she pushed me hard.

As we were changing our shoes, she said, "Someday I want to open up my own studio and keep all the money. When I teach lessons through someone else's studio, I only get a part of the money and I am sick of it."

"When will you be ready to open up your own studio?"

"When I win something big in ballroom dancing! Then people will respect me and want to take lessons with me," she replied.

"When you eventually open up your own studio, I know what you can call it."

"What?"

"Dancing Sensation."

She laughed and said, "I like it."

"I have faith that you will be successful and open up your own studio and I can help you because I understand business and know how to do marketing," I said.

"Great. I don't know a lot about marketing, so you can handle the business aspect."

"Deal."

Then we laughed together.

On the way home, I talked to Olga about Christmas, since it was coming up soon. I was eager to set plans for Christmas Eve and Christmas Day.

"I want to introduce you to my parents and my family on Christmas," I told her. "Would you be able to come with me to my grandparents' house on Christmas Day?"

"Okay."

"My parents and the rest of my family congregate at my grandparents' house each Christmas. Your parents can come, too."

"Even though my father is Christian, I identify mostly with my mother's religion, so I am Jewish, but I still like to celebrate Christmas. I like to get gifts," she said, smiling.

"Speaking of gifts, I would like to bring you the Christmas gift from me on Christmas Eve. Would it be okay if I come to your house the night before Christmas Day?"

"Yes, I think my parents would love to have you over for dinner."

"Great," I said. "I look forward to spending our first Christmas together." I kissed her cheek when I stopped my car at a red light. I was feeling romantic. "Christmas is my favorite time of year, Olga. I am like a little kid. It keeps me young."

"I got a Christmas gift for you, Martin. Do you want to know what it is?"

"No, I'd rather wait. I like surprises."

"Okay, but I'll tell you that it is nice."

"I'm sure it is, Olga."

So Christmas plans were set. In love and primed for Christmas giving and receiving, I was happy. I popped a Christmas music CD into my CD player and sang "Chestnuts Roasting on an Open Fire" so freely that Olga laughed at me with great hilarity. But I didn't mind. I was in a festive mood. When I dropped her off at home, I was singing, "Hark the Herald Angels Sing." I shouted out, "Glory to the new born king."

Then I left to go home. Five minutes later, I was attacked in my mind by thoughts of sexual relations with other women and a temptation to spurn Olga. I was appalled, but every man struggles with lust at some point. These thoughts hit me like a ton of bricks, but I prayed for the Lord God to strengthen me and help me to stand still in faith, waiting on

God to deliver me from the claws of temptation. As promised in the Bible, God makes a way of escape for the believer.

Chapter Seventeen

Christmas Eve

Christmas is always a special time to me, but my first Christmas with Olga was particularly special. I called it "the Christmas of young love." During the prior month leading up to Christmas, my heart had opened up to the touch of love like never before. I opened up myself to trust Olga. I didn't want to hold anything good back. It felt as if love was carrying me on wings, not so much because Olga was doing anything special, but the love of Christ poured into my heart in a deeply spiritual, personal sense and it changed my outlook.

On the day before Christmas, I sent an e-mail to Olga, expressing my feelings:

> Dear Olga,
>
> Thank you for being wonderful to me! You give me your acceptance as a special person. You accept me for who I am and I appreciate it very much. I care about you.
>
> Martin

On Christmas Eve, like Santa Claus with his sleigh, I loaded up my car with the big gift and a supply of small gifts in a shiny red bag. Then I drove to Olga's house. I had Christmas music playing in the car. I was singing along, loosely and freely. I arrived without needing Rudolph the Red-nosed Reindeer to lead me. We did not have a white Christmas. Actually, it was warmer than usual.

I was looking forward to spending Christmas with Olga. I brought a carton of eggnog to drink. But since Olga didn't have a fireplace, I didn't bring any chestnuts to roast over an open fire.

When Olga opened the door for me, I couldn't hold back my happy feelings.

"Merry Christmas!" I shouted with my arms full of gifts.

Olga's eyes became very wide when she saw the big box I was carrying with one arm. The moment for me to give her my big gift finally arrived. Giving a gift to a woman is something I cherished. I felt like I was being Jesus Christ-like because He was such a generous giver. Elevating my giving to a sense of heavenly nobility showed me where my heart was. I had "no strings attached" to the gift. I had a pure motive.

"What's that?" she asked. "Oh, let me help you!"

She took the big box from me and placed it on the floor. She was smiling. Her parents came out of the kitchen to greet me. I gave each of them a wrapped gift. They were surprised and told me that I didn't have to give anything to them.

I said, "I want to."

Olga said, "I want to open my gift now. I can't wait. Is it okay if I open it?"

"Sure," I replied, appreciating her enthusiasm.

She tore open the Christmas wrapping paper and saw that the gift was a laptop computer. She was so thrilled that she stood up and hugged me with passionate sincerity. It warmed my heart.

"Thank you! Thank you!" she said.

"Merry Christmas, Olga!"

After many Christmas Eves without a girlfriend, I deeply

appreciated having a girlfriend with whom to share Christmas. Only lonely people can understand what I am saying. After having so many lonely Christmas seasons like I had, the sensitivity about having someone special cannot be taken for granted. Often, people who would be very generous on Christmas and appreciate a "special someone" don't have a significant other, for whatever reason. The loneliness makes the heart long for the warmth of Christmas love and romance.

No one saw it with their eyes, but my heart must have been burning with the brightness of love and appreciation. I was happy about giving the laptop computer to Olga.

Unexpectedly, she gave me a watch with my name engraved on it. It was an expensive-looking watch with gold trim.

"You didn't have to get me such a nice gift," I said to her.

"It's not as nice as the computer, but I had it engraved."

"I see that. Thank you."

Her parents opened their gifts from me. I gave her father a toolkit and a flashlight. I gave her mother something flowery and delicate for her collectibles. I couldn't even tell you what it was, but it looked nice. I tried to customize my gifts to the tastes to the person receiving them.

Also, I had a gift for Olga's dog. When I pulled it out of the bag, Olga laughed. It was a thick rope with a ball on the end of it. The words "Dogs Love Christmas, Too" were embroidered on the rope. Still laughing, Olga gave the toy to her dog. She patted him and kissed him as well.

What a great Christmas!

I had dinner with Olga and her parents. The food, which was Russian, was delicious. I complimented the mother on her cooking several times. There were some awkward moments of silence because her parents didn't speak much English, but I asked them to teach me Russian words. They taught me to say "thank you" and "how are you?" in

Russian. It was not an easy language for me to pick up phonetically.

During dessert, Olga said to me, "I love the computer you gave me."

"I'm glad."

"Now I can go on the Internet from anywhere in the house, as long as I am near a phone jack."

"Right," I remarked. "What are you going to do with your old computer?"

"I am going to put it in my mother's room."

"Are you going to keep the printer in your room?"

"I haven't thought about that yet. Yeah, maybe I will keep the printer in my room. Or, if I keep it in my mother's room, I can take my laptop into her room to print stuff off. This is wonderful."

"And you can play DVDs on the computer. I thought that it was a cool feature to have."

"It is better than anything I thought you would get me."

When her parents left the kitchen, Olga and I kissed each other. It was innocent and sincere. We were overcome by the beautiful feelings of Christmas and I kept thinking that this was a Christmas Eve that I would never forget. God had blessed me so much and God allowed me to open up and show my generosity, which had been hidden in my heart, like an unlocked treasure, for years.

Olga and I spent the rest of the evening watching a movie – a modern adaptation of the classic "A Christmas Carol," by Charles Dickens. As I sat back watching the movie about Scrooge, I was thinking about how a person would have to be without love to be so stingy. To live a life without love of others was sad to me. Scrooge had a cold, hard heart. His stinginess was simply a symptom of his sinful nature. By being broken and recognizing his own need for something greater than himself, he went through a conversion – a spiritual conversion, in a sense. I had recently learned that the author Charles Dickens may have been a born-again Christian.

But the story in the Bible about Jesus was still the greatest story ever told and the only reason to celebrate Christmas. Everything about the birth of Christ Jesus was remarkable, especially as it was fulfillment of prophecies. Born of a virgin, Jesus has not left the humanscape of the world, not even after all these centuries and generations. No one can get rid of Him, even though believers die and leave this earth. The power of Christmas to endure is amazing.

I had a wonderful, peaceful feeling.

As I was leaving Olga's house, I said, "Thank you for sharing Christmas Eve with me. I had a great time."

"Me, too."

We hugged for several minutes. I didn't do anything crass or inappropriate. I saw each moment as an opportunity to prove to Olga over and over again that I was a gentleman. I wanted her to know that I wouldn't take advantage of her and I wouldn't ruin a special time like Christmas with anything crude. My heart was open to her and I appreciated her.

"Merry Christmas!" I uttered for the ump-teenth time, as I strolled out the door.

"Thank you, Santa Claus," she said to me, joking.

But I responded with a serious remark.

"I hope you see me as more real than Santa Claus."

"Of course! Don't be silly!"

"You're the silly one," I said to her, smiling.

"Oh, you!" she said, pretending to pout. Then she broke out laughing.

"I'll see you tomorrow at my grandparents' house. I e-mailed you the directions this morning."

"I know. I got them."

"Can I say Merry Christmas to you one more time before I leave?" I asked.

"Sure."

"Okay. Merry Christmas!"

"I have never seen you so happy, Martin. You are like a little kid."

"The Christmas spirit can do this to me."

"I like it," she said. "You're cute."

"If I could fly like Rudolph the Red-nosed Reindeer, then I would fly into the air right now. She thinks I'm cute." I swung my arms and twirled around.

Olga laughed and covered her mouth with her hand.

Before I left her, I said, "I am going to go look for a star in the sky. Maybe I'll run into the Three Wise Men."

"Good luck."

"Maybe I'll have a better chance of running into the Three Stooges."

"You mean, the Three Scrooges?"

"Ah," I said, breaking out into boisterous laughter. "You're right. There are Scrooges all over the place in this town. I'll probably find more than three without a problem. And you know what?"

"What?"

"Those Scrooges can't have the Christmas gift you gave me. I really like the watch you gave me, Olga. Thanks again."

"See you tomorrow. I love you, Martin."

Then she closed the front door of her house. But her words "I love you" hit me so hard that I thought I was going to fall over. Hearing her say those three magical words struck me as unique and touching. She was responding to me. I had worth, I told myself. I could be a man. I could inspire feelings of love in a woman. This was what I had been waiting for. Love was turning into the air I breathed.

As I strolled to my car, I looked up and admired the star-studded night sky.

"What beautiful multitudes of stars!" I whispered to myself.

The stars seemed to congregate in clusters, as if the stars were getting ready to go to church and praise God for all His awesome powers and control. I was reminded that God knows where each star is, as He created them in what the world refers to as the Big Bang. Science is now proving that the Book of Genesis is more on the mark in the creation story than society wants to admit. God created science, so there is no contradiction just because science shows us how things work. The fact that God created the earth with His spoken word must have created a bang.

But the birth of His Son Jesus to offer salvation for each person to accept or reject as a free gift was a bigger bang to me than any goings-on at the time of creation.

In all my smallness of being, I was filled with an awesome love, not just for Olga, but for God Himself. He had blessed me and I was able to "bless" another person like a son imitating his father. If I was a prince, then I would have to be the most humble prince in the world because, when God opened the floodgates of heaven in me, I was overcome by gratitude for how good God is.

When I arrived home, I needed to express myself in all my freedom of speech and constitutional right. My spirit poured out of me as words onto the paper in a journal, which had beautiful paintings by the "painter of light" Thomas Kincade:

How does Olga really know that I love her? She must know the difference between true love and counterfeit love. True love is unselfish, sensitive, generous, compassionate and faithful. Counterfeit types of "love" are selfish, insecure, impatient, lustful, deceptive and unfaithful.

My love for Olga is genuine. Being in love with her comes naturally to me. My love for her is peaceful. My love is a blessing from God, who is omniscient, omnipotent and omnipresent. God is love and He proved it. I humble myself to the power of love.

The world is polluted by greed and ambition, but love survives. The world is full of men who are fakes, cheaters and liars. But love can change a person's heart. Eternal love touches the soul and opens up new possibilities.

How does Olga know that I am trustworthy? How can Olga be confident that I will remain faithful to my commitment to her? How does Olga know that I think about her all day, every day? Will I be understanding and gentle when we have challenges and problems to face? Will God answer our prayers and bless our relationship with deeper love?

I want Olga to know all about me and I want to know more about Olga's inner beauty that God has put in her soul like a candle eternally shining with a majestic glow. I want to be true to Olga. I need God's grace to be different from the typical men who are fakes, cheaters, smooth-talkers, flirts and liars. Corrupt human nature, with its denials, frivolities, unpredictability, paradoxes and blind spots, is powerful and persuasive. But true love supercedes the base qualities of human nature.

God's love, freely given to me, is the secret ingredient that has transformed me.

I want to give Olga the answers to the questions about me. I want to express myself to her with words from the deepest part of my being. I want to share meaning with Olga.

I stopped writing at this point. But I planned to write more in the journal and eventually to give the journal to Olga as a personal testament of my awakening love, rooted in God's love.

Before I went to bed for a peaceful night's sleep, I opened my Bible and read the story of the birth of Jesus again. God had kept His promise. I knew that I know. I couldn't prove it to anyone and I am not interested in shoving the Truth down anyone's throats. God offers the free gift of salvation to everyone. People need to be open to God's ways and be ready to forsake their own ways.

I prayed that the true meaning of Christmas not be lost on anyone alive today. I was so in love that I even loved humankind and I didn't want to see one person perish or needlessly suffer because they reject God, who is the author of peace on earth and good will to all other people of all races.

"Merry Christmas, God," I said, finishing off my prayer. "Cool story. I can't wait to see how it all comes in the end You have promised."

I smiled peacefully. I believed that God had a sense of humor, too, as well as a sense of adventure.

Chapter Eighteen

Christmas Day

When I woke up on Christmas Day, I pinched myself to make sure that I was really living in a bubble of an emotional high. I didn't want to confuse it with one of my many daydreams through the years. I was putting myself out on a limb to feel exhilarating emotions, though I was risking getting hurt.

Olga and her parents met me at my grandparents' house. Everyone in my family, including my parents, my siblings, my uncles and aunts, were very friendly and welcoming to Olga and her parents. I was pleased that my family was embracing Olga so readily.

Olga brought porcelain angels to my grandmother as a Christmas gift. In a move that surprised me, my grandmother kissed the angels.

"Did you see that, Olga?" I asked. "My grandmother kissed the angels you gave her. I have never seen that before."

Olga smiled and wrapped her arm around me.

"This is like having a big family again, Martin. Most of my family is still back in Russia. I like being here."

"I am glad you came. Did you use the new computer last night?"

"I stayed up until two o'clock in the morning, doing stuff on the laptop," she replied.

"Did you get enough sleep? Are you tired?"

"I slept late. I told my mother not to wake me until eleven-thirty this morning," she explained. "I am a night person. Not a morning person at all! I hate waking up early. I am grouchy in the morning." Then she laughed.

"I am a night person, too."

My mother said to us, "Please sit down and eat."

My mother and my grandmother served enough food to qualify as a feast. Olga's parents seemed to enjoy the food and the conversation. My grandfather was talking to Olga's father about life in Russia.

"Very difficult," I heard Olga's father say to my grandfather.

At the same time, my father was asking Olga about her dancing. My father usually showed interest in a person who had artistic abilities, especially when it related to music.

"Do you do your own choreography?" he asked.

"Yes, I do."

"Do you have your own music?"

"I dance to music that I hear off the radio."

"Have you thought about having music specially recorded for your music?"

I interrupted, "Dad, I don't think Olga wants to talk about it now. It's Christmas."

"I am not saying anything bad, am I?"

"No, but you sound like you are interviewing her for a job," I said.

My father laughed lightly and said to Olga, "Sorry, maybe I was."

Then my sister said to Olga from across the table, "I think I know you."

Olga raised her hand and replied, "You know, you look familiar, too."

It turned out that Olga went to the same college as my sister two years earlier. Then she transferred to another college. My sister and Olga talked for nearly a half-hour about college life and career plans. It was ironic to me that my sister had met Olga almost two years before I did. Was it destiny?

As my father was talking to me about some music he was studying, I caught bits and pieces of the conversation between them.

Olga would say, "I didn't like her."

Then my sister would say, "She flunked out of school."

A few minutes later, I'd catch the phrase, "She is dating a new guy."

Then I'd hear Olga say, "I didn't trust her old boyfriend. He seemed like a jerk."

I classified their conversation as "girl talk" – not something I was particularly interested in. But I was relieved to see Olga relaxed and at home around my family. My mother talked to her, too.

In fact, my mother complimented Olga on her hair and her fingernails. My aunt complimented her outfit. My grandmother complimented her on the smoothness of her skin. My father complimented her on how well she spoke English. My family treated her like a princess.

The treatment continued when my family showered Olga with gifts, which she wasn't expecting. She unwrapped the gifts and handed the wrapping paper to me. I then shoved it into the trash bag. Olga held up each gift, while people in the room said "ooh" and "ah." I felt like I was on a game show on television.

After opening all the gifts, Olga went around the room, kissed each member of my family and said "thank you." I would have never believed that all this was possible. Having been the lonely guy on Christmas for so many Christmas Days, seeing this new reality was special to me. I had never met a woman who had taken such an interest in me and shared a love with me.

Growing up, I had felt like the ugly duckling and I didn't know for certain if a woman would truly love me. Or would

I be loved for the wrong reason? Or would I misunderstand something as love when it wasn't? As a man aware of his imperfections in thinking, I wanted to be sure and my feelings felt sure for Olga. I had a peace about how our relationship was progressing.

Christmas was memorable.

However, after she went home with her parents and I went home to stay in my room, I had a need to pray about what was unfolding in my relationship with Olga. Even though I had a sense of peace, something deep inside me was not right. Something was unsettled. But I couldn't put my finger on it, figuratively speaking. I couldn't understand what was lingering underneath, leaving me to feel like a question persisted at all times.

At first, I didn't understand what the nagging question was. I tried to stay focused on the good times with Olga. I talked to God about it.

"Dear Lord, things are going well with Olga. Thank You. Thank You for a special Christmas. I needed it. My loneliness was ripping me apart before I met Olga. I feel like my life is changing. I don't feel 100 percent comfortable, but this is probably my emotions adapting to a new reality. Please don't ruin it for me!"

I was expressing doubt in God's love without realizing what I was truly saying. How could I say "Please don't ruin it for me" to God? How foolish was I? Did I trust in my own wisdom more than in God's wisdom?

I continued to talk to God, "I love Olga. I want us to have a long-term relationship together. Look at how great I feel. This can't be wrong. Things are going too well with her. I don't want this to end. Please make it last. I pray, in Your holy name. Amen."

Sadly, I was trying to justify my relationship with Olga to God. Doubt lingered in my heart. I wanted to overcome it. Did I have an agenda that would take me farther than God wanted me to go? What would God do? How much freedom would He give me?

I was so sensitive to anything that tried to disturb my inner peace. There was no human explanation for it. My peace was a confidence in God. But could I trust God completely? I wasn't sure if I had ever been tested to the full extent of trusting God. How would my character respond?

Moreover, I didn't understand how people can live in their tumultuous lives and ignore their true needs. Don't people sense their own spiritual needs? Unmet, ignored spiritual needs can put a person in constant turmoil. I had accepted Jesus because I didn't want chaos, turmoil, hatred and greed to rule my life. I had a rational reason to put my faith in God; it's called freedom.

I was concerned mostly about my spiritual life. I didn't know much about Olga's spiritual life – or if she had much of one. But I believed that she was a good person and I was using this as justification to pursue a deeper love with her.

I ignored the warning signals that were crossing my mind. I ignored the Bible verse that says a Christian should not become "yoked" with an unbelieving person. I was not married to Olga, but marriage was up for consideration, indeed.

A distraction was more fun. On the day after Christmas, I focused myself on finding a musical concert to which I could take Olga. I tried to think of a singer that she liked. The singer Marc Anthony came to mind. Olga had danced to some of his songs, I recalled. So, I went on the Internet and discovered that he was performing in New York City at Madison Square Garden on New Year's Eve.

I said to myself, "Wouldn't it be great to do something memorable on New Year's Eve?"

The idea of traveling to New York by train and seeing Marc Anthony at Madison Square Garden was interesting to me. I hoped that Olga would be agreeable to it. First, I had to find out if tickets were available. Amazingly, tickets were still available, yet they were expensive tickets.

"It's time to live it up a little," I convinced myself, charging the tickets on my credit card.

Hoping that Olga would love the idea for New Year's Eve, I planned to tell her on our next date, which was later in the day. We had plans to go to the museum of science to see a 3-D movie.

I was very excited to present the idea of going away to New York for a trip on New Year's Eve. My adrenaline was pumping. I didn't want to stay outside in the freezing cold to watch the ball drop in Time's Square on New Year's Eve, but a musical concert with a singer whose music made the dancing sensation Olga want to dance sounded perfect. Actually, it didn't take much to get her to want to dance. Try breathing!

Chapter Nineteen

Unfolding Plans

I had everything planned out – when I would tell Olga about the trip to New York to see Marc Anthony, what I would do to set up our travel arrangements and where we would stay in New York.

I picked up Olga to go to the museum of science and I made sure that I was playing a Marc Anthony CD when she stepped into my car.

"Hello, Martin," she said to me. Then she kissed me on my cheek.

"Do you recognize this song?" I asked her, pointing at the CD player.

"Yes, of course. It's Marc Anthony."

"That's right."

"Do I get a gold star for answering the question correctly?"

"No, but you get a kiss from me."

I kissed her softly on her lips.

"That's better than a gold star," she said, flattering me.

"Guess who is going to see Marc Anthony!"

Olga took a deep breath and blurted out in a high-pitched voice, "Me?"

"Yeah, and me, too," I said. "I got two tickets for you and me to go see Marc Anthony in concert on New Year's Eve."

"That's awesome. I didn't even know he was coming to town," she said with a quizzical look on her face.

"He isn't," I stated dryly. "We are going to him. We have to go to New York."

"New York?" she screamed. "Great! I'd love to go to New York."

"Good. I'll order two train tickets."

"Where will we stay?"

"I have already made reservations at a hotel in New York."

"You are such a planner, Martin."

"Good plans?"

"Yes, good plans."

She giggled with excitement. If I could say so myself, I hit a homerun with this idea to take her to New York and spend New Year's Eve at a Marc Anthony concert in Madison Square Garden.

As I was driving down the road, Olga said, "Your idea is so romantic, Martin."

Her tone of voice conveyed to me her passion. I learned that, if I wanted to make a good impression on Olga, I had to do something out of the ordinary, as well as spontaneous and romantic, to score major points with her. The computer had pleased her, but this New York trip seemed to be sending her off into orbit of thrilling happiness.

"What am I going to wear to the concert?" she asked rhetorically.

I started to laugh.

"What are you laughing at?" she asked me.

"Just that we aren't leaving for a few days, but you are already concerned about what you will wear to the concert."

"That's a woman for you," she remarked, using her sense of humor.

"I'm learning."

"Not too much I hope."

"Just about you."

"Good?"

"Good," I affirmed for her.

When we arrived at the museum of science, I asked Olga to walk fast because we were slightly late. I hated to be late and I wanted to get inside and buy the tickets. Olga wanted me to slow down my walking pace, but I was tense about being late.

However, when we reached the ticket counter, the person at the window told me that all the tickets had been sold out. I was not only disappointed, but I was also angry. We had come all the way into the big city for nothing. This was ruining my plan and I didn't like it. I became moody and inadvertently stopped talking to Olga.

After a few minutes of my silence and obvious distraction, she asked me, "Are you upset with me?"

"No, not at all."

"I could have been ready earlier."

"It's not your fault, Olga. I haven't been here in a long time and I didn't realize that tickets would sell out so quickly."

"I could have told you that, Martin," she said. "But you didn't give me all the details of what we are doing. You mentioned the museum, but I didn't know you wanted to buy tickets to the 3D show."

"I wanted it to be a surprise," I said, still moody about missing the movie.

"Well, we tried."

"We can come back another time," I said.

"I am not too interested in the movie. It's okay."

Then we returned to my car and I drove us to a suburban area to get something to eat. I had a particular restaurant in mind. Yet, when we arrived, the restaurant was in the process of closing.

"Why are you closing so early?" I asked the man at the door.

"We close early today."

The man closed the door in my face. I was annoyed. My plan for us to eat a late dinner was foiled. This didn't help my bad mood.

Gently putting her hand on my back, Olga said, "It's okay. Maybe we can get a cup of coffee at a café down the street."

"I should have called ahead and found out that this restaurant closes early."

"Martin, you don't have to put so much pressure on yourself," she said. "Relax!"

"It is sometimes difficult for me to relax when things are going wrong."

"But we are going to New York on New Year's Eve. All this other stuff today is nothing. This New Year's Eve could be the best I have ever had in my life."

"I am glad to hear that, Olga. I will do all I can to help make it special for you."

"And I want you to enjoy it, too, Martin," she stressed.

"Being with you will be what's amazing to me!"

She smiled and we walked hand-in-hand to the café down the street. As soon as I started to eat the large chocolate cake at the cake, I told Olga, "I feel better now."

"I don't want to touch the chocolate cake. I want to lose weight."

"I probably should eat healthier, but it's tough to give up chocolate."

"If I am going to become a champion dancer in the United States, I need to become skinnier."

"But you are already skinny," I said.

"Maybe skinny for every-day life, but not for ballroom dancing."

"You want to be in better shape. I can understand that. I have spent a lot of time exercising and working out myself."

"When I get in better shape, I hope to get a dance partner," said Olga. Then her eyes seemed to glaze over, as if she was lost in thought. The mention of a dance partner had a spark to it, indicating to me that she thought about it often. But she was still unaware of the potential effect on me as a love interest. I still wasn't sure how I felt about her partnering with another man to dance, requiring practices for several hours a day. Could it really remain platonic and on a professional level? I listened to what Olga had to say about her dreams to dance with a professional-level dance partner and conquer the world of ballroom dancing.

Then she said, "But I don't care about being famous. I don't need people to recognize me on the street and come up to ask for my autograph."

With a twisted smile, I asked, "But will you give me your autograph when you become a world champion of ballroom dancing?"

"You can have as many autographs as you want."

"Thank you," I said, raising my voice in mock sincerity. "I will get as many autographs I can and then sell them for a profit."

She grimaced and replied, "Than forget it!"

I laughed and nearly fell off my seat.

When we finished our coffee, I said, "Just a few more days 'til we are in New York. Just imagine – Madison Square Garden with thousands of fans. It's going to be incredible."

"I wish I had time to take a dancing lesson with a New York-based teacher while I am there."

I quickly replied, "No, we won't have time."

Reluctantly, she conceded. I took her home and sang my whole way home.

As planned, I purchased the train tickets for the both of us to leave the morning of New Year's Eve. I confirmed the hotel reservation a second time. I tried to think about every detail.

Then I prayed, "Heavenly Father, keep me true to Your Word and Your desires. Help me to abstain from falling into failure. If Olga is the woman I am to marry, then I want us to grow in love before we dive into sexual intimacy. I want a greater romantic relationship with a woman than what most men settle for. Most men just want to get a woman in bed and they don't care about the future. You have called me, Lord God, to a higher calling of integrity and love. True love waits. Help me to be strong! I know temptation will come, but, with You, Lord, I can win all battles. In Jesus name. Amen."

I was already counting down to New Year's Eve in New York in advance. It was another opportunity for a romantic interlude with Olga. I did not want to be a hypocrite. I wanted to go to New York with a clean conscience and honest motives. No matter how decadent and permissive the people around me would be, I had to remember that I had given my life to Jesus because of who He is. If God didn't exist, then I would fall into sin at every turn. My faith was a risk.

Chapter Twenty

Fun Starts in New York

The train ride to New York on the morning of New Year's Eve was almost mystical, as if the train was traveling through the clouds on the way to a magical city. Ever since I was a boy, I have enjoyed train rides. There was something about being on the rails at a steady, fast pace, yet slow enough to see the scenery. And in every tunnel, there was a light at the end. Whether I could see it from my seat or not didn't matter. Believing that the light was there was the real faith.

While Olga listened to her radio on headphones, I read a book. It was nice that we were comfortable enough with each other to be silent, yet know we were together. The silence didn't separate us like strangers. I had never felt this type of closeness with another person on a train.

When we arrived in New York, Olga went wild with excitement. "I feel comfortable in New York," she said.

"How can you feel comfortable here? Look at all the big buildings. This place is huge," I said skeptically.

"New York reminds me of Moscow where I grew up."

"Look at all the traffic and all the yellow cabs," I said.

"I don't mind."

"Yeah, but you don't have to drive here. All we have to do is walk down the street from Penn Station and we're at our hotel."

"Everything is so close," she said.

"You can say that again."

"My uncle lives in New Jersey, but he has an office in New York City. He says that he loves working in the city. He makes a lot of money as a chiropractor. But he works six days a week, twelve hours a day. He used to be married, but he got divorced."

"Oh yeah. What happened? Working too much?"

"His wife joined a cult and left him."

"A cult?"

"Yes."

"A religious cult is dangerous. It deals with mind control and dictating behavior, sometimes violent or oppressive behavior. It is evil and Jesus condemns it."

"My uncle says that his ex-wife is nuts for joining a cult group," she said.

"I feel sorry for her. I pray that she finds the true God someday. She won't find the fulfillment she needs by looking in a cult religion."

"My uncle told me what she said when she was leaving him. She felt empty inside herself. She wasn't happy. She needed something more and my uncle couldn't give it to her. He didn't know exactly what it was. She couldn't explain it to him well enough. She was empty and in search of satisfaction. Money couldn't help her. My uncle is rich, but his money couldn't save his marriage."

"Sorry to hear that," I remarked. "Marriage is a God-given institution that should not be treated so lightly. But I think I understand the emptiness that your uncle's wife was experiencing. It is a spiritual emptiness that can only be filled by Jesus." Deep in thought, I looked down at the ground and rubbed my chin.

"Whatever it was, she moved out and my uncle moved back to live with his parents, who are old and sick. My uncle loves cars. He trades in his car for a new car every six months."

"What does he drive now?"

"He drives a Lexus."

"A far cry from what I drive."

"I would like to drive an Audi someday."

"If I had the money, I would buy you a sports car, Olga. I'm being honest."

"The thought is what counts."

I lifted her hand and kissed the top part of her hand, as we stood on the corner of a New York street.

When the light changed, we started across the street in the crosswalk and Olga asked, "When are you going to buy me the Audi?"

"You're already asking?" I laughed.

"Just checking," she replied, playfully teasing me.

We checked into the hotel. Olga was standing next to me while I was signing the paper and registering my credit card. The lobby looked older than what I expected. The drapes were yellowed and the rug was dirty.

When we went to the elevator, Olga said to me, "The woman at the desk was giving me dirty looks."

"Are you sure?"

"Yes. She was probably jealous of me."

"Why do you think that?" I asked.

"Well, she is working on a New Year's Eve and I am checking into this hotel with you. She may have liked you."

"Don't say that, Olga."

"Women get jealous easily."

"There is nothing to be jealous of."

"That's what you say," quipped Olga, rolling her eyes.

Carrying our own bags, we went upstairs to our room. The hallways were dingy-looking. There was a strange smell as well. I led the way down the hall to the room. I put the electronic key into the lock of the door, but it wouldn't work. I tried again, but it still didn't work.

"It's not working, Olga."

"Let me try."

She fiddled with the lock using the electronic key. Nothing!

I said, "I'll call security to come up and let us in."

I used the telephone next to the elevator to call the front desk about being unable to get into the room. Within five minutes, two security guards came upstairs. One had the air of nonchalance. The other seemed to be arrogant.

When the arrogant guard opened the door, he said, "Lucky I made it here! Otherwise, you two would be sleeping together out here in the hallway." When he smiled, I saw his crooked teeth.

Olga whispered under her breath, "I don't think so."

As the security guards whistled their way away, Olga and I went into the room. I closed the door behind us. We were not impressed with the way the room looked. The rug was horrendously dirty. The walls were shabby. The bathtub was filthy.

Olga said, "This place is disgusting."

Continuing to look around the room, I said, pointing, "I think those are bullet holes in the wall."

"Let's get another room, Martin."

"Maybe we could clean it up."

Annoyed, she shot back, "I don't want to clean it up. I want a new room. I won't stay here. Call the front desk *now*." Her tone was fierce.

This was the first time that I had heard her use such a fierce tone of voice and demand something so harshly.

Wanting to appease her, I replied, "I'll call the front desk and ask them to change us to a better room."

"I thought that you would have picked a better hotel than this one, Martin."

"I have never been here before, Olga. I thought that it would be a nice hotel."

"I would expect better."

"Me, too."

Then I called the front desk and asked for a change of room. What they told me was a surprise.

"Yes, we will change your room, sir," said the front desk attendant. "I am sorry. We mistakenly put you into a shuddered room that is scheduled to be repaired."

"Now that you mention it, this place needs lots of repairs."

"If you come back to the front desk, I will give you a key to another room. I am sorry for the inconvenience."

"That's okay. Thank you for being accommodating."

Olga was looking at me intensely. She wanted to know what was going on.

I told her, "They put us in the wrong room. This room is supposed to be repaired. We shouldn't be in here."

"I am annoyed," she stated. "I think that the hotel should give you a free night because of this inconvenience. I would complain to the hotel manager, if I was you."

"I don't want to complain. The guy at the front desk was very helpful. He will give me a new key to another room."

"I am telling you, Martin. If you complain enough, they will drop the bill. You could get a free night."

"No, I can't do that. If the hotel refused to give me another room, then I would complain, but I just want to get settled. Don't worry about the money!"

I went downstairs and secured the new key. Then I led Olga to the new room, which was two floors up from the first room. Olga looked like she was tired of lugging her suitcase with her, so I helped her. Anything to help my girlfriend! It was nice to have a girlfriend.

Olga complained about this second room, too, but I was able to calm her down and agree to stay in it. She may have expected us to stay in New York's most expensive hotel, but we could only stay in a place that I could afford on my modest salary. I wanted her to understand it. But she seemed to think that I was being stubborn for not giving her what she wanted.

I was starting to get angry that things were off to a bad start on New Year's Eve. Olga was in a bad mood. The hotel was putting us in a lousy room. The massive size of New York was making me feel out of place. I wanted to ask God to help me out, but I had no opportunity to pray. I knew that Olga was not a Christian and I didn't want to offend her by my praying or talking to her about my spiritual need for God, who fills the natural emptiness in my soul.

When Olga went into the bathroom, I sat down on one of the two beds. The room was a standard-sized hotel room with two double beds. A nightstand with a lamp on it was between the two beds. I looked on the shelf of the nightstand and I saw the Gideon Bible, which is in every hotel room in America.

As soon as I saw the Bible – I didn't even open it – I was reminded of the Bible verse in which Jesus said "Do not commit sexual immorality."

Many years earlier, I had learned what the Bible said about sex. It had stuck with me, as if it had gelled with my soul. I was willing to believe the Bible and obey God. There would be no human reason to abstain from sexual relations, but God, who is holy and righteous, commanded to stay away from sex outside of marriage. If Jesus had never said it, then I would have never thought of it. Jesus also said that those people who love Him will follow His commands. Tough words, but I was dedicated to true love. I was willing to wait.

When Olga came out of the bathroom, she said, "There is no hairdryer. We should go buy one."

"Do we have to go outside?" I asked, uninterested in going back outside and walking the streets of New York.

"Yes, Martin, unless you see a shopping mall in this hotel room that I don't see."

Her sarcasm was more biting that what I would have expected.

"Okay. We'll go find a store and buy a hairdryer," I said.

But I didn't talk to her the whole way down. I looked away from her. She didn't need to be snappy about the hairdryer. However, I tried to calm myself down. I didn't tell her that she was getting on my nerves. I didn't want to ruin the evening. I was hoping that the dinner and concert would be much improved. When we walked through the hotel lobby, we saw a restaurant.

"Is it okay with you, Olga, if we go to the hotel restaurant later?"

"What kind of food do they serve?"

Looking at the menu, I said, "It's Italian food. Northern Italian food, which I like better than southern Italian food."

"What's the difference?"

"Thicker red sauce from southern Italy."

"I'm fine with the restaurant."

"Good. We have a plan," I said, clapping my hands together.

"Again with the plan? You love to make plans."

"And I like it when the plan goes right."

Then a strange thought crossed my mind, but I didn't share the thought with Olga. There is a difference between having "a plan go right" and having the "right plan." I didn't know why this thought intruded on my mind at this time, but it was glaring to me.

When we walked out of the hotel, Olga started to dance on the sidewalk. My attention shifted to focus more intensely on her. She was doing ballroom dancing moves, manipulating her hips seductively. She was getting the attention of men on the sidewalk as well.

"People are looking at you, Olga," I mumbled.

"Good. I like it," she replied, playfully. Then she rushed up to me and kissed me. She had a way with me.

Around the corner we found a shopping mall. On our quest for the hairdryer, we entered the department store. It had "Clearance Sale" and "Going Out of Business" signs all over the place. Half the store was empty, but it was busy with customers, who apparently were seeking good deals.

Olga and I found a hairdryer quickly and I thought that we were going to leave right away. But Olga decided that she wanted to look around the store. She drifted into the shoe department. The area was a mess. People had thrown shoes all over the place.

Olga said, "I want to buy a new pair of slippers." She picked up two different pairs of slippers and asked me, "Which pair would you like better on me?"

"Both look fine."

"You're no help," she said with a hint of humor.

"Thanks. I'm glad to be here, too," I said. "Can we go now?"

"Wait."

Still looking at the slippers, she said, "I think I will get this pair." She held a pair of black slippers up in the air. I barely looked at them.

"Great!" I said. "Let's pay and then go back to the hotel."

"You aren't easy to shop with, Martin. Do you know that?"

"I am the type of guy who comes to a store for a reason, buys what I need and then leaves."

"I like to look around."

"I noticed."

"Good for you."

Our banter was half playful, half getting on each other's nerves a bit.

When we left the store and went down the street, Olga started to dance again.

I said to her, "You are an impulsive dancer, Olga. When the impulse hits you, you need to dance."

"Dancing is in my blood," she replied. "I could never give it up. I will dance until I die."

"If I am still dancing at eighty years old, I will be dancing slower than I dance at my age now."

"I want to take dance lessons with ballroom dancing teachers in New York," she said.

"Do you know any?"

"Not yet! But I am looking for them on the Internet. It is easy to come to New York by train. I would like to do it monthly."

"That could get a little expensive, don't you think?"

"But it is doing what I love to do," replied Olga, lifting up her arms like she was going to receive a bird into her arms. "Dancing."

She must have felt as free as a bird when she danced. Her love for it was immense. It was a source of her pride. She wanted to conquer everything there was to conquer in ballroom dancing. But, as I would learn later in our relationship, her love for dancing was more complicated than I thought. I would have to adapt.

Chapter Twenty-one

Romantic Dinner in New York

Something changed when we returned to the hotel. We changed our clothes and went to dinner at the Italian restaurant on the hotel. Her crankiness left her. More patience settled into my soul. Forgetting the past few hours, I was enjoying our time together as soon as we entered the elegant restaurant. Olga looked beautiful and I was proud to be seen with her.

However, something happened at the restaurant that punctured my good mood temporarily, as if the world was offended that I was happy. Also, it showed that happiness is an elusive state of mind that rises and falls.

The host at the restaurant was instantly focused on Olga.

"I hope you don't mind my saying so, young lady, but you are a beautiful woman. I see many pretty ladies from all around New York come into this restaurant, but you stand out as among the most beautiful I have seen in a long time."

Flattered, Olga giggled and batted her eyelashes at me, as if she was waiting for me to become jealous of the attention she was receiving from another man.

Disrupting the host's flurry of compliments on Olga, I asked him, "Could we get a basket of garlic bread?"

"Young man, when you are with a young lady as magnificent as the one you are so fortunately with, you must be more subtle," said the host.

"Thanks for the advice," I replied flatly.

Still standing at our table, the host asked Olga, "Are you Italian?"

"No, I'm Russian."

"Oh, Russian!" he beamed. Then he said something to her in Russian. She laughed.

I asked her, "What did he say?"

"Something very funny! Something naughty!"

With a serious face, I said, "I'm going to have to learn Russian and take boxing lessons."

I was getting annoyed with the host.

I asked him, "Don't you have other things to do? It is New Year's Eve after all."

Olga scolded me, "Don't be rude, Martin."

All I said next to the host was "Merry Christmas!" as I grit my teeth.

Then I leaned toward Olga, as the host was walking away, and I said, "I want to go to another restaurant."

"Don't be silly! I like it here."

Because the host had gushed with flattery all over Olga, we stayed at the restaurant. If the tables were turned and a hostess had offended Olga, then you can be sure that we would have changed restaurants immediately. Olga used her emotions as a compass for what we did as a couple.

"Martin, are you jealous?" she asked.

"No."

"The man probably wanted to date me."

"Do you want to date him?"

"No, of course not," she replied, grimacing. "I am with you."

"Good."

"How do you think I look today?"

"Fabulous!" I replied in a serious tone.

"I'm glad."

I changed my tone to be more upbeat. "Olga, you are an incredibly beautiful woman. The host is right. You stir my emotions and I think about you all the time. I am wild about you, Olga. Your hair, your dreamy eyes, your full lips, your fine figure – all of you come together like a picture-perfect sculpture. I am attracted to you and you make me feel wonderful."

I wrapped my arms around her.

Then she commented, "Don't mess up my make-up."

I pulled away from her.

"Don't be like that," she said.

"I'm sorry. I don't want to mess up your make-up."

"Come closer to me!"

I smiled and said, "That's what I like to hear."

"Do you?"

"Definitely."

We kissed. Then we ordered drinks and appetizers. When we received the drinks, I toasted. We raised our glassed together.

"I toast *us* on a very special New Year's Eve. To love and remembrance!"

"That's romantic, Martin," said Olga. "Short and sweet."

"Thank you."

A party was taking place on the other side of the restaurant, separated by partitions. The people at the party were playing loud Russian music. I assumed that Olga would have liked hearing music from her motherland.

"You like this music, Olga, right?"

"No, it's traditional Russian music. My father likes it. I don't. I like more modern music. I have always liked Western music more anyway."

"I see."

Then the waiter came to our table and we ordered dinner. I ordered chicken and Olga ordered pasta with shrimp.

While we waited for the food to come, I continued to tell Olga how beautiful she was.

"You are amazingly beautiful, Olga."

I was tempted to fantasize about her and think of us in bed together. Her dress was tight and somewhat provocative. I ran my hand up and down her back. I kissed her neck and held her hand. My emotions were pouring forth unrestrained on her. However, not at any point did I lose control or my sense of what is morally right. I may have indulged my fantasy a little too much, but I told myself that I was in love and it isn't unusual for a young man to find the romantic embrace of a young lady as appealing.

Olga was all mine, I told myself. No one and nothing could come between us. I had never wanted a woman to love me as much as I wanted Olga to love me. I was confident. I believed everything would work out for the best. I still believed that God would give me what I considered "a break" and allow my dream to come true. I viewed my sincerity and my years of emotional suffering from loneliness as justification for having free reign to have romantic success with Olga, yet without consciously violating the Word of God, which stands uniquely in the universe of man and woman.

Maybe it was a contradiction, but I wanted to stay true to the Bible because I knew deep down in my heart that self-indulgence leads to a myriad of problems and harm. I wanted the best that God had to offer, while still pleasing Olga and keeping us on track to a thrilling and fulfilling romance for a long time.

When the waiter brought the food to our table, the smell of Olga's pasta dish prompted me out of my deep-thinking stupor. Olga probably didn't know why I looked so serious, but my mind was working like a jack-hammer and I was thinking about my plan for success.

As we began to eat, I asked Olga, "Are you looking forward to the Marc Anthony concert?"

"Uh-hum," she replied with her mouth full of food.

"Did you know that Marc Anthony married a former Miss Universe?"

"No, I didn't know."

"Yeah, and I read somewhere that he filled up a hotel room with dozens of white flowers and then proposed marriage to her."

Wiping her mouth with her cloth napkin, she said, "Now, that's romantic."

"I would think he could have lots of women, but he loves this one woman and I respect him for his monogamy, you know, his faithfulness in marriage," I said.

"Women throw themselves at him."

"I would think it is a burden to have women throwing themselves at me."

"You would love it, Martin. Come on!"

"In the beginning, it may be interesting, but I am interested in one woman, one relationship and building on that."

"Come on, Martin," said Olga, not believing me.

"I'm serious. I enjoy our relationship, Olga, much more than if a group of screaming groupies came running through that door and ran up to me, asking me for my autograph and tearing my clothes off."

"You really enjoy our relationship that much?"

"Yes, I do, Olga. You mean the world to me and I care deeply about you."

Then I pulled a small gift out of my pocket. It was a small teddy bear with the words "Love Ya" on it. Olga smiled, kissed me and put it in the center of the table.

"You always have nice little surprises for me, Martin," she said.

"I know that it isn't expensive."

"It doesn't matter. It is the thought that counts," said Olga.

Chapter Twenty-two

Concert at Madison Square Garden

After dinner, Olga and I walked to Madison Square Garden. The light wind was blowing Olga's hair up. The air was cold, but I was warm with satisfaction from being in New York on New Year's Eve. Entering the arena, I said to myself, "I'm actually here." And I was walking into the world-famous building with a pretty woman.

Madison Square Garden was huge. I figured that our seats were somewhere in the back, so I was shocked when the serious-looking man with the flashlight pointed me to seats on the floor of the Garden. I was ecstatic. Olga and I ended up sitting in seats in the middle of the floor.

"These are wonderful seats," she said to me, her eyes opening wide in amazement.

"Nothing is too good for you, Olga," I replied, smiling.

She kissed my cheek.

After we sat down in our terrific seats, I looked up and saw the ceiling, which I had seen on TV many times. Being in Madison Square Garden was almost surreal to me. It was a place of history and championships. As I continued to look up, I saw that large supplies of balloons were held by nets.

I looked at Olga and said, "There are balloons up there.

They will come down on us at midnight when we ring in the new year."

"I am already having a great time, Martin," she said. "I am glad we came."

"You are the most beautiful woman in New York," I said spontaneously.

"No, I'm not."

"Yes, you are."

"Who said?"

"I said."

I kissed her.

Then I asked her, "Are you thirsty?"

"Not yet."

"Okay. Well, just let me know when you are thirsty and I will get you a drink," I told Olga.

A few minutes later, a man and a woman sat down in the seats directly in front of us. This couple couldn't keep their hands off each other. They were rubbing each other's backs and nibbling on each other's ears. I didn't know if they had met a week earlier or had been dating for years, but they had a spark of romance they weren't afraid to display in public. I tried to look away from them while I waited for the show to start, but I couldn't help but notice them. The girl was pretty, but she was plain compared to Olga, in my opinion.

Before Marc Anthony performed, a comedian came out on stage and warmed up the crowd with jokes. He did a great impression of NSYNC, dancing and singing like them, except he exaggerated everything for comic effect. I was rolling in laughter.

After the hour-long comedy routine, it was time for Marc Anthony to perform. I can't tell you how loud the place became when he was announced. Marc Anthony is an international superstar. When he walked out on stage, the place was so loud that I thought the roof would blow off. Women, including Olga, were screaming.

Marc Anthony launched into his first song and he drove the crowd into a wild frenzy. The music was upbeat and intoxicating. I thought women were going to take off their clothes and charge the stage. The adrenaline was increasing. Everyone, except me, was dancing.

Olga was dancing up a storm with each song. Eventually, she bumped her hip into me and said, "Dance."

"I don't have much room here to dance," I said.

The woman on the other side of me kept hitting me by accident. If I started to dance, I would hit her and she would have probably ended up on the floor and wanting to sue me. No thanks!

I watched Olga dance just as much as I watched Marc Anthony sing. Olga's body moved with passion and precision. I was extremely attracted to her. She looked wonderful. She was smiling and happy. I felt like a dream was coming true. But something was missing.

I didn't know exactly what it was, but something was missing. For all the outward appearance of our relationship, something was still lacking internally. I didn't have confidence yet that this woman was the one for me to spend the rest of my life with in marriage. We were still getting to know each other. I wasn't in a hurry, but I knew enough that superficial happiness was not a replacement for deep, abiding love.

As we approached midnight, Marc Anthony stopped performing and waitresses passed out glasses of champagne. It was a nice touch. I didn't want to drink it, however, because I was concerned that it would give me a headache. I was not a drinker. But Olga persuaded me to drink, so I did.

Then, the big screen in Madison Square Garden showed Time Square and the dropping of the ball to indicate the coming of the new year. Marc Anthony counted down. 10-9-8-7-6-5-4-3-2-and-

HAPPY NEW YEAR!

Fireworks exploded in the Garden. The balloons were let loose. They floated down over the crowd. Then Marc Anthony broke into singing. But the best part of ringing in the new year at midnight was kissing Olga.

I leaned down and gave her the biggest kiss on her lips I ever had. Our lips caressed each other with alternately light and aggressive movements. I didn't want to stop kissing her, but I stopped and said, "Happy New Year, darling!"

"Happy New Year to you, too, honey," she said to me.

Then we embraced in a hug that seemed to wash aware all my past hurts. It was like being reborn and starting life fresh. I was in love and happy.

I said, "I'll never forget this time with you."

Then I noticed that the two people in front of us were kissing frantically and soon left together. The thought that they were leaving to go have sex with each other crossed my mind. But I quickly put it out of my mind. The temptation of having sex with Olga was lingering in the background for me. I didn't want to embellish any thoughts that may weaken my resolve.

We didn't leave yet. Marc Anthony performed for another half-hour. People were going wild, dancing in the aisles and screaming. He did two encores and left the audience craving for more.

It was an unforgettable night! An unforgettable New Year's Eve!

Olga and I didn't leave Madison Square Garden until close to 1 a.m. I was thirsty. We stopped at the smallest Dunkin Doughnuts shop I had ever seen in my life. This Dunkin Doughnuts shop could only fit four people and it was smaller than the average ATM vestibule. But I bought myself a cold drink.

It was a great night, but trepidation started to sink into my soul, as we walked to the hotel. Olga and I clearly liked – or even loved – each other. From a human perspective, it would make sense to "make love" with each other. I was at a crossroads. My desires were telling me to get into bed with her and let nature take its course.

On the other hand, my conscience was fully awake and instructing me to make the right moral choice, based on the Word of God. An important choice was waiting for me in the near future. I walked into the hotel and went up to the room with Olga, knowing I had to make the decision. No one else could make the decision for me.

After we went into our room and closed the door, making the decision didn't become any easier, but my true character would be revealed in privacy.

Olga kicked off her shoes and, as she wrapped her arms around me, said, "I love this type of living the good life."

"This is high living," I remarked.

Then we fell onto the bed and kissed each other passionately. I was on top of her. She kept her legs together, but, as I kissed her neck, she seemed lost in thought, yet sensitive to my touch.

After a while of kissing and caressing, she said, "I will go change and then we will go to bed."

She stood up from the bed and walked to the bathroom. Then she closed the door. This was time for me to pray. I needed guidance. At the rate I was going, I was going to tear off Olga's clothes and take full advantage of the opportunity. She was at the height of appreciation to me. She was also well primed for loving after the Marc Anthony concert. I could easily justify sleeping with her and make her believe that it was the climax of a marvelous night in New York.

For a guy who had had a great deal of trouble getting girls to go out on dates with me – let alone go to bed with me – this opportunity to sleep with a young woman was coming amazingly easy to me. I couldn't trust my emotions, so I turned to God at 1:35 a.m. to ask Him for guidance, while Olga was stripping off her clothes in the bathroom.

I prayed, "Heavenly Father, in Jesus name, I need Your help. I am being tempted in my flesh to have sex with a woman I am not married to. I know this is wrong to You, but my desires are strong. I need You to show me what to do, what is right. Please give me the strength to live for You, Lord, and to avoid a mistake that would affect me for the rest of my life. I don't know if Olga is the woman I will marry, but I believe the best thing to do is wait. Now I depend on You to strengthen me in the face of this sexual temptation. In Jesus name. Amen."

Seconds after I finished my prayer, Olga came out of the bathroom. All she was wearing was a silver-colored nightgown that went down to the middle of her thighs. It revealed the top of her breasts as well. Her legs were bare and she had wiped off her make-up.

When she sat down on one bed, I immediately switched to the other bed.

Her face expressed confusion. She asked, "Why did you go over there?"

"I'm going to sleep on this bed," I said.

"I thought that we would sleep in the same bed," she said, pulling down the bed's cover. She leaned back on the pillow.

"I am very attracted to you, Olga, but-"

"Then let's sleep in the same bed," she said. The temptation to jump on her and have wild sex all night long hit its peak at this moment. She wanted me and she was welcoming me into the bed.

But God must have stepped in and strengthened my spirit to stay away. In my heart, I knew that I was choosing selflessness over selfishness, morality over immorality, Jesus over self. The decision was not easy, but I knew the best things in life are not always easy.

I wanted to explain to her why I was choosing to sleep in a separate bed.

"Olga, we have only been dating for a few months and I

feel like we are still getting to know each other. Sex is very important to me. God created sex and I don't want to abuse it. I want our relationship to continue to grow. If we have sex too soon, then history tells me that the relationship could break down quickly. I want us to last. Does that make sense, Olga?"

"Yes, I guess so." She didn't sound convinced.

"And I want God to bless our relationship. I have a sense of morality and I don't sleep around with different girls. I don't want to use you for my own selfish purposes. I also think that waiting is a sign of sincerity and love. I hope you understand."

"I think I do," she said.

"Good," I said, relieved. "I am attracted to you, but I think we should wait. God will let us know when the time is right. I am a Christian and waiting is what I believe is the right thing to do. I hope I am not ruining your night."

"No, I have had a great night. This has been the best New Year's Eve I ever had," she said with a sincere tone.

"You make me happy, Olga. Thank you."

Then I turned off the light. I was in one bed and Olga was in the other. The light in my heart was still shining. Within a few minutes, I was sleeping. It had been a long day and I needed rest. I had a peaceful sleep. My conscience wasn't bothering me.

The irony was that I was in a city full of sin – and justification for sin – on New Year's Eve. The city would have encouraged me to dive right into the sexual escapade. But I was choosing Jesus.

I took a stand on the Word of God. I recognized sin for what it is in all its ugliness. I put conscience before pleasure. I put morality before self-justification. God's grace was protecting me. The allure of the city didn't overtake me. There might have been eight million "naked" stories in New York, but I was fully clothed in the righteousness of Jesus Christ, who, according to the Bible, resides in the heart of each spiritually born-again, spirit-quickened believer.

I chose Jesus Christ in New York.

Chapter Twenty-three

Like Iron in My Soul

On New Year's Day, I felt great. I was benefiting from making the right moral decision. No guilt! No regret! My love for Olga was increasing. I believed that we had taken a step forward toward a real, long-term commitment.

She and I took a train back home in the early afternoon. Olga looked tired and she was quiet for most of the train ride. Periodically, I held her hand, wanting to convey to her my emotional availability to her.

In my mind, I was thanking the Lord God for strengthening me on the previous night to resist temptation. The Holy Spirit was like iron in my soul to keep me strong, walking in the ways of the Lord. I could have made a mistake and ruined my future relationship with my wife, but I chose Jesus. He strengthened me from within. His power was yet again proved to me to be real.

My relationship with the Lord Jesus Christ was preeminent in my life. My inner peace and joy emanated from this relationship. Even though a relationship with a woman was fantastic for me, I had to keep the proper perspective and priorities.

However, I did not make my priorities clear to Olga. Again, I was secretly afraid that, if I revealed too much about my faith in Jesus to Olga, then my relationship with her would collapse because she would be "turned off" by my living faith, which is very different from the religious appearances that people put on.

When we arrived back to our home state, I drove Olga home and gave her a big hug in front of her house. The air was chilly, but the warmth of my love was keeping me warm on the inside.

"I love you, Olga."

"I need to go to sleep early," she said. "I am very tired."

"I had a great time."

"So did I, but I will be able to remember more of it after I get more rest," she remarked.

"Understood."

On the next day, Olga was refreshed and she called me.

"Martin, thanks again for a wonderful time on New Year's Eve at the Marc Anthony concert. It was amazing."

"It was."

Then she said, "I told my parents all about the trip."

"Oh, yeah?"

"My parents think that you are a decent man."

"Thank you," I replied.

I appreciated that her family recognized that I was "decent." It was a signal that my character was making an impact on people. I stood up for integrity and I abstained from the dangerous, sexual escapades that cause problems. Caring for Olga, I also had made sure that she was safe in New York.

After I finished the conversation with Olga a few minutes later, I wrote a letter to Olga and planned to send it to her in a fancy envelope.

Dear Olga,

I feel a connection with you, Olga. It runs deep into my soul and affects everything in me. I am sitting here thinking about how to describe and prove my love for you. But I must admit that I am finding it difficult to describe and prove my love perfectly in words.

Words fail me.

This kind of love is new for me and I am just learning about it. Love is much more than I thought it would be. Love is more than just thinking about you. Love is more than just spending time with you. Love is even more than just feelings.

You may be surprised to find out that I think love is greater than just feelings. Most people seem to think that love is a feeling. When a person has "the feeling," then he is in love. When he does not have the feeling anymore, then he is not in love. I see this as a superficial way to look at love. Infatuation is based on feeling.

However, love is based on so much more and I am experiencing this love so dramatically, so genuinely for the first time in my life. Thank you, Olga, for being in my life and sharing in this blessing of true love. I have waited for a long time. It was worth the wait.

Love is spiritual, pouring out from God's love for us. This love is amazing! My love for you, Olga, makes me want to dance. You are the dancing sensation. I only want to dance with you.

This love gives me courage, confidence, strength and freedom. I am free to love you in an honorable and responsible way that is greater than you ever thought possible.

Sincerely,
Martin

I started to do two things – (1) think more about whether Olga is the woman for me to marry and (2) plan a trip to Virginia Beach, Virginia in order to visit the *700 Club*. I struggled in knowing whether I truly knew what God wanted me to do or not, but I took steps out in faith.

I had four reasons why I should marry Olga. She and I were comfortable with each other. She was beautiful. She and I loved each other. And God could use Olga to refine my character by testing me and motivating me to be a strong man of integrity, work ethic and commitment. At the same time, I had three reasons why I should not marry Olga. She didn't know Jesus, so she was not a born-again Christian like me. She wasn't settled as much as me, as she was younger than I was and she was still trying to figure out her career decisions. And she had exhibited an overt attitude about accepting sex before marriage.

In my earnestness to keep the relationship going, I told myself that Olga would eventually accept Jesus as Lord and Savior, if I had patience. I also told myself that I could help her to get settled in her career, so her transition would be easier with me. Moreover, I overlooked her attitude about sex, writing it off in my mind as the natural inclination of an unsaved person who is spiritually lost. Because I loved Olga, I didn't want to give up on her. The thought of Olga going to hell troubled me.

The Bible states that the only way a person can get into heaven is through faith in Jesus Christ. I loved Olga enough to want her to go to heaven, too. My eternal destiny was sealed by the Holy Spirit. I will spend eternity with God. Praise Jesus! I know that I know. I have no fear of death. I wanted Olga to share in eternal life as well, just as my father prayed for years for my mother to accept Jesus whom she stubbornly resisted. My parents had had a difficult marriage because my father was focused on Jesus while my mother was focused on "self."

I could understand my father's love for my mother and how her rejection of Jesus – and, subsequent, rejection of him – hurt him deeply. I had watched for years as my parents could not relate to each other spiritually. My father had given his life to Jesus *after* he married my mother.

Because love was inspiring me to be committed to Olga under stressful circumstances, I was willing to wait and continue to pray for her salvation in Jesus Christ. This had nothing to do with wanting to control her. It had to do with wanting the best for her. Not only would Olga have a more adventuresome, exciting life on earth after surrendering her life to Jesus, but she would spend eternity in heaven. All questions about death would be answered in the person of Jesus Christ.

However, instead of searching for Jesus, Olga was much more interested searching for a male dance partner. I have never met a male dance partner who walks on water like Jesus did, but Olga was fooling herself into thinking she would find a dance partner who practically walks on water – or, that is, dances on water without sinking. Olga's expectations were high. Subconsciously, she was looking for a savior that would help her become a world champion ballroom dancer.

Chapter Twenty-four

The Dance Partner

Olga called me and said, "I have found a partner. He is Russian and he has been dancing since he was ten years old. He specializes in smooth dancing, but he said he is willing to learn Latin dancing. We are going to meet this Saturday afternoon and try each other out."

"Okay," I said.

"And I have more news!"

"Okay."

"I have left Bill's studio. I told Bill to go to hell."

"You did?"

"Yeah. I was fed up with Bill. I didn't like his comment to me last month at the party. He didn't give me enough lessons and he didn't help me to get a partner. I don't need him anymore. I have been looking on the Internet for a dance partner and I found Michael."

"This Russian guy you mentioned?"

"Right. He dances at another studio and he wants to introduce me to the owners Austin and Cathleen. He says that it is a much better studio than Bill's studio. He used to work for Bill years ago. He said that Bill doesn't know what he is doing. Bill is a terrible businessman. I will like it much better at this new studio. And Michael invited me to a dance party on Saturday night. Isn't that wonderful?"

"Wait!" I said. "I thought that you and I are going out this

Saturday night to the movies."

"Oh, that's right. But you do understand how important this is to me, don't you, Martin?"

"Yes, but-"

"I know what I can do. I can go to the dance party for an hour and then meet up with you afterward and we can still go to see the movie. Is that okay?"

"Well, I guess. I appreciate that you are making time for us to be together." I tried to say it as sincerely as I could. I didn't want to sound sarcastic.

"Great!" she said. "I'll call you when I am about to leave the party."

"Sounds good."

"I am so excited. I could have a partner."

"Oh, Olga, I can get my money back from Bill for the lessons I have not taken, right?"

"Oh, yeah. Bill will give you the money back. He'll only keep the money for the lessons you have taken with me."

"Good. I'll call Bill and get my money back. I hope your telling him to go to hell doesn't ruin my chances of getting my money back."

"If it does, I'll cause great trouble for Bill. He insulted me. I want to get him back."

"Nothing like revenge to start the new year," I remarked jokingly.

On the next day, I left a voice mail for Bill, informing him that I will no longer be taking lessons at his studio. I told him that I was aware about Olga's leaving him. Then I politely asked for a refund of the money I had paid ahead of time to take lessons with Olga.

Later in the day, he called me back and said, "I am not going to give you your money back, Martin. That is not my policy."

"But Olga said that it is your policy," I said.

"I only give money back within three days of a person signing on for lessons."

"That's a little detail that Olga forgot to tell me," I said, as I was getting annoyed.

"I suggest that you continue to take lessons at my studio."

"But Olga no longer teaches ballroom dancing at your studio."

"I have other young female teachers. They will treat you right. They can teach just as well as Olga. They are cute, too," said Bill.

"But Olga is my girlfriend, besides being my teacher."

"To be honest with you, I was never completely comfortable having a teacher and student who are dating," he said. "I generally don't want my teachers dating my students because, if you break up with the girl, you won't take any lessons."

"It's all about business, isn't it?"

Bill laughed and replied, "This is the real world. We don't just dance for the art of it. We are in it to make money."

"Olga is in it because she loves dancing," I said. "I don't think she cares about the money much."

"Olga is a nice girl, but she has trouble focusing and committing to one path of action. I'll leave it at that."

"I don't really need your opinion about Olga."

"Okay, but I hope you still take lessons with another one of my teachers," said Bill. He told me to take as much time as I needed to decide. Regardless of my decision, he wasn't going to give me any of my money back.

Another waste! This was the second time that Olga had propelled me to leave a dance studio and lose money. I didn't know whether to be angry or understanding about it. I felt that I had to show Olga my understanding about her position. She was emotional about it. But I had learned my lesson. I was going to be more careful with my money – at least, that is what I told myself at the time.

On Saturday, I waited for Olga's phone call. I spent the time talking to God, asking Him for guidance and asking

Him about what I should do and how I should interpret my emotions. I was troubled that Olga was off at a party dancing with a stranger. But dancing was her life and she couldn't be stopped. If I asked her not to do it, she would have resented me. She wanted a dance partner more than anyone or anything else in the world.

The temptation was to distrust Olga, but I kept telling myself to trust her. The one I didn't trust was the guy named Michael. For all I knew, he could have been trying to seduce her. All men struggle with lust and I started to think of Olga as slightly naïve about the power of lust.

What would stop her from suddenly being overcome by the thrust of lust? What would stop her from succumbing to the seductive touch of a handsome man who wanted to make her feel good? Sex is easy to justify in our society that has turned away from Jesus. *Playboy* magazine founder Hugh Hefner, shock jock Howard Stern and KISS band member Gene Simmons seem to have more influence on people than Jesus does today, according to the media. They have persuasive points about the "goodness" of sex in all forms and fashions.

In that case, nothing would stop Olga from agreeing to a "fun" and "fulfilling" session of sexual pleasures with any dance partner. This line of thinking made me insecure and angry. As an idealist, I wanted to meet a girl, fall in love and get married without all the strings of emotional and sexual baggage. In this way, I was probably being somewhat naïve.

It was difficult for me to believe that God, being who He is, would create people to engage openly or covertly in sexual selfishness, sleeping around with different people and treating marriage like it is a stamp of approval of a life of sexual immortality. This didn't register with me as what God intended when He created people. And when Christians engage in sexual indulgence outside of marriage, then no wonder the atheists in the world believe there is no God.

Gushes of these thoughts flowed over my mind like muddy waters, as I waited for Olga to call me. It was seven o'clock, then eight o'clock and then nine o'clock on Saturday evening. No call from Olga! I was becoming concerned.

By 10 p.m., I still didn't hear anything from Olga.

"It's not like her to fail to keep a promise with me," I told myself. "Maybe she is in trouble. Maybe her car broke down. Maybe she hurt herself dancing."

I became nervous, imagining that Olga was in a car accident or hurt.

Ten-thirty. Nothing.

By 11 p.m., my thought pattern had changed. I started to think of Olga as having a fun time with Michael. Did he like her? Was he making a pass at her? Was she kissing him? Did she view me differently? My insecurities flared up. All the rejections from women from the past resurfaced in me.

Then the telephone rang. It was ten minutes after eleven.

"Hello."

"Martin," said Olga.

"Olga, are you okay? Where are you?"

"Yes, I am okay. I am even better than okay. I am doing great," she said.

"Oh?"

"I have been having so much fun dancing with Michael. He is great. I think we are going to become partners. Isn't that great?"

"Yeah," I said with no enthusiasm – not even feigned enthusiasm.

She sounded very happy.

I said to her, "We had a date planned for tonight. It's already after eleven o'clock."

"I'm sorry, but I lost track of time while dancing."

"I thought that you were only going to stay an hour, Olga."

"But I was having fun dancing. Don't you believe me?"

"Yeah, I believe you, but I was getting concerned that something bad had happened to you."

"You knew I was with Michael."

"I don't know Michael," I said sharply.

"Why are you using that tone of voice with me?" she asked, conveying to me that she didn't like my tone.

"I thought that you would call me earlier." I wasn't going to let go of the fact that she was three hours late in calling me. She purposefully didn't call me, I was thinking.

"I can still meet you now."

"It's too late to see the movie, Olga."

"We can hang out."

"No," I said. "I am tired. I am going to go to sleep."

"Well, if you want to lay down early to go to sleep, I understand."

"Have fun dancing more with Michael tonight," I said.

Then I slammed down the telephone. I was furious.

"It's done," I whispered to myself.

I did not call Olga for a whole week. And she didn't call me either. I assumed that we had broken up. She had been out dancing with another man. A ballroom dancer is still a human being with all the weaknesses of human nature, whether sexual, intellectual, emotional or physical.

Olga may have been a dancing sensation on her way up in the dancing world of the United States, but I wanted to love her for herself, not because she was a dancer. Yet, dancing was her true love – a fertile area for her to find herself, her strength and her meaning. I felt like I was in the way.

We were like two dancers both trying to lead. It didn't work.

Chapter Twenty-five

Reconciliation

After a week of no communication between Olga and me, I started to miss her. My heart began to ache with a sense of separation and loneliness. Without question, I loved Olga and I was having a hard time accepting that she and I would not be together.

I was angry and I told God that I had no power in myself to overcome my own anger, but I needed His grace to help me. I asked God to search my heart for anything wrong and set me straight. Eventually, I was feeling motivated to call Olga and communicate about our feelings.

When I called her, I simply said, "Olga, it's me."

"Hi," she said in a low, serious tone of voice. "I didn't know if you would call."

"I have been upset all week."

"I know," she said. "I kept asking my mother why you weren't calling, Martin. I don't know why you stopped calling."

"Yeah, I didn't like how you forgot to call me while you were dancing with the guy Michael." A hint of irritation was in my voice.

"But I did call you. How can you say that I forgot to call you?"

"You called me hours late."

"I told you that I lost track of time. I was still willing to go out with you. You were the one who didn't want to go out later. You said you wanted to go to sleep."

"I was angry."

"Not fair, Martin," she asserted. "You sound like you thought I was off on a date with another man."

"Well-"

"I wasn't and you know it," she said, raising her voice. "I was doing what is my life's passion. I was dancing with a new partner and Michael has asked me this week why I seem upset. I told him that you weren't calling me all of a sudden."

"I missed you, Olga."

"You did?" Her tone changed.

"Yes. Very much so! That is why I called," I said. "I love you and I don't want to end our relationship. I would like us to give it another try."

"Let's forget about what happened and get back to where we were before last week."

"Sounds good to me."

So we were back in our relationship. Our reconciliation was solid. I realized that I might have overreacted to Olga's calling me late and dancing with another man. I was unfair to her. I didn't want to end our relationship on a misunderstanding or an emotional moment that would fade away. I was glad that we were "boyfriend" and "girlfriend" again.

I could plan our trip to Virginia and help her with her college work. For the next month, I was at her house three times a week helping her study for tests and figure out complex issues. We sat in her kitchen and talked. I was trying to get her to think about the issues, but she had to change the subject and talk about something with dancing at least once every fifteen minutes. She could be easily distracted from college work.

When I told her about the trip to Virginia, she was thrilled. I told her about the beautiful beach, lined with hotels and restaurants. The idea of a "getaway" appealed to both of us. I was planning to reserve a suite with two rooms. But I had a few surprises in store for Olga in Virginia.

I prayed fervently about whether I should ask Olga to marry me while we are vacationing in Virginia. This was a monumental question. I desperately wanted to know whether marrying Olga was part of God's plan for my life.

As I continued to pray, I started to sense in my spirit what God was conveying to my heart. The first thing was that I should wait on the Lord and I should wait for a confirmation in my heart from God while in Virginia. The second thing was that I should bring Olga to the *700 Club* taping in Virginia Beach and see how she reacts to the Gospel of Jesus Christ being stated openly in a TV studio. The third thing was to offer an opportunity to Olga to accept Jesus as her personal Lord and Savior. She had to confess to God that she was a sinner and in need of God's forgiveness, based on the death and resurrection of Jesus two thousand years ago. These three things were the criteria I needed to consider in making a final decision.

At an emotional level, the idea of asking Olga to marry me on Virginia Beach was phenomenally romantic. I wanted to enjoy every moment of it. If I ended up not asking her to marry me in Virginia, would I be disappointed? Would I have lost a good opportunity? I wished that I could be sure of what God wanted me to do before the Virginia trip, but He was silent on the issue after I sensed He wanted me to wait on Him. I could not rush God. However, in preparation for going ahead with it, I bought a diamond engagement ring. I hid it in my bedroom.

One day, as I was thinking about the possibilities of Virginia, Olga called me and she sounded like she was crying.

"What's wrong, Olga?" I asked.

"My knee hurts," she replied. "When I came back from dancing practice, my knee started to hurt and it is bothering me. I don't think I will be able to dance tomorrow. I am scared that it is serious. I have had knee problems in the past."

"Olga, I will pray that God heals your knee."

"Thank you" was all she said in response.

"Do you have another practice with Michael tomorrow night?"

"Yes, I do. If my knee hurts tomorrow the way it is hurting now, then I won't be able to dance. It hurts me more not to dance than it is to have a painful knee."

It was ironic that dancing was practically Olga's whole life, but she was one serious knee injury away from never dancing again. She had put her trust in something - dancing – that couldn't guarantee her long-term happiness. She needed the Lord God more than she knew.

After I hung up the phone, I prayed for her.

"Heavenly Father, in Jesus name, I ask You to heal Olga's knee. By the stripes of Jesus, Olga is healed. By the stripes of Jesus! Praise Your holy name, Jesus! Thank You for offering Your healing power to us. You healed people two thousand years ago when You were on earth. You are still healing people today, but doubt can get in the way of healing. Get rid of all doubts in me, Lord. I want to believe You completely. Heal me from my unbelief! In Jesus name. Amen."

When I called Olga the next night, the first question I asked her was "How is your knee?"

"Fine," she replied, matter-of-factly. "I was able to dance very well tonight."

"Great!" I said, thinking about how God graciously had answered my prayer for her healing.

"But there is a major problem."

"What?"

"Michael and I had a fight and we aren't dance partners anymore." She said it in an even tone, but then her voice suddenly cracked when she said, "I don't have a partner anymore."

"What happened?" I asked, feeling empathy for her.

"He wasn't doing what I wanted him to do," she admitted.

"What do you mean?"

"I wanted him to work more on Latin dancing, but he wanted to do smooth-style dancing too much. I was annoyed with him and I told him so."

"What did he say?"

"He said that I am too demanding. I told him that I want to be a world champion more than he did and that he wasn't going to get in my way of becoming a world champion ballroom dancer. I will do whatever it takes!"

"I know you would, Olga," I said in a supportive tone of voice.

"Then his girlfriend came to the lesson and she wanted to dance with him, so he cut our practice short. I don't care if he wants to spend time with his girlfriend, but he shouldn't let it get in the way of our practice. If we are to become champions, we need to work hard."

"It seems that he is not as dedicated to it as you are. He seems to want to have more of a personal life."

"He can have his personal life, too, but when he is with me, he needs to work hard. I told him what I was thinking and he said that he didn't like my attitude. So what? I didn't like his girlfriend's attitude either," said Olga, upset.

"So you won't be dancing with Michael anymore?"

"No," she replied. "But I have a lesson with Austin, the owner of the studio where Michael brought me to. I want you to come to the lesson with me, Martin. I don't want to be alone. The lesson is at Austin's house."

"Why isn't it at the studio?"

"Austin has a dance studio in his basement," she said.

"For private lessons?"

"Yes."

"How convenient for him to have a private lesson with pretty girls!" I said sarcastically.

"He lives with his fiancée. He is a good man. He isn't trying to seduce me. Are you jealous?"

"No, I just don't like guys who play games with women and make demands on them for sexual favors."

"Austin is not like that. He has a beautiful fiancée who lives with him. They are getting married soon, I think, and he is a family man. He is close with his parents."

Olga defended Austin, but from a Christian perspective Austin was a sinner. He was sinning against God by living with a woman *before* marriage. Olga had no qualms about it. I did have a concern about it. But I didn't say anything to Olga. I figured she wouldn't understand why I would have a problem with a man and woman living together before marriage.

Once, I told my mother that God's judgment will fall on a man and woman who live together in sin. She laughed at me and said that I believed "religious tradition" - as she put it – too literally. "Times have changed, Martin," she said to me. I have news for my mother. God hasn't changed. This would have been news for Olga, too, but I kept it to myself.

On the following weekend, I accompanied Olga to Austin's house in a wooded area of a wealthy neighborhood. In the yard, as I was looking at the gigantic house, Olga told me that Austin was from a wealthy family. I followed her into the side door, which was unlocked.

"He leaves his door unlocked?" I asked.

"He told me that he keeps the side door unlocked for students to come in and out," she said. When we stepped inside the hallway of the house, Olga said, "I will go change in the bathroom. I will be right back." She left me standing alone in the corridor of this big, strange house.

As I was looking at the paintings on the wall to pass the time, a woman with strawberry-blond hair opened a door and walked into the hallway. She was wearing a mini-skirt and no shoes.

She yelped. "Oh, my God!"

"I'm sorry to frighten you. I am here with Olga for a dancing lesson with Austin."

"Oh, of course," she said, calming down. She rubbed her neck.

"This is a nice house."

"Thank you."

She stared at me. The silence was awkward.

Then she said, "Austin is a great ballroom dancing instructor. He was my teacher."

"Was he?"

"Then we fell in love and we are getting married this summer," she said proudly.

"Congratulations!"

"How did you meet Olga?"

"Through ballroom dancing as well."

"How nice!"

Then, as if she suddenly lost interest in talking to me, she turned and went back into the main area of the house. She didn't say goodbye to me.

Olga came out of the bathroom and was ready to dance.

I said to her, "I met Austin's fiancée a minute ago. It was a strange conversation."

"What did you think of her?"

"She seemed nice."

"Austin used to be her teacher."

"I know. She told me."

"I think that she was after him for his money."

"Don't say that too loud! She might hear you," I said.

"I don't care. I don't like her."

"When you don't like someone, watch out world!" I stated with a hint of humor.

"I don't need to put up with any crap. If I don't like

something, then I say it and I am not afraid to make a change," said Olga. "It's my right."

Olga was now claiming her right to control.

Minutes later, she was downstairs dancing with Austin in his huge dancing studio, which was lined with floor-to-ceiling mirrors. The wooden floor was top-notch quality. The sound system was high-end. Clearly, Austin had spared no expense to build a state-of-the-art dance studio in his house. No wonder he charged a high price for taking a lesson with him! My sense was that he believed that he was worth it. Even just looking at him, I could sense from the way he carried himself that he was a man of pride. He seemed impressed with his dancing expertise.

I would be more impressed by a man's character than by a man's dancing expertise. However, Olga would think the exact opposite, I believed. She valued a man for his dancing ability much more than valuing a man for his character of integrity, commitment, honesty, generosity, kindness and patience.

Yet, I didn't feel comfortable to talk to Olga about my impression of her view of integrity vs. dancing. How big could the differences be between Olga and me? I hoped for the best, which meant tiny differences. New experiences were the tools to reveal more truths about each other.

How would we respond as individuals? How would we respond to conflict? How would we respond to disappointed expectations?

I hoped for the best.

Chapter Twenty-six

LITTLE DIFFERENCES

The differences between Olga and me started off as little. They were revealed during two musical concerts that we attended. I never would have thought that stubborn qualities about me would be revealed at a Sting concert and then at an NSYNC concert. And I will put my hand on a Bible and swear to God that I only went to the NSYNC concert because Olga liked the singing group. These were the days when Justin Timberlake was dating Britney Spears.

First, we went to the Sting concert. The tickets only stated that Sting was performing. But, in fact, a jazz singer came out on stage to open the show for the first hour. Olga hated her singing. She was restless in her seat next to me.

"Let's go take a walk. I can't take this woman's singing," Olga said to me.

But I didn't want to get up. I didn't mind her singing and I didn't want to stand in the outer corridor. Also, we were seated in the middle of a long row and I didn't want to disturb everyone by slugging my way out of the row.

"She won't be singing for much longer," I said. "I don't want to go anywhere."

This wasn't the answer that Olga wanted to hear.

When Olga was teaching me in the dance studio, she was in control and I complied to virtually everything she said. I gave her full freedom to teach me the way she wanted to teach me. But, in everyday life, I didn't agree with everything she wanted to do. If her love for me depended on whether I agreed with her 100 percent of the time, then it would become an issue.

Yet, I tried to be polite and soothing.

"Sting should be coming on stage to perform soon. Please wait!"

"I don't like to wait," she shot back at me.

I was on the verge of saying "I've noticed" but I didn't. I held my tongue. I didn't want to stir her up. She forced herself to sit still, but her eyes wandered.

The jazz singer continued to blast out her voice like a fire-breathing dragon. I was waiting for glass to break in the auditorium. Her style of singing was markedly different from Sting's style.

Olga asked, "Why did Sting choose to have her open his show?"

"He must like jazz," I replied.

"Can you get me a drink?"

"Now?"

"Yes."

"Can I get it at intermission?"

"I'm thirsty."

"Oh," I said sighing.

"Why are you making that sound?"

"I just want to relax and listen to the music," I said.

"Hey, we got here early because you wanted to come early."

"I don't like to be late for a concert."

"We came too early."

"I didn't know how bad traffic would be."

"Are you going to get me my drink?"

"Okay."

Annoyed, I stood up and bothered about fifteen people so that I could get to the concession stand and buy Olga a drink.

When I reached the concession stand, I realized that I forgot to ask Olga what she wanted to drink. Since I wasn't going to go bother the fifteen people again to ask her, I guessed and bought her lemonade. If she didn't like it, I would drink it, I thought.

When I went back to the row, I asked fifteen people to stand up while I walked back to my seat, intensely focused on not spilling the drink. I disliked this aspect of a concert in a big auditorium. When I reached my seat, I gave the cup to Olga.

She looked at it and said, "Why did you get me this?"

"You wanted a drink."

"You didn't get me what I wanted."

"You didn't tell me what you wanted to drink," I said.

"Yes, I did."

"No, you didn't."

"Yes, I did."

"Do you want me to drink the lemonade?"

"No, I am thirsty."

"Good."

Either I had not listened carefully enough or Olga had expected me to read her mind. We had gotten on each other's nerves. And we had a loud jazz singer belting out her tunes as a soundtrack for our petty fight.

Olga and I didn't talk to each other until the jazz singer left the stage and Sting came on the stage with his guitar. As soon as he started to sing a song I recognized, I felt better.

I turned to Olga and said, "I'm sorry about the drink. I probably didn't hear you say what you wanted."

With a humorous tone, she said, "You loved the jazz singer, so you didn't want to leave. That was it, right?"

"No, not at all."

"You can make things difficult, Martin."

"Bothering all these people to stand up in this row wasn't part of the plan. I liked being in my seat and I was waiting for Sting."

"What do you care about the other people? They don't care about you. Bother them to stand up. So what?"

"And I didn't want to stand in a long line at the concession stand."

"Was it as long line as you expected?" she asked.

"Not as long as I thought it would be."

"So there."

I rolled my eyes.

Sting did a magnificent performance for two hours. Olga and I ended the day in a good mood. On the way home, Olga didn't stop raving about how good Sting was. We took a crowded subway to a bus stop and then boarded a crowded bus. Unlike me, Olga didn't like public transportation, as if she was haughty and didn't want to associate with "the unwashed masses."

For the second concert a week later, we didn't take a bus or a subway. I persuaded Olga to take a regular train with me. She disliked it, but it was less than an hour ride. I think she was trying to keep me pleased enough because I was the one who paid for the two tickets to see NSYNC. If she got me upset and constantly complained, then who knows what I would have done with the tickets? Olga was careful with me. I could tell.

The reason I was adamant about taking the "party train" to the concert was that the stadium was far away and I didn't know the way. It revealed that I didn't like to drive somewhere on an uncharted route. If most men will just get in their cars, drive off and refuse to admit that they are lost to their girlfriends or wives, then I am different. If I know I am going to get lost, I am either going to map out a route in detail or, if the distance is long, find an alternative way to go.

Olga started to poke fun at me because this idiosyncrasy I have about traveling long distances in a car to an unknown location.

"We could have driven to this stadium, but, no, you don't

want to drive, Martin."

"I like the train. We are on the party train."

"You were afraid we would get lost, but I told you I know the way."

"I like the train," I repeated.

"Whatever!"

The train was slower than I expected, but, as someone who likes train rides, I was fine with it. Olga was restless, but she read her magazine. We were surrounded by teenage girls, who wore outrageous clothes. They must have thought that the boys from NSYNC would come into the audience and invite them backstage. Teenage fantasies!

When we arrived at the stadium, Olga and I immediately realized that it was cold out. We had miscalculated the weather. A cold front swept into the area. The temperature must have dropped twenty degrees from what it was earlier in the day. Olga, who was dressed lightly, was freezing. I didn't have a jacket to cover her.

Expressing my frustration, I said to her, "I didn't plan correctly for this concert. I should have brought a jacket or a blanket."

"I am cold."

"And we had to come to a concert at our outdoor stadium? What a day!"

When we walked into the stadium to find our seats, the opening band was playing. The screaming of the little girls in the audience was deafeningly loud. I wanted to turn around and go home, but I stayed for Olga. I hugged Olga to keep her warm, as she shivered. Then I bought her hot chocolate.

"To warm up your insides," I said to her, handing her the cup of hot chocolate.

She sipped it and said, "It tastes terrible."

"Sorry, I can't do anything about that."

Our date started to improve when NSYNC came out on

stage and performed. I recognized more songs that I cared to admit. The girls in front of me, behind me and beside me screamed for NSYNC like wild banshees.

By the end of the night, my ears were ringing.

When the concert ended after a spectacular array of fireworks, Olga asked me, "How are you?"

I replied, "I am so ready to go to Virginia Beach."

"Is it warm in Virginia?"

"Yes."

"It better be," she said, hugging me to stay warm, as a cold breeze blew by us.

Chapter Twenty-seven

Virginia Beach, Virginia

The Virginia trip was a critically important juncture in my relationship with Olga. I had intentions to ask Olga to marry me, but I also had a sense that I still needed to wait on the Lord God to guide my heart. I remembered how He had made an impression on me to talk to Olga about salvation in Jesus Christ and to see how Olga reacts to being in the studio at the *700 Club*. I was getting impatient and I wanted to make a move.

The last thing I packed before driving to Olga's house was the little box with the engagement ring in it. I hadn't looked at it since I bought it, but this ring carried with it deep meaning for me. If Olga would accept it, it would mean vindication and a new beginning for me. Anxious, I hid the ring in my luggage, which I intended to keep closely by my side at all times on the train.

As planned, I drove to Olga's house and picked her up so that we could go to the train station together. Without any wasted time, I loaded her luggage into my car and I prodded her to move quickly.

"I don't want to be late for the train," I told her.

"You are always early," she replied.

Driving down a main street five minutes away from Olga's house, I slowed down at an intersection and then took a left turn, which I had done more than once in the past.

Seconds later, a police cruiser with its lights flashing was pursuing me down the road. I immediately pulled over.

Olga asked me, "What's wrong?"

"I don't know," I replied. "I wasn't speeding. I don't think my rear lights are out. I can't think of anything I did wrong."

After stopping behind my car, the officer stepped out of his cruiser and approached my side of the car. He approached with the same cautious manner that I had seen many times on television.

"Do you know what you did wrong back there?"

"No, officer," I replied, trying to sound respectful.

"You made a left turn at the intersection. It is a violation to make a left turn at that intersection."

"It is?"

"Didn't you see the signs?"

"No, I'm sorry."

With a sarcastic tone, the officer remarked, "There are only four signs at the intersection saying 'No Left Turn.' A red line is also through a left arrow just in case you didn't read the sign."

"I'm sorry, officer. I really didn't see the signs. I am going to catch a train down to Virginia with my girlfriend here and I guess I am preoccupied in trying to get to the train station on time," I said, sounding nervous.

"Okay. I'll give you verbal warning, but if you ever make the wrong turn again, you will pay a price for it."

"I understand," I said. "Thank you."

As he walked away, Olga said, "He was nice to let us go. He could have given you a big ticket."

"I know."

"Now you're tense, Martin."

"I made a bad decision to take a left turn. I honestly didn't see the signs because I was preoccupied with myself. You know, my plans and all the contingencies! I wasn't focused on what I should have been watching."

"Don't be too hard on yourself, Martin."

"Thank God that the police officer didn't keep us for twenty minutes while he writes up a ticket. We might have missed the train," I said.

I was careful to drive under the speed limit and watch for traffic signs all the way to the train station. To my relief, Olga and I arrived at the station on time and boarded the train with fifteen minutes to spare. But I was still tense.

Olga and I asked the train's conductor to show us to our cabin. When he stopped in front of a room that looked like an over-sized closet, he pointed inside of it. I looked at it and couldn't believe that this small room was a cabin for two people. I asked the conductor if there had been a mistake. He said there was no mistake.

"Where are the beds?" I asked.

"Folded up," he replied. "When you want to go to bed, I will unfold them for you."

"These are certainly tight quarters. Can I upgrade to a bigger cabin?"

"The train is full. We have no room for upgrades." Then he walked away.

Olga said to me, "I don't like this cabin. I want something bigger."

"This is all we can have, according to the conductor."

"I am not happy," she said.

Olga's happiness could go up and down like a roller coaster. I accepted the vicissitudes of her moods.

Later, I slept on the top bed and Olga slept on the bottom bed. I woke up at 2 a.m. and looked down. Olga was gone.

"Where could she have gone?" I asked myself. "In the dining car?"

After getting partially dressed up, I walked to the dining car in a sleepy haze and found Olga sitting in a seat while she was talking to the dining car attendant and sipping a cup of either coffee or hot chocolate.

When she saw me, Olga said, "I couldn't sleep, Martin. I hate the cabin we have."

"I'm sorry about that."

"I have been talking to Gary here," she said pointing at the dining car attendant who walked away from her as soon as I stepped into the room. "Gary told me that he thinks I am beautiful and he asked if I have a sister just like me." Then she laughed.

Drowsy, I was in no mood for joking or laughing.

When I didn't laugh, she asked, "Martin, are you in a bad mood?"

"No, but I am tired. Do you know what I mean?"

"I am not tired."

"I'll sit here with you until you get tired and want to go to bed."

"I can't take that cabin, Martin."

"Will you stay up all night?"

"No, I guess not, but I want to talk to Gary more. He has been telling me stories about people on this train. He has been working on trains for fifteen years. He has a girlfriend in Virginia. He is divorced."

She gave me more information than I needed to know. Giving up on trying to persuade her to go back to sleep, I returned to the cabin and fell asleep quickly. I dreamt that I was on one train, but Olga was on a different train. The train I was on was headed up into the sky, which was cluttered with puffy, white clouds. The train that Olga was on was headed full-speed to a mountain with no tunnel opening. I could see what was happening. Then I woke up, shaken. It was 9 a.m. and the sun was shining outside my window. Olga was sitting on the bed below me, looking into her purse. I was relieved.

"Good morning, Olga."

"We're in Virginia."

"Great."

Two hours later, Olga and I were at the hotel – the Cavalier Hotel on Virginia Beach. It was a grand hotel with "southern comfort" charm to it. Set on a hill overlooking the beach, the Cavalier looked majestic. I considered it a perfect spot for proposing marriage. The surroundings seemed right for a romantic mood.

While Olga was looking around the hotel, I checked in and asked the manager to lock the engagement ring in a security box next to the front desk. I wanted it to be safe while I made a final decision during the week on whether to ask Olga to marry me or not. Also, I worked out a plan with the hotel manager for me to change our room for the last night. I wanted to be in the "Presidential Suite" with Olga on the last night of our vacation. I planned to sleep on the sofa while Olga slept in the bed. Despite the romantic majesty of the hotel, I remained firm on my moral stance.

I planned to go to the *700 Club* at CBN on Tuesday morning and I should have extended an invitation to Olga to join me, but I didn't. I balked. Even though I knew God wanted me to take Olga with me to the TV studio to hear a Christian news broadcast, I became afraid that Olga would immediately have serious doubts about me.

My mother had criticized my father harshly years earlier for working as a volunteer for an affiliate of the *700 Club* in our hometown. My father was a counselor to help people deal with their problems through prayer and trusting in God. Nestled in Virginia with Olga, I was afraid of receiving the same treatment that my father received from my mother. So, as my mother often told my father, I backed off of inviting Olga to visit the Christian Broadcasting Network with me. But I wanted to go myself.

On Tuesday morning, I went to CBN and had a tremendous time being in the audience of the *700 Club* and listening to Pat Robertson, as well as his son Gordon, talk about the issues of the day. I also had the opportunity to walk around the campus of Regent University, where the American Center for Law and Justice is located. I looked at the whole place as a testament of God's power. God was using modern technology to spread the good news about Jesus Christ all over the world. I saw what can happen when people believe in Jesus and take steps of faith forward to success in God's plan. I was inspired and I wondered more seriously what God's plan for my life is.

However, I still had made the mistake of not inviting Olga to accompany me. I lost the opportunity to see how she would react to the Christian worldview that I embraced. This exposed my failure to use the courage in my heart.

When I returned to the hotel in late morning, all I told Olga was that I visited a local TV station. She didn't seem to care. Then we went to the beach. The question – "Should I ask Olga to marry me?" – persisted in my mind for hours. I decided to make a decision by Wednesday night.

On Tuesday night, I took Olga to dinner at a fine restaurant called Orion's. It is easier to talk about God when things are good – when rich food is on the table as if in a feast. To unsaved people, including people who incorrectly think they are "Christians," God is wishful thing; God is terminology for the impersonal power of the universe; God is off doing his thing while people do what they want to do; God is malleable and subject to people's different views.

Unsaved people think that people created God, therefore, control God. They think that old-fashioned, creative men wrote the Bible in a conspiracy to harmonize society. They think that any book that mentions "God" in it is comparable to and just as authoritative as the Holy Bible. Unsaved people live in dangerous, spiritual darkness, but Jesus loves them all and will let them know somehow that He is alive and He desires a personal relationship with every single person today.

I bent to what I thought Olga could accept.

"What do you think about Jesus?" I asked her, as I poked my fork into a bacon-wrapped shrimp appetizer.

"Oh, I don't know. He was a good man, I guess, and started the Christian church, but I don't believe in Him," she replied in between her bites of food.

"What do you mean?"

"You know, that I don't believe that He is the Son of God."

"Are you sure that Jesus is not God?"

"No, I am not totally sure," she admitted, sounding tentative.

"Then there is a chance that you could believe in Jesus one day."

"Maybe," said Olga.

That was it. Subsequently, my impulsiveness took control of me. I decided for certain that I was going to ask Olga to marry me. Her "maybe" was enough for me at the time. As long as she wasn't closing the door completely on believing that Jesus is the Messiah (as Sid Roth tells Jewish people all the time on Messianic Vision, www.sidroth.com), then I had hope that she would find her Savior in Jesus. She would become a "completed Jew," as Sid Roth would say. There is power in the blood of Jesus.

Impulsively, I let my mind and heart get carried away with romance. On the next day, Olga and I moved to the Presidential Suite. She was thrilled about it. The suite was very spacious and had an all-marble bathroom.

I waited for "the perfect time" to "pop" the question to Olga. While she was taking a shower, I went downstairs and picked up the diamond ring. Minutes later, I was back in the room and I waited for Olga to come out of the bathroom. I turned on a mini-tape recorder I brought and I played romantic music to create an emotional mood in the room. When she came out, she was fully dressed in a nice outfit that highlighted her shapely figure.

Pouncing on the opportunity, I said, "Please sit down, Olga. I have something to give you."

"Another gift?"

She sat down at the foot of the bed. Expectations were running high. The romantic music was playing. A cool breeze was blowing through the window, making the curtain dance. The stage was set for a dramatic moment.

Without hesitation, I knelt down and said to Olga, "I love you with all my heart and I want to spend the rest of my life with you. Will you marry me?"

Then I presented the diamond engagement ring to her. Opening the small box unveiled the ring to Olga in all its magnificence. This was an incredibly beautiful diamond ring with rare quality.

Olga froze. She said nothing for almost ten seconds, which seemed like eternity to me. I hung on the silence, thinking, "Oh, no!" Time seemed to freeze as well for me.

I waited.

Then, as if she flipped a switch, she said, "Yes."

She threw her arms around me. I responded by saying, "I love you, Olga."

We were engaged. The moment had tremendous impact on us. Olga immediately wanted to tell people. When we went to the restaurant to eat, she told the hostess and the waiters. Celebration was in order. I was happy that she was happy. *I was really going to get married.* All the past years of failure with woman disintegrated.

Olga and I still slept separately and we did not engage in sexual relations, just because we got engaged to be married. Marriage is the threshold to sex, not an engagement. My conscience was clear on this point because the Word of God to all people is clear on this point. In God's kingdom, there is something holy, something special about the marriage vows and union.

Even though I had made a promise to give myself to Olga

in marriage, I was still aware that, as a born again Christian ensured heaven after death, I belonged to the Lord God. I had given my life to God years prior to promising to give my body and soul to Olga.

I was going to live and grow in the relationship with Olga following the guidelines in the Bible. My engagement did not give me free reign to rewrite the rules of morality. Marriage meant that I would have to depend on God more than ever. I knew that I couldn't have a successful marriage without God. No way!

I was thinking about all these points on the train ride home the next day. Olga asked me why I was quiet. She wanted to talk about the wedding, but I said, "We have a lot of time to plan for the wedding. I would rather start next week. For now, I am still on vacation." In fact, I was in a dream world of my mind's own making. In a daydream, I could control consequences and the future.

The one thing that Olga and I agreed on was to wait to tell our parents until we arrived home. Having taken the "sleeper" train ride back home over night, we arrived at home at 7 a.m. We went to my house first and told my parents. Then we went to Olga's house and woke up her parents to tell them the good news about us. Olga's mother seemed extremely happy. Olga showed off her diamond engagement ring.

I got what my impulses wanted - a bride-to-be with a shapely body and what I hoped was an undying love for me. I based my marriage proposal on Olga's "maybe."

Chapter Twenty-eight

Engagement Party

My parents had a birthday party for me, but it turned into an "engagement party," since it was a week after Olga and I announced that we were getting married. The occasion would have been fine, but the problem was that none of Olga's family was invited. Olga was not happy about it, but, for the most part, she hid her irritation from my family.

My grandparents, cousins, aunts and uncles showered Olga with compliments and gifts. Hearing them made me proud. My family had not seen me with many beautiful girls, so I have to admit that it boosted my confidence to present the beautiful, dancing sensation Olga to them as my bride-to-be.

"Olga, you are so pretty," my aunt said to her.

Olga was dressed in a black outfit with white, frilly trim. Her make-up was perfect and her hair had curvy style. Her beauty seemed to reflect on me. Even if I told myself that my vanity was not something God would be pleased with, I couldn't help myself from enjoying the fact of having an outward show of my success as a man. I kept telling myself that God had finally given me a "break" after years of failure and rejection with women. I let my feelings rule my thinking. I was in love and, amazingly, a beautiful woman was in love with me. I wanted to show it to the world, even if I was ignoring my spiritual blind spots.

The engagement party was fun. We ate great food and had a big cake. Everyone took pictures of the two of us. We opened the gifts in front of everyone. I heard the "oohs" and "ahhs." The funniest part of the party was when Olga opened up a gift from one of my aunts. She took out the gift and held up what looked like a see-through, red scarf. It took a few seconds for Olga to figure out that it was a sexy nightgown.

Smiling, I said to everyone, "That's more a gift for me on our wedding night than for her."

I was essentially telling people that I was focused on our wedding night as the night of intimacy and becoming "one flesh." Written on my heart, I had a biblical perspective, no matter how sexy a piece of lingerie was.

Olga was quiet. In fact, she was quiet most of the time at the engagement party. She smiled politely and kissed the cheek of the older people, but she was unusually quiet. I thought that she would take the party in stride as I was doing.

My sister's boyfriend asked us, "When will your wedding be?"

"We haven't set a date yet," I replied. "We have to look around. I am not in a hurry. We'll find a place and set a date."

My aunt then asked, "Did you take Olga with you to pick out the diamond ring?"

"No," I replied. "I bought it on my own. I am a romantic and I wanted to surprise her."

"That's nice."

Olga stared at the engagement ring on her finger. She seemed to gaze into it, as if looking at her own reflection in the ring. The ring sparkled on her finger.

"I like diamonds," she said intensely.

"I hope you don't like them too much."

She said in a joking fashion, "I think I like them too

much."

We laughed. Then she continued to stare at the diamond ring, as if it had a spell on her. To me, the ring was simply a small outward expression of my commitment to her. The real commitment was in my heart, which I had opened up to the Lord Jesus Christ. No matter what anybody else did or said, I wanted to do the will of God. But I was still subconsciously trying to serve two masters. I was still trying to control some aspect of my life with Olga. It made me feel good.

The engagement party was a success to me, but not to Olga. When we left the party and walked across the parking lot, she did more talking in the next ten minutes than she did all through the party. She had evidently bottled up how she felt and now she was letting it out like a wild tiger.

"I can't believe that your mother turned your birthday party into an engagement party without telling me. I could have invited my family. I would have liked to have had my grandmother here today."

"I am sorry, Olga. I don't think my mother did it on purpose."

"Oh, yes, she did."

"I think my relatives simply brought engagement gifts of their own accord. My mother couldn't control it."

"And I am appalled that one of your aunts would give me the red thing. It is see-through. I was embarrassed."

"My aunt has a sense of humor. She didn't mean to insult you."

"She should have treated me with more respect," said Olga. "I think more of your family could treat me with more respect."

"They respect you. Why are you saying these things?"

"And I didn't like the restaurant that your mother picked. Couldn't she have picked a nicer restaurant?"

"This is a nice restaurant and the prices are affordable. She can't afford to take us to the most expensive restaurant in town," I said, defending my mother.

"If she knew it was an engagement party, then she should be willing to spend more money for her son."

"My mother is very generous. I don't want her to go broke to give us a party."

"I am going to be your wife, Martin. Don't you care how I feel?"

"Of course, but I think you are being unfair to my mother."

"No, I am not," she said staunchly.

Later in the day, I thought about Olga's edgy attitude. She seemed different – more demanding and critical. I was surprised. I didn't understand why she was so sharp in blaming my mother. I also thought that she went too far to expect my mother to pay a huge amount of money for a party at an expensive restaurant. I was appreciative that my mother and father were willing to have any party at all.

I was struggling with my sense that Olga was violating the Bible's principles and indulging her irritable emotions. I did not have a good grasp of how far Olga could go. In my helplessness, I prayed for Olga.

"Heavenly Father, in Jesus name, I ask You to get through to Olga and show her the truth in You. Olga needs to be saved. She needs to know You, Jesus. This is her only hope in life. If she plans to criticize everything and everyone, she will never be happy. She was very irritable today and I think she was a little irritated at me, but I pray for her. Bless her and comfort her! Reveal to her the truth. I love her with all my heart and so do You. Use me as an example of Your grace and love. Father, You continue to mold me to be more like Your Son Jesus. May Olga see Jesus in me! I want Your light to shine through me, separating from the darkness. In Jesus name. Amen."

In short, I had become engaged to a woman who was not a Christian. Right after the engagement, she slowly started to change. I sensed minor signals about her change, but I thought she was going through a phase. Besides, my love for her was huge and I continually told myself that I would endure through all things for the love of my life. I was a Christian believer and I believed that love was enough to make a marital commitment work well.

I wanted to prove to Olga that a Christian has endurance and a positive outlook on life. I hoped from the depth of my being that my Christian witness to her would be enough for God to get through to her heart and convince her to give her life to Jesus Christ, who is God. Full of hope, I lived each day with a sense of inspired energy.

Chapter Twenty-nine

Dancing Sensation

I found a new way for me to exercise my love for Olga and my faith in God, as well as my natural creative talent. Knowing that Olga was committed to dancing as a lifetime interest, I decided to help her get a small "ballroom dancing" business started. I developed the plans myself and then I presented the idea to her.

"Olga, I want to help you start your own dance studio now," I said. "The future is now. I can be the business manager while you teach the students."

"I love the idea," she said, radiating with a positive reaction.

"I have already developed a plan. It entails my developing a Web site. Will you be able to rent space at other studios to teach students?"

"Yes, I'm sure I can."

"Great," I said. "And we're going to call it Dancing Sensation."

She laughed.

I said, "We can create marketing brochures with the tag line of, you know, 'Become a Dancing Sensation! Take Lessons with Olga.' How does it sound?"

"Fabulous! I can make extra money by teaching."

"It will take time to build up the business, but I would be committed to it and, five years from now, we could have a good dance studio business going."

"The other dance studio owners are going to hate us because we will be competing with them."

"I realize that the ballroom dancing scene is very competitive between studios," I said. "But I am not going to back down because other studio owners won't like that I take business from them. You are a great dance teacher, Olga. You will care more deeply about how the students dance. All the other studios seem to care about is how much money they can make off the students. Since I have lost money at both studios I've signed up with, I know."

"The idea of having my own studio is thrilling," she said, clapping her hands. "You are amazing to do the work to help me get it started. I know I can make it successful. I can teach much better than most of the teachers I have had in America. But I need a name."

"What do you mean?"

"I am not well-known yet. I need to win a major dance championship in order to command top dollar. Without being famous and making a name for myself, the most I can charge a student is probably $50 a lesson. But once I win a championship or two, then I can charge $75 a lesson or more. People will pay it because they want to take lessons with a champion. I want to be a ballroom dancing champion more than anything in the world," said Olga.

"I'll see you after your practice," I said, waving goodbye to her.

While she went to practice dancing by herself at a studio, I went to the mall. I found a store that customizes messages on hats, so I ordered the words "Dancing Sensation" to be stitched on the front of a black hat. I wanted to surprise Olga with it.

When I saw her later in the day, I noticed that she looked unhappy.

"You don't look happy," I said to her without mincing my

words. “You look like you are brooding.”

“I am not happy.”

“But we are getting married and –“

“It’s not that,” she claimed. “I am not happy about my dancing situation. I need to win a championship, but I don’t have a partner. I am not making enough money to pay for lessons with a top coach so I can become good enough to get a first-rate partner. I am depressed.”

I said, “Look, if it will help you, I will help pay for some lessons with a top coach. I don’t have a lot of money, but I can pay for some lessons. Then, when you start making money or you get your own partner, I can stop paying for your lessons. I need to save up money for us to live together after we get married, but I think I can afford some lessons today.”

The expression on Olga’s face changed dramatically. She looked happy. She hugged me and thanked me profusely. I gave her the hat with “Dancing Sensation” stitched on the front of it. She laughed. Then she went off to call a dance coach in order to make an appointment.

She called me later and said, “I have made an appointment with one of the best coaches in town. His name is Chris. He won championships in England.”

“How much does he charge for dance lessons?”

“He charges $350 for five lessons.”

“Wow!” I blurted out. “That’s a lot of money.”

“Bit it makes me happy, Martin,” she said slowly.

“Okay.”

“You’re the best.”

“I hope you can stretch out the five lessons over a long period of time.”

“Oh, yes, I will probably take one or two lessons per month.”

“Good. Thanks for being reasonable.”

“I am so excited,” she said. “I have to go out with my

mother to buy new dancing shoes. I also need to go look at new clothes. I have lost six pounds and I plan to lose more."

"But please don't force yourself to lose too much weight too fast."

"I need to get skinnier."

"You are skinny, Olga."

"No, I am not."

"Your body looks fine."

"To be a ballroom dancer, I need to be skinnier. I need to lose another ten pounds."

"But don't starve yourself."

"I won't, but I need to eat less and exercise more."

"Make sure you are doing what is healthy for your body," I said. "I care about your physical health, as well as your emotional and spiritual health."

"Thank you, Martin."

Even though I was trying to be a positive influence on Olga's life, I realized later that I was not praying as consistently or fervently as I should have been. I felt that I could handle the situation, so I wasn't actively seeking God's guidance. What's more, I was unconsciously defying Proverbs 3:5. I was leaning on my own understanding.

Moreover, although I was still saved by the blood of Jesus and sealed for eternal life by God, I was not acknowledging the Lord in all my ways. I don't exactly know the point it started to happen, but I was getting off course and I was using "love" as the justification. However, was the quality of my love self-centered or selfless? The tests would come soon in our relationship.

A few days later, I gave Olga a check for $350 so that she could take her coveted dance lessons with the coach named Chris. The thought crossed my mind that this guy Chris might be a sleazy character, but I put it out of my mind because I wanted to continue to trust Olga. As far as I knew, I had no reason to distrust her. I believed that Olga considered our relationship to be important and special as I did. I believed that love was filling her up in such amazing ways that she was letting go of her selfish ways and giving herself completely to our relationship.

Meanwhile, I worked quickly to set up the Web site for Dancing Sensation. I reserved the Web site URL and I paid a Web site developer to design the Web site. I also paid an Internet service company to host the site. I sunk about $250 into the Web site during the first week. I felt good about what I was doing. I couldn't wait to show Olga.

At the end of the week, when she called me after her lesson, she was excited.

"Martin, I loved my first lesson with Chris. He is a great dancer. I learned new things. He worked me out hard."

"Good. It sounds like we got our money's worth."

"Certainly! And he thinks I am good enough to compete in a competition in less than two months."

"Already?"

"Can you believe it? I will need to take more lessons than I thought."

"You do?"

"I will need to take at least one lesson each week and I will need to practice three or four times a week. I want to win the championship."

"I know you will win, Olga," I said, wanting to encourage her.

"I wouldn't have this opportunity without you, Martin. Thank you for paying for the lessons. I will need another $350 next month. My five lessons will run out in a month. I have booked my next lesson for next Tuesday."

This was exactly what I didn't want to happen. I should have been saving up money for the wedding, but Olga had a short-term focus and she wanted to dance with all her heart. Fearing that disappointing her would ruin our relationship, I quickly agreed to continue to financially support her dancing.

In the back of my mind, I was thinking, "I hope God is on board with this." It is frightening to make a decision or take an action when there is no assurance that this is what God wants done. But I had been affected by rejection and failure with women for so long that I was drifting away from waiting on the Lord.

Wanting to change the subject, I said to Olga, "I have good news. I have set up the Web site for Dancing Sensation. I paid a designer to design it. I have paid an Internet company to host it. And-"

"But I cannot start teaching with my studio now," she said, interrupting me.

"Why not?"

"Because Chris is a professional, I will be qualified as an amateur. I will dance Pro/Am with Chris. As an amateur, I cannot be paid for teaching lessons to students."

"Oh. I didn't know that."

I was disappointed. All of my work and investment in the Dancing Sensation Web site was for nothing. It was too late to get my money back. The Web site would have to remain as a stagnant site on the Internet, adding to the list of static, pointless Web sites that exist.

If I had been more patient and had waited to develop the Web site until Olga's dancing plans were ironed out, then I could have saved myself the trouble, the time, the effort and the money. I paid a price for impatience, even though the idea seemed good.

Chapter Thirty

Surprise on Anniversary

Still getting over the sting of the Web site failure, I tried to get myself on an emotional high by focusing on our one-year anniversary. I made plans – and again opened up my checkbook – to have a special evening with Olga. The key element was surprise. All I told her was that I wanted to take her out for our anniversary – exactly one year from the day of our first date.

When I walked into Olga's house, I said to her, "You look stunning."

She was wearing a black outfit with a sparkling, diamond-like belt around her waist. The diamonds looked real to me, but she said they were fake diamonds. They enhanced her appearance. As usual, her hair looked perfect.

I kissed her on her cheek and said, "Happy Anniversary." Then I gave her a dozen red roses in a beautiful bouquet.

She smiled sweetly and said, "The flowers are beautiful."

"We better be going. We have reservations."

"Where are we going?" she asked.

"It's a surprise. You'll see when we get there," I replied, smiling.

"Always a surprise with you," she remarked, as she smelled the roses.

Then we stepped outside together. It was a beautiful evening – cool with a gorgeous sunset. I wanted to enjoy every moment. I felt aware of God's goodness to me. The sunset was like raspberry and vanilla ice cream in a swirl.

Olga and I walked down the walkway. Olga started to turn to the left; whereas, I turned to the right. She was headed toward the spot where I usually parked my car. But she was going to be surprised.

I said, "Follow me."

"Where did you park?"

"Please just follow me," I said, smiling and waving my arm. I was asking her to trust me.

Looking curious, she followed me around the corner. I took her hand and we walked down the street. I didn't say a word. Yet, I could see her reaction coming on slowly. She put her hands in front of her mouth.

Then, swinging her arms up, she shouted, "No." She sounded like a child who was overcome by surprise to the point of where she couldn't believe it.

"Yes, it's true," I said, still smiling broadly.

"A limousine?"

"Just for us!"

"That is wonderfully romantic on our anniversary," she uttered, still in shock.

It was a black, stretch limo with a contemporary, sleek styling. The limo driver held the door open for Olga and me. The vehicle was extremely comfortable inside. We had access to a TV, a radio and a mini-bar. Olga was so excited that, like a child, she pushed all the buttons.

"Take it easy," I said. "You don't know what all the buttons do."

"This is the first time I have ever been in a limo."

"It won't be the last," I said. "We'll get a white limo for our wedding day."

Olga virtually jumped on me and kissed me. Then she moved quickly around the limo, unwilling to stay in any one spot for more than a few seconds. She looked excited, but, as a Christian, I was not going to take advantage of the opportunity for selfish reasons. I believed that romance requires patience and waiting. If I had gotten the limo in order to get her into bed for pre-marital sex, then my motive would have been slanted and tainted. But I had gotten this limo to show her how much I love her.

I wanted her to know that I wanted the best for her. She accepted the limo with open arms. How would she like something better than the limo? Faith in Jesus Christ is infinitely better than a limo ride. Being adopted into God's family – through faith in Jesus – is eternally more significant than being a passenger in a stretch limo. I viewed this limo ride as the beginning of Olga's acceptance of the "royal" treatment I wanted to shower on her, reflecting God's love.

While Olga was focused on the limo as "the thing," I was focused on the "giver" of the thing – the Creator of the universe. Without the love of God flowing through me, I wouldn't have given freely and openly to Olga. I was giving to her with no expectation of anything in return, except for perhaps her appreciation. I did not want to compromise the future of our marriage by making a mistake and rushing into sexual relations, simply because our emotions were soaring.

The limo took us to a fine French restaurant and the driver waited outside. I escorted Olga into the restaurant, which was very elegant.

"I love this place," she remarked.

After we sat down and looked at the menus, she ordered lamb and I ordered filet mignon. I thought that it was interesting for Olga to get lamb because Jesus is known as the Lamb of God. Her lamb at the restaurant tasted good and was nourishment for her body, but the Lamb of God would be nourishment for her soul. I was getting excited that God was moving to open Olga's "spiritual eyes" and "save" her soul. Nothing would have been more pleasing to me.

With Christ, she would enjoy true freedom – freedom

from sin and death. She would have access to the God who can help her and comfort her. She would gain a more positive perspective on life and learn of her purpose in life. The benefits of welcoming Jesus into her life would be countless.

With a heart of love, I wished the best for Olga.

Religion would be very different. Religion would bind her, making her focus on outward expression of piety, rather than inward relationship with Christ. Religion creates hierarchies and can cause a person to be intolerant of others. Religion cannot free a person from sin or death. Religion can actually put a person in violation of God's immutable laws. And why would people want to be "religious" and live counterfeit lives when the riches of Christ are available to them for the asking? I was not desiring Olga to become religious. Instead, I was hoping the love of Jesus would transform her and put her on the right path in life. It would bring us closer in intimacy. I believed I was acting on faith.

But was my heart in the right place? Where was I compromising in my own life? Or did God have me on a path of particular experiences to mature me? Or was God on the verge of testing me? Could God trust me? Was the "success" in a romantic relationship – something I had been craving with all my being for several years – going to change me for the better or for the worse?

As I sat in the restaurant, I was feeling nothing but positive. A harpist was playing near us. The smooth, soft sounds of the harp seemed to float on the air like angels humming. The music, the food, the atmosphere – all of it blended into a memorable time for us.

"This is as perfect as it could be on earth," I said to Olga. "Everything has been wonderful tonight."

"The food was incredible."

"I can't believe that you got a limo. I never expected it," she said.

"I wanted to surprise you."

"Well, you did."

As she sipped her water, I looked into her deep, dark eyes and wanted to convey to her my feeling of love for her. I felt that my love for her was like a never-ending fountain.

"I love you, Olga," I said to her gently.

"Oh," she uttered, touching my hand. "I love you, too."

It was good to hear her say it to me.

"I wasn't expecting the harp music, but it's interesting," I said.

"Yes, I like it."

Then she looked at the engagement ring on her finger.

"You still like the ring?" I asked.

"Of course! I never knew that I would love diamonds so much. I want to get a wedding ring with diamonds on it, too."

"I thought that a wedding ring is just a plain gold ring."

"It doesn't have to be. I saw an ad for a ring with diamonds on both sides of it."

"How much does that cost?" I asked.

"I don't know," she replied.

This reminded me that she had a tendency to want something but not know the cost of it. I didn't say anything about it. I didn't want to ruin the evening. If I said anything about the importance of knowing the cost of something, it would have ruined the romantic mood. I was not stupid. I didn't see myself as a "preacher" who had to correct her every little thought. Nonetheless, I was starting to notice a pattern that she didn't make an effort to evaluate the cost of something before setting her heart on it. If she wanted something, the cost seemed to be negligible. What would be the biggest price she would pay to get her heart's desire?

I looked out the window and I saw the limo driver standing outside the limo. Unlike Olga, I was aware of how much the limo was costing me, but I was happy to pay it. The evening was memorable and incredibly special. Olga and I reluctantly left the restaurant and returned to the limo.

After we climbed back inside and the limo driver closed the door, Olga said, "Let's go party! I don't want to go home."

"Oh, the plan was to go out and have a romantic dinner," I said. "I didn't plan to go any place else."

Olga was disappointed. I didn't want to go out and drink alcohol.

With her sad eyes, Olga looked at me and stuck out her pouting lip.

"Here comes the lip," I said with a hint of humor.

"Planner!" she said sharply.

Then we both broke out laughing. Nothing was going to ruin this incredibly special and dreamy evening of romance. Olga backed down from her desire to "party" and she hugged me during the ride back to her house.

"I love you" was the last thing I said to her before she exited the limo in style.

Chapter Thirty-one

The First Competition

Olga worked extremely hard in practice to prepare for her first U.S. competition. She practiced dancing by herself four times a week and she worked out at the gym three times a week. As time moved closer to the competition, she started to take two lessons a week with her coach. I was giving her a check for $350 every three weeks. Wanting to be the supportive fiancée, I gave her the money without making a big deal of it. I wanted to keep a lifestyle of giving.

Once I said to Olga, "God loves a cheerful giver."

She nodded, smiled and accepted the check. Then she talked to me about her dancing, which some people could argue was her god. I wouldn't have said it. I felt that she was on the verge of giving her life to the real, living and all-powerful God. How marvelous it would be for her! She could let go of all the nagging things that bothered her. Give it to the Lord! Set herself free from the entanglements of human nature – greed, impatience, jealousy and all the rest!

I was interested in Truth.

I told her more than once, "The Jewish people are God's chosen people. This is what the Bible says. Everything that is happening in the Middle East today was predicted by the Bible thousands of years ago in God-inspired prophecies."

I was pure in my motive, judging no one and accepting all

into God's family of repentant believers, but I had a conviction. It was a deep abiding belief in the Word of God that examines the souls of people. The Bible explains human nature perfectly. Experience and evidence prove it. Sin is real in human nature and people don't know what to do with sin. Sadly, sin is the root of many people's problems, but people refuse to admit it or confess it to God, based on the shed blood of Jesus.

Scripture verses from the Bible churned in my mind throughout the days. Bible verses came to my consciousness automatically in situations. No effort on my part! This made me believe that the Holy Spirit brought things to my attention and I had a choice in believing it or not. My conscience would alert me when I was going outside the will of God, but God still let me have free will. The Bible is the revealed will of God for all people – of all races. I know that I know.

Did my conviction in God and the Bible make me a suitable mate for Olga?

What a question! It crossed my mind in the days leading up to the first dance competition that was Olga's main focus. I was secondary to her during this time period. I had a habit of thinking of important things and *not* sharing my thoughts with Olga. It was fear that she would reject me, if she knew the truth about my faith in Jesus, who is the only way to heaven. To paraphrase, God says, "Take it or leave it."

I felt like Moses. God has a purpose for me. I am a spokesperson for God – an ambassador for Christ. God wrote His laws on the tablet of my heart, enlivened by my conscience, which had been regenerated when I asked Jesus to become my personal Lord and Savior. As a changed person, I was privileged to be sensitive to God's desires. More importantly, God was sensitive to my desires, like a father sensitive to a child's desires.

When I went to the dance competition to see Olga, I was thinking about my relationship with God.

I sat down in the back row and slouched down in the chair. My presence was a show of support for Olga. I didn't see her on the floor, however. I assumed that she was still getting ready in another room. I imagined that Olga was dancing on the floor, which was huge. Plenty of room for Olga to shine in her dancing!

A family was sitting in front of me. The young child was trying to run onto the dance floor, but the father was holding her back. The child screamed and cried, but the father scolded her and said, "Wait!" The child didn't like to hear the word "Wait." Even though the child struggled to escape, the father held her tightly. I believe he knew that she would get hurt if she ran across the dance floor where strong dancers were moving fast. The child didn't seem to understand her father's love, which was trying to protect her.

Minutes later, the announcer announced Olga's name. I applauded along with the large audience. Olga walked out onto the floor with her head held up. She was wearing a sparkling outfit. Her hair was pulled back very tightly on her head. It looked uncomfortable, but she had to look like the other girls.

The music began with foreboding power.

I whispered a prayer to God, "Help Olga, Lord! Please bless her dancing!"

Olga and her coach launched into dancing like fireworks exploding. They danced five different routines consecutively. The music was powerful. Olga danced sensationally to me. She was truly a dancing sensation. When she finished, the crowd applauded and shouted words of praise. It was a shining moment for her.

I rushed down to the edge of the stage and, after Olga was congratulated by several people, I walked up to her and said, "You were wonderful, Olga."

"Thanks."

"I am proud of you," I said sincerely.

"I hope I win."

"All the dancers have been good."

"But I want to win," she said pointedly.

"I think you have a great chance to win."

"You do?"

"Yes."

I realized that she didn't quite like my complimenting the other dancers.

"We are all very competitive with each other," she admitted to me.

"I've noticed," I replied with a light tone.

"I want to introduce you to a couple of people, Martin."

She introduced me to a woman who turned out to be fifty years old, but she looked like she was thirty-five years old. Dancing apparently kept her young-looking. Her name was Maureen. Then Olga introduced me to a woman who was a doctor. She didn't look like a doctor in her ballroom dancing outfit, but I took Olga's word for it.

Olga's coach called for her. "Olga, Olga, come out to the center of the floor with me. They are about to announce the winners."

Olga and four other women walked onto the floor and stood in line. The spotlight shined on them. It was inevitable that four of the five women would walk away displeased about losing. If Olga lost, I knew that she would be emotionally crushed. I was feeling the anticipation.

"And the winner is..." said the announcer. After a short pause, he said Olga's name. Olga's face turned pink with relief. Her friends screamed joyfully from the sideline. Her coach hugged her. Olga gave a smile that was brighter than any smile I had seen on her since the limo ride. She was clearly emotional. I was happy for her.

I shouted to her, "Congratulations! I love you!"

"I was only going to accept first place," she said to me a minute later. "I am glad I won."

"Wonder if you lost?"

"I would have run in the back and cried."

"Well, you won, so you don't have to cry," I said. "Now you can take things easy."

"No." Her tone was forceful.

"No?"

She said, "I can enjoy this winning first place, but tomorrow I need to start getting ready for the next competition."

"Already?"

She looked at me harshly and remarked, "You do want me to win, don't you?"

"I do," I insisted. "I am very happy that you just won. I thought that you would get a break before the next competition. We haven't been able to go out and go to a movie together because you have been busy with dancing."

"No rest for the weary in the dancing world."

"I guess not."

"I am going to go dancing with Chris and his other students at a club. Can I call you tomorrow, Martin?"

"Sure," I replied. I didn't tell her that I had been wishing for the two of us to spend time together after the competition. She was enthusiastic about going to a club to dance with the other trained dancers.

"And Chris invited me to go dancing at another club next Saturday night. If I want to be better known in the dancing world, I need to go to these ballroom dancing parties. Chris will introduce me to people, especially potential dance partners for me."

"He'll be introducing you to male dance partners?"

"Yes, isn't he nice to do it?"

"Oh, he's a peach," I said with biting sarcasm.

"What's that tone for?" she asked me.

"Nothing."

"What are you thinking, Martin?"

"Nothing."

"I don't believe it."

"Just go and have fun with your friends at the club! We'll talk tomorrow."

I kissed her goodbye. I made my desires and my feelings subservient to her desires and her feelings. Like a "good boy," I complied with what she wanted. I wanted my patience and my trust to be a Christian witness, even though the temptation to be annoyed with her was knocking on the door of my soul. I was careful not to harm the trust I had with her.

Besides, I had no control over her and I wanted no control over her. True love does not involve controlling another person. Selfishness is the thing that could pollute love. I was unwilling to pollute my love for Olga. Humbling myself, I put my trust in the Lord to give me the strength to let her go on her own and slip away into the seduction of dancing at a club late into the night.

Olga loved dancing. She was a sensation. This thought replayed in my mind over and over again on my way home. I was in bed before midnight, while my fiancée was dancing with the world. God knows when Olga went to bed.

Chapter Thirty-two

MORE DIFFERENCES

Planning a wedding is not easy. Planning a wedding between a Christian and a non-Christian is particularly difficult. I wanted to do what the Lord God wanted. Olga wanted to do what she wanted. I won't say that what Olga wanted was "wrong," but there was an unstated, friendly battle for control of decisions. The first major sign to me that this battle was underway was the choosing of the reception site for the wedding.

Olga had a couple of choices and I had a couple of choices for the reception. Honestly, I tried to make it a joint decision, but I initiated the conversation.

"We need to consider cost, style, size, quality of food and location," I said.

Olga didn't say anything, but I think she disliked that I was outlining the criteria, which I had read in a wedding planning book. Some men do not like to get involved in the details of the wedding day, but knowing that Olga wouldn't weigh costs, I had to be involved, I thought.

Also, planning events was something I did for work, so I believed that I could easily adapt my planning skills to the wedding. Moreover, it would take work off of Olga's plate and she would have more time to focus on dancing. I've heard other women complain that their boyfriends don 't help plan for a wedding. Women couldn't accuse me of being one of those uninvolved boyfriends.

But Olga was still quietly resentful about our picking one of my choices.

"This is the place you wanted all along, Martin," she said to me.

"No, that's not true. I could have easily gone with one of your choices. But one of your choices was much too expensive and the other choice was poor quality. You said it yourself. What's the problem? I thought you liked the reception place I showed you. It is within our price range. It looks elegant. The location is near the city."

"That's it. It is near the city. You weren't really open to having our wedding reception outside the city. Admit it!"

"I admit it," I replied. "Location is important to me. I wanted to be in a central location. There are people coming from the north, south and west. This location is convenient for all of them."

"You don't have to choose a reception place just because the guests would like it."

"They're our guests," I said, throwing up my arms.

"And they should be glad they are invited."

"I will be glad if they come," I said.

"And I want to see the whole invitation list before we send out invitations."

"Okay," I said. "I will have the invitations done at a print shop near my work."

"I want a small wedding," said Olga. "No more than fifty people."

"But my mother wants to invite more people. I have a big family."

"My family won't pay for more than twenty-five people."

"Fine. My mother already said that she would pay for my side," I altered Olga.

She didn't respond.

"Olga, I think we need a break. This wedding planning

has been causing us stress. I want to suggest to you that we have a getaway weekend. Just the two of us! We'll stay in the city and go to a dance club. How would that sound?"

"Sounds okay," she replied blandly. Her mind seemed to float off to think about something that she wasn't revealing to me.

"By the way, I have to go to California next week for work. I leave on Monday morning at 8 a.m."

"September 10th?"

"Right."

"How long will you be gone for?"

"Until Thursday."

"You'll be partying," she said with humor.

"No, I will be working hard all day and going to sleep early." I was serious. "My company works me very hard when I go out to California. They have me work twelve-hour days."

"Better you than me."

I went away to make arrangements for our "getaway weekend." I booked a suite with two bedrooms at an old hotel in the city. Again, I was planning to sleep in a separate bed from Olga. This had nothing to do with my attraction for her. It was simply my faith in Jesus Christ being exercised, somewhat like a bodybuilder is faithful to lift weights and eat right. Yet, I was doing it for the soul. Sex can destroy. Reality proves it. The world is littered with broken relationships.

I wanted to use wisdom and I will never forget a phrase that a Christian minister said on radio many years ago – "When it is wise to wait."

When the weekend rolled in like a break in the clouds letting sunshine through, Olga and I checked into the hotel. Olga's facial expression showed her feeling when she saw the separate bedrooms. I thought that she was going to mutter, "Here we go again with the Christianity," but she didn't.

I couldn't read her mind, but I sensed that she was somewhat disappointed. I tried to ignore this sense I was having about her. I had a strong belief that she had to see me on more than one occasion show her that I stood for moral integrity. I was being tested and I wanted to pass the test.

We went to dinner at a nice seafood restaurant. I was looking forward to the conversation with Olga. I liked having conversations with her.

"Olga, thank you for joining me on this getaway weekend. I felt that we needed a break from the treadmill of life we have been on lately. It is great to spend time with you and just hang out."

Sipping my glass of wine, I turned and looked out the window at the stunning sunset. Without looking at her, I said, "My life has changed because of you, Olga. I am not lonely anymore. I am able to be open and free with my giving. I appreciate you, my love."

"I am glad that you don't feel lonely," she said.

"We are going to have a fantastic wedding."

"How do you know?"

"Because I am going to pray for God's blessings on our wedding," I replied immediately, looking into her eyes. "You know that I am spiritual."

Olga sipped her drink and looked away from me.

I continued, "I am really looking forward to our wedding night, too. We will get intimate and start a new life as husband and wife. I love you, Olga, and I respect you. My love for you means more to me than I ever thought possible. I want to prove my genuine love to you by waiting for intimacy with you. We are in the engagement period and we don't have to rush things. God created marriage as a blessing to people and I want the best in marriage. In fact, I want to make a toast." I lifted my glass and then Olga lifted her glass. "To our future marriage – may it be the best God has to give us!"

Carefully, I tapped her glass with my glass. I smiled, which compelled her to smile back at me. Without any forced effort, the words "I love you" slipped out of my mouth again. I was all about love.

We ate and then took a taxi to the dance club. She wanted to dance. No surprise there! This wasn't ballroom dancing, however. This was a techno music club. Even though I am a Christian, I didn't want to be "a stick in the mud." I could dance and slip into the crowd. My faith in Jesus still remained dominant in my heart, but no one on the outside could see it.

As soon as we walked into the club, Olga said, "I want a drink."

She asked me to get her an alcoholic beverage. For myself, I bought a Pepsi.

When she saw me return with the drinks, she remarked, "Only Pepsi."

"I took the Pepsi Challenge at the bar."

Olga looked confused. She didn't know what I was talking about. This reminded me that she had only been in the U.S. for four years. I couldn't expect her to be familiar with all aspects of American pop culture from years ago.

The music was pounding and methodic. People were pouring into the club, as if they were coming to breathe new life. Machines were pumping white smoke into the club for atmosphere. Through the smoke, I saw physically attractive women wearing skimpy clothes.

I turned to Olga and said, "You are the most beautiful woman in here, Olga."

"Please!" she replied, not believing me. "But some of the girls do look cheap in here."

It was no surprise to me that she was evaluating different girls in the room.

"I haven't been to a techno dance club like this in a long time. I used to go with friends from college."

"I feel comfortable in a club like this."

"Funny, I don't," I said.

"Then why are you here?"

"Because you wanted to come here," I told her.

"Do you want to leave?"

"No, Olga, I didn't mean it that way. I wouldn't come here all the time, but I am fine right now."

"I wouldn't come here all the time either. It would get boring."

"At least we agree on that," I said.

Then, suddenly, four "go-go girls" jumped up onto four dispersed platforms and started to dance. They were wearing knee-high boots and small outfits. Men were staring at them from all around the club. I was thinking, "I wonder if these girls get tired of dancing like that all night."

Olga grabbed my hand and pulled me onto the dance floor. She danced in a sensual way, letting her body go.

"Relax, Martin," she said to me.

Letting my body move impulsively to the music, I gradually worked my way into comfortable dancing movements. The only problem was that people kept bumping into me or stepping on the back of my feet. But I persisted on the dance floor. Unlike ballroom dancing, this type of dancing was unstructured and free-flowing. My emotions carried me.

The surprise of the night came when I bumped into a woman. I said, "I'm sorry."

The girl turned out to be one of the go-go dancers who had come down from her platform and was walking through the crowd. I soon found out why.

"Come up to the stage with me," she said to me.

"No, thanks," I replied, continuing to dance in my spot in the middle of the crowd.

The go-go dancer said to Olga, "Make your boyfriend come dance on the stage."

Olga wanted me to go up on stage. "Go ahead, Martin."

"No, I don't want to."

Getting my message, the go-go dancer walked away, in search of another guy to bring up on stage. She found another guy within seconds. The guy – or whom I referred to as "sucker" – was all too willing to dance like an idiot on stage.

Olga leaned closer to me and said, "You should have gone up on stage and danced with the girl."

"Wouldn't you have been jealous that I was dancing with another woman?"

"No."

She shook her head and started to spin away from me.

Then a guy walked by me and handed me two glow sticks. They were fluorescent yellow. I yelled out to Olga, "What am I supposed to do with these?" But she couldn't hear me.

So, I began to imitate what other people were doing with the glow sticks on the dance floor. They were waving them, twirling them and shaking them. With one glow stick in each hand, I waved them like a madman. The music was becoming more aggressive and I was shaking my whole body to the beat. I wasn't holding back.

Olga and I danced for three hours at the club. We left at 2 a.m. We walked back to the hotel, which was only a block away. Olga seemed nonchalant, but I was intensely vigilant about muggers.

"Martin, you are so intense," said Olga.

"Walking down a city street at two in the morning isn't the same as a walk on the beach."

"Nothing is going to happen."

"It's true that God will protect us, but I still need to be vigilant. When I let my guard down, something could happen."

It was dark, but I caught a glimpse of Olga rolling her eyes, as she tossed her head back and sighed.

"I didn't say anything about God," she said. "I mean that

there are other people on the street, too. Everyone is leaving the clubs. It is safe to walk down the street."

"You have a thought-provoking perspective on the world, Olga," I said, too tired to think of anything else.

When we reached our hotel room, Olga said, "I want to watch TV. Do you want to join me?"

"I had fun tonight at the club, but my legs are killing me. I can't believe that we danced for three hours."

I sat down on the chair next to her bed, where she was sitting. She used the remote control to turn on the TV. She picked a channel that was showing a movie with a man and woman in bed with each other. My assumption was that they weren't married.

She asked, "Don't you want to join me on the bed?"

"Listen, I am so tired that I should go to my bed," I stated. "If I sit down on your bed, I will fall asleep."

"That's okay."

"You'll be more comfortable without me."

"How do you know?"

"In just a few more months, we will be married and we will have an exciting wedding night and we'll have fifty years to share a bed. Right now, I am exhausted and I can barely keep my eyes open." I was honest with her.

"I don't want to wait to our fiftieth wedding anniversary to have sex, Martin."

I laughed and replied, "You are a joker, Olga. You are only twenty-two years old. You have lots of years ahead of you. I will make up for this waiting after we get married. If we truly love each other, then we will wait because true love waits. This is part of God's plan of intimacy for our lives. A monogamous marriage between two committed people is the best relationship."

"You have never been married, Martin. How are you so sure?"

"I know Christian couples who have been married for

years and are very happy," I replied. "And I believe the Word of God."

She didn't say anything in response.

"Good night, Olga. See you tomorrow morning. We will go for a nice breakfast," I said gently. Leaving her room, I closed the door, took a deep breath and then went to my room. I needed to pray. As soon as I closed my door, I knelt down next to the bed and broke out in prayer:

"Heavenly Father, in Jesus name, thank You for keeping me morally strong during this time of extra temptation. If You weren't holding me true to Your Word and Your law, I would give in and go back into the other room and have sex with Olga. But I know You created sex for the rich joys of marriage. The world has hijacked sex and turned it into a cheap, counterfeit impostor that does not deliver the true promise of love. You are the Creator of love and I want Your best. I ask You to help Olga to understand. She will not understand me if she doesn't understand the reasons why I act. Show me how to deal with her! I commit my relationship with Olga to You, Lord God. May Your will be done. You have changed me for good. Make me a witness of Your work in my life. In Jesus name. Amen."

I went to bed without an assurance about Olga, but I trusted God. Just before I fell asleep, I was thinking about the verse that says God works all things for good for those who love and obey Him. This settled my mind. I didn't have to worry. Whatever was going to happen in the future, God was still in control and He could work anything and everything for a higher purpose.

I believe God impressed on my heart that my relationship with Olga would result in growing my character to the next stage of maturity. Resisting temptation was a way for my character to be refined and grow. I was taking a risk, but I was sure that God had not abandoned me.

On the next day, I bought an expensive breakfast for Olga.

More importantly, I intently listened to Olga talk about what was on her mind. Of course, it was ballroom dancing that was on her mind.

In between bites of her pancakes, she said, "I am happy that I won the local dance championship and I believe I can win the next one, too. I am also happy to have such a good coach in Chris. Now, if I can only get a steady partner, then everything will be complete. Chris says that I keep getting better. I should be better in the next competition than I was in the last one. My mother is going to come to the next competition. I want to show her how good I am. She expects the best from me. I better win. I think about dancing all the time. It is hard to think of anything else. I think of the wedding, of course, but I think of myself dancing at the wedding in my wedding dress. My mother and I are going to buy my wedding dress tomorrow. I want something that is going to stand out."

"Whatever dress you choose, Olga, you will look amazingly beautiful."

I kissed her.

"I believe what you say, Martin," she said. Then she broke out laughing.

"I wish you would believe everything I say."

"Fat chance," she said, again laughing loudly. "If I agreed with you on everything, life would get boring."

"Life could never be boring with you, Olga," I said, smiling. "You are one in a million."

"I have to get you back out on the dance floor, Martin."

"Please eat your pancakes!" I said, using a humorous tone to change the subject abruptly.

"Okay. Okay, you don't want to talk about dancing right now."

"You are a great ballroom dancer, Olga. I am not. Let's face reality."

"You are not as bad as you think, Martin."

"Listen, I am a sinner, and no religion can convince me

that I am not. In fact, I am worse than I think I am."

"You don't always have to mention religion."

"I don't feel like I *always* mention religion," I said.

"We won't talk about it."

I agreed to drop the subject. This might have been a mistake.

Then I told Olga my big surprise. She had no idea that I was planning a trip for us.

"Olga, I have a big surprise for you. I am planning a trip to Florida for us."

"But I have my competition."

"It will be after your competition."

"Great. I want to lie down on a beach in Florida."

"No, I made plans for us to go to Disney World."

She didn't seem enthusiastic.

"You're the planner, Martin." Her tone was less than flattering.

Chapter Thirty-three

September 11th

Two days later, my little issues with Olga seemed absolutely pointless in light of the tragedies that struck New York and Washington D.C. I was in California on a business strip on the day when the world changed. September 11th happened. Nothing more needs to be described. Everyone remembers where he or she was on September 11, 2001 when the news broke.

My heart broke along with the hearts of hundreds of millions of people. I fell to my knees and prayed fervently for the families of the victims. The attacks were obviously the work of terrorists.

With all due respect to the victims and their families, the reason I bring this up is to share two conversations I had with Olga during this week. After I heard the news on TV, I went to work and got permission to call my fiancée using an office telephone.

"Olga, it's me," I said with gravity in my voice. "I heard about the attacks in New York and Washington D.C. about an hour ago. A plane has also gone down in Pennsylvania."

"It is terrible, Martin."

"It is."

"Come home."

"I can't. All the airline flights are canceled."

"Don't take an airplane! Take a train home or drive a car,"

she insisted.

"Across country? I can't Olga. I will wait here in California until it is safe to fly."

"It is not safe to fly on an airplane."

"Olga, my faith is in God. He will protect me on a flight home. This is a time when faith is important. Without God, there is only hopelessness. But, as a Christian believer, God is with me. I will pray about what the right thing is to do."

"If there is any risk, don't take the airplane. Take a car, I tell you."

"If God puts it in my heart that I shouldn't board a plane, then I won't board the plane. But I will face this dire situation with courage. This is not about me. It is about thousands of people in New York who have died or are feared lost. The focus should not be on me and my little life. The focus must be on something much bigger. I can't help the people across the country, but I can pray and that is what I will be doing all week."

"Do you have to work today?"

"I am hearing that the company may give us the day off. Everyone is shaken up," I replied.

"Are people scared?"

"I think there are a lot of emotions swirling around in people. This is an incredibly difficult time in our nation's history. I don't think we, as Americans, have felt this vulnerable for a long time. The United States was built on principles from the Bible. Really, God blessed America and raised up this country as the best country in the world. As a nation, we have ignored Jesus for decades and it has left us vulnerable from dark spiritual attacks," I explained.

"I don't know why anyone would cause such death and destruction."

"Olga, I am sorry, but I need to get off the phone now, but I will call you later from my hotel room and we will talk more. Is that okay?"

"Yes, I understand that you are at work."

"Faith in God is what will get me home safely. Not to worry!"

"But God lets bad things happen to good people."

"It depends on how you define 'good.' God also allows good things to happen to sinful people like us. His protection is a good thing. I will not live in fear. God did not give me the spirit of fear. He has given me the Spirit of power and truth. I appreciate that God answers prayers. I'll talk to you later, Olga."

My company let all the employees have the day off, so I returned to my hotel room and watched the news coverage. Every so often, I had to say a prayer. It was my way of dealing with the situation. Humanity was helpless in the face of death. Only God is bigger than death.

One particular prayer has remained with me. "Heavenly Father, I pray for the families of the victims. We have experienced an unthinkable national loss today. The powers of evil have made an impression in this world of good and evil. Even though our society ignores Your Son Jesus and takes His precious name in vain as a swear, You are still God of the universe. As a nation, we have ignored You and Your Word, but we expect Your protection. Forgive us for our short-sightedness, but please have mercy on us! You are good, God, and I know You love everyone and You don't want to see a single person perish. Help the families of the victims."

Tears were coming out of my eyes.

After a brief pause, I continued in fervent prayer, "Father, You have given humanity free will. To me, it is dangerous to give people free will because people can choose and do choose to turn away from Your ways of life. But I trust You in Your eternal wisdom. I believe Your heart is hurting today, too, Lord, because man has chosen his own way of violence and hatred. Your Son Jesus told us to love our enemies. We could never do it in our own strength, but the Bible says You sent the Comforter, the Holy Spirit. We need You today, God. As a nation, we may need You more today than we have in a long time. Have mercy on us and comfort the families of the victims of the horrible attacks. In Jesus name, I pray. Amen."

My personal relationship with God made all the difference for me. I could go to Him for anything and speak my heart truthfully. I was not afraid. I sensed His presence like subtle warmth in my soul. His love was shining.

Just before calling Olga later in the day, I read a part of Psalm 23 to myself, "The Lord is my shepherd, I shall not be in want. He makes me lie down in green pastures. He leads me beside quiet waters. He restores my soul. He guides me in paths of righteousness for his name's sake. Even though I walk through the valley of the shadow of death, I will fear no evil, for You are with me; Your rod and Your staff, they comfort me."

A spiritual boldness was rising up in me.

Then I called Olga. "Hello, Olga, it's Martin. I have been watching all the media coverage all day. I have been praying for the families of the victims."

"I don't understand how this could happen," she said somberly.

"As a nation, we let our guard down and we underestimated what terrorists would do. God is love and He wouldn't command anyone to kill innocent people. God is the God of forgiveness. It is His nature to forgive, but it is also His nature to judge and be the standard of supreme justice. Jesus paid the price for human sins. The Bible says that the only way to heaven is through Jesus Christ."

"The Bible was written by men a long time ago. It is just another religious book. Each religion has its own book."

I became bolder.

"The Bible is not just another religious book. The Bible is

the Word of God. The difference between Christianity and other religions is that God came in the form of a man and died on the cross. Then He was raised from the dead. All the prophecies of the Jewish Bible, the Old Testament, came true. Read the book of Isaiah!"

"The Jewish Bible is not the same as the Old Testament of your Bible," claimed Olga.

"I am not an expert on the Jewish Bible, but the books of Moses are in the Christian Bible."

"Martin, I know you are emotional, but you call yourself a Christian only because your parents are Christians."

"No, that is not true," I replied. "My parents gave me more reasons to reject Christianity than they did for me to believe it. I would have abandoned Christian faith if it was not for one thing - Jesus is alive, spiritually-speaking. God has blessed me so much and He has answered my prayers. There is something more to God than human nature wants us to admit. I don't fear death, Olga. If I die today, I will immediately be in the presence of Jesus in heaven and I want Him to say, 'Well done, good and faithful servant.' As we saw today, we never know when death will come for any of us. My faith in Jesus gives me confidence. Jesus was either a liar or really the Son of God. You know what I believe."

After I said it to Olga, I realized that my tone of voice was more impassioned than I would have planned. Olga was silent on the line.

Then I said, "God is still in control."

She remained silent.

"Olga, I better hang up," I finally said. "My calling card is starting to run out."

"Okay. I'll see you when you come home."

"Sure thing."

My stay in California was extended three days because the airport was closed. When it opened over the weekend, I was one of the first people in it. Understandably, security was extremely tight. My co-workers were with me and they were nervous.

One of them said to me, "You don't seem nervous, Martin."

"I am not nervous. I have faith that we will get home safely."

My attitude of faith seemed to rub off on them because they gradually calmed down. I was the first to board the plane and I said words of encouragement to them all.

"God is in control," I whispered.

Hours later, we landed in the airport safely. As the plane was landing, the passengers broke out into thunderous applause. It was tremendous. I also found out upon arrival that armed U.S. marshals had been sitting near me.

After arriving home, I went to see Olga at her house. As soon as she opened her door, I hugged her and told her that I loved her. We were reunited and that was all that mattered. We needed each other, I felt.

"I am glad to be back with you," I told her affectionately. She hugged me tightly.

Chapter Thirty-four

THE SECOND COMPETITION

A month later, Olga said to me, "As President Bush says, we should move forward with our lives. We can't change the past. My way of moving on is through ballroom dancing."

"My way of moving forward is trusting in God," I said sincerely.

"Dancing is more fun," she stated with humor.

"Maybe, for a while." I wasn't in a joking mood.

The time for Olga's second ballroom dancing competition of the year arrived sooner than I expected. The difference with this competition from the first competition was that Olga's mother was in attendance at the competition. She missed the first competition because she hadn't been feeling well.

With a supportive attitude, I went to the second competition to see Olga dance with her coach. The competition was intense, but, as soon as she finished her routine, I thought Olga did well. She danced five distinctive dances. I took pictures with my one-time-use camera.

Her mother said something in Russian to her and I could see that Olga was bothered by it. She walked away from her mother before her mother stopped talking.

"What's wrong, Olga?" I asked.

"My mother says that I was too slow on the dance floor."

"I think you did fine."

"My mother has high expectations."

Then her coach grasped her hand and escorted her out to the center of the dance floor. As if on cue, Olga forced herself to smile and appear that everything was fine.

"And the winner is…" said the announcer. Guess who?

Olga won first prize for her overall performance, but she didn't rank first in each of the five dances. Subsequently, her mother berated her in Russian for failing to be ranked first in all the dances. She was yelling at Olga in Russian. Olga translated it for me. Her mother was apparently merciless.

Crying, Olga ran to the ladies' room. Her tears were making her blue make-up run down her face. Her mother followed her. I couldn't do anything, but I was sympathetic with Olga. I considered it unfair for her mother to berate her. Olga won first prize. Who cares if her scores weren't perfect?

While Olga and her mother were in the ladies' room, I looked around the ballroom. The female dancers were dressed in skimpy outfits, revealing more of their body than they would probably feel comfortable doing on the street. Also, everyone hugged and kissed each other in an ostentatious way. The ballroom dancing world is a touchy-feely culture. Yet, ironically, the competition between the dancers is extremely fierce. My sense was that dancers had to smile to show confidence in themselves – not because they were happy or that they liked the other people. Superficial, outward appearance was the measuring stick of their existence.

I was thinking about how I had surprised Olga with the news of our planned trip to Orlando, Florida. Once she gets to Disney World, she will love it, I told myself. My view was that she didn't understand Disney. I wanted to introduce her to the dreamland that is Disney World.

It was becoming customary for me to create a dream-like plan whenever I felt that Olga needed to get away from the realities of her life. This was my way of cherishing her. I wanted her to have nice things in life and to see the world. In my opinion, one of the best things we could do was to create memories of us together. This would help bind us together tighter, I thought.

When Olga returned from the ladies' room, she said, "My mother won't let it go. She is angry with me because I didn't rank first in every category."

"That's ridiculous. You won first place," I stressed.

"I need to win a national championship before my mother will be happy."

Olga was emotionally shaken.

"You will someday," I said, trying to assure her.

"I need to get myself ready."

"What can I do to help?"

"I need to take more dancing lessons."

"Okay."

"I'll need another check from you."

"That's fine," I said without hesitation, even though I knew it would stretch me financially.

"I am going to show my mother that I can get better."

I saw the driving force of her mother as unhealthy for Olga. Her mother was reinforcing a negative self-image. I didn't know if her mother quite understood the impact she was having on Olga, who was sensitive.

I remarked, "When we get to Florida, we can put all this behind us and relax."

As I was about to kiss Olga on her lips, she pulled away from me and said, "I have to go say goodbye to some important people in the dancing world. They might be able to help me."

She darted away, as if she had been shot out of a slingshot.

While waiting, I sat down at the empty table and watched the cleaning crew clean up the place. Dance music was still being piped through the speakers. With the door now open, a cold breeze was blowing into the hall.

Minutes later, Olga returned to me and said, "Tim said that he knows a guy who would be a good partner for me." She seemed excited, as if she had thrown off her mother's berating. But I knew Olga well enough to know that she didn't forget negative things like that.

"That's great, Olga."

She and I walked out of the hall together. As she went to her car and I went to my car, we waved goodbye to each other. Her mother followed her to her car. I didn't say anything to the mother.

I stepped into my car, inserted the key and tried to start the engine, but it wouldn't start. Before I could alert her that I was having car trouble, Olga drove off. I was left alone in the parking lot with no cell phone and no assistance. The temperature was dropping and I didn't have a warm jacket.

"Great!" I muttered sarcastically.

I walked down the street to a pay phone and called roadside assistance. Then I waited for the tow truck to find me. I used the time to think about my life. I seemed to be on a treadmill. Tensions were high at work because of the slumbering economy. Rumors of lay-offs persisted. I hadn't talked to Olga much about the issues at work. I hadn't wanted to worry her.

Our relationship was hitting what I would call a "dry spell." It was getting stagnant, which was something I dreaded. I also wondered if Olga was starting to take me for granted, or if I was taking her for granted. An uneasy feeling wouldn't leave me.

As I watched for the tow truck to drive up, I started to think about how I was a Christian and Olga was not a Christian. A pesky Bible verse floated across my mind like a balloon. To paraphrase it, the verse said, "Do not marry an unbeliever!" I had taken this as a holy suggestion. I told myself, "God didn't mean it so strictly. He means, in general. Olga and I are different. We have an understanding with each other."

But then a doubt entered my mind. Do we really have a good understanding of each other? What are the bounds of our understanding? I felt a need to talk to Olga about it. So, this was bothering me, as well as the concern that Olga would think I am taking her for granted.

"Flowers!" I uttered to myself, as the cold breeze blew at me. "I'll giver her flowers and an 'I love you' note."

The tow truck then arrived. The driver was a wild character. He spoke very loudly and seemed to say whatever came into his mind. No self-editing!

"What do we have here? Car problems?"

"That's right," I replied.

He opened the hood and within a minute determined that he could not fix my car.

"Got to be towed."

"How am I going to get home?" I asked.

"I'll take you home," he said.

The conversation in the truck gave me a sense of where his priorities were.

He said, "I've been married three times and I have a new girlfriend. She has a daughter. A good kid! My ex-wives didn't understand me, but we had fun. I used to be a big party animal. The biggest! The women loved me. It's better to have women love you than hate you."

"I'll try to remember that," I said.

"What you have to do to be successful with women is sweet talk them and be confident. Women dislike men who lack confidence. They want a man with direction. Someone reliable and caring! Fake it! All men want one thing – great sex. It's a natural drive we have. Do you have a girlfriend?"

"I am getting married. My fiancée Olga is a dancer."

"Get as much sex as you can before you get married," he

advised. "Marriage can ruin the sex. None of my marriages lasted more than three years. I had to look outside the marriage for good loving when the romance dried up."

"I see."

"I am not really a tow truck driver," he said. "I am only doing this on the side for extra money. I work in distribution during the day." He kept talking, but I wasn't listening to him. I didn't understand his attitude about marriage and sex. Was he so negative and cynical that married life held no spark for him?

Spiritual emptiness personified! The broken marriages were a symptom.

Then I asked him, "Did you get married in a church?"

"Yes," he replied. "The last wedding was a fantastic church wedding with lots of flowers. The minister gave a great speech and blessed us."

"What happened to the blessings?"

"Ah, that's only for the wedding day."

"It's interesting how people invite God to the wedding, but not to the marriage," I said, ending the conversation about marriage. He didn't talk to me anymore.

I went to bed after 1 a.m. I didn't know if Olga was at a dance club or not.

On the next day, I brought flowers to Olga and I wanted to talk to her about how we understand each other, but all she wanted to talk about was dancing. I couldn't steer the conversation to a deeper level about our relationship. The details weren't important. Giving up, I postponed the heart-to-heart conversation we needed to have to a future date.

Chapter Thirty-five

WINTER VACATION

The weeks flew by, leading up to the day of departure for Florida. The thought of being in Florida motivated me for weeks. When the day finally arrived, I was thrilled. I hadn't been to Florida in many years and this would be the first time that I went to Florida with a girlfriend. I had worked out the whole plan on my own. Believing that Olga would love what I was planning, I carefully planned the hotel, the transportation and the park visits. This Florida trip was my Christmas gift to her. All my work to plan for it was part of the gift.

However, tension grew between us before we left our state. Early in the morning, it had snowed. Three or four inches of snow had accumulated. I was concerned about whether our flight would be canceled.

As we were standing in front of my house with our suitcases in the snow, Olga said, "You are quiet, Martin."

"I am thinking about whether the airport will close down because of this snow."

"It stopped snowing hours ago. I'm sure they cleaned off the runway."

"I hope so."

"You really want to go to Florida, don't you, Martin?"

"You don't?"

"I want to dance."

"You'd rather dance than go to Florida?"

"All I think about is dancing."

"I thought that you would take a break from dancing during this vacation."

"No way! I am bringing my dancing shoes. I will be working out in the hotel gym, too."

I didn't respond.

A few seconds later, she said, "You aren't happy."

"When I am vacation, I leave the rest behind."

"You want me to be a world champion ballroom dancer, don't you?"

She seemed to be heaping guilt on me.

"Yeah." I was less than enthusiastic.

Then Olga shook a small tree next to me and caused snow to fall onto my new suitcase. I looked at her with perplexity.

"What did you do that for?" I asked.

"Don't take it so seriously! It's just snow."

"I don't want snow on my suitcase."

"It will melt."

"This snow is getting to me," I said, trying to avoid an argument with Olga. I yelled out, "I need to go to Florida."

She rolled her eyes and sighed, as the taxi arrived. We loaded the suitcases into the trunk and left. The taxi slid on the icy roads all the way to the airport. Desperately wanting to get on the plane and fly to Florida, I was quiet for most of the taxi ride, as if my brooding silence would melt the snow on the airport's runways.

Remarkably, there was no delay in our flight at the airport. Like soldiers falling into line, we boarded the plane. The flight attendants gave us bags of peanuts and cups with lots of ice cubs. I wished that the plane was a time machine and we'd be in Florida in an instant. Yet, the flight wasn't very long and I was able to read a magazine from cover to cover.

Olga and I took the shuttle from the Orlando airport to the

hotel, which was located on the grounds of Disney World. We checked in and then hopped on a long golf cart to be driven to our suite. The driver was extremely friendly.

I whispered to Olga, "I wonder if Disney tells people like him to be extra friendly."

"Probably."

Olga looked disappointed when she saw that I had picked a suite with two separate bedrooms. I was still taking moral integrity seriously. I was not treating the words of Jesus lightly. This was important to me. God had been good to me for many years, blessing me in school, work and home life. To ignore His desire for my life was the epitome of being ungrateful. Knowing that the Holy Spirit is extremely sensitive, I didn't want to consciously and deliberately sin. Self-gratification was not a good excuse.

But this didn't mean that I avoided fun. Within an hour of checking into the hotel, I was in the outdoor pool, as the sun set and the spotlights from Disney rolled across the darkened sky.

Treading water in the middle of the pool, I said to Olga, "This is terrific! To be in an outdoor pool, while it is snowing back home, is incredible. The water is so warm. This is the first time that I have ever taken a vacation in wintertime and I think it's great."

Then I swam under a mini-bridge that cut across the pool. At the same time, Olga was swimming around the edge of the pool. When I swam up to her, she started to splash water at me playfully.

"Oh, yeah," I said. I splashed water at her in return. She squealed.

It was a good time.

"Olga, do you want to get something to eat at the hotel's restaurant?"

She nodded.

After we changed into dry clothes, we went to eat at a

restaurant called Olivia's. The food was fantastic.

"What great food!" I said to Olga. "This is a great start to our vacation. Swimming in the pool and eating this food! Tomorrow, we will go to Disney World's Magic Kingdom. Then we'll go to Epcot Center on Tuesday."

"I have to buy a bathing suit," Olga informed me.

"What? You have a bathing suit with you."

"I don't like the bathing suit I have. I want to buy one down here."

"Okay. You can probably buy one in the hotel's gift shop."

She replied, "I already looked in the shop while you were checking us in. They don't sell bathing suits. They told me to go to another place."

"How far away is it?"

"They said I have to take a bus."

"I hope we can do it quickly. I don't want to waste time. We have lots to see at the Magic Kingdom."

"I want to sit in the sun after I buy my bathing suit."

"You'll get sun while we are walking around the park," I said.

"Don't expect me to do much walking!"

"Olga, we have to walk to get to places."

"I wouldn't mind sitting by the pool."

"Please don't do this to me, Olga. We came all the way down to Orlando, Florida. There is much to see. I want to show you so much of the place. I was here many years ago and there are new things for me to see. I don't want to miss anything important."

"You are like a little child sometimes, Martin."

Her tone sounded sharp and slightly bitter.

I joked, "Disney World can do that to a man."

On the next day, I went with her on a bus so that she could buy a new bathing suit. What I hoped wouldn't happen ended up happening. We spent two hours – two wasted hours, in my opinion – searching for a bathing suit for her.

Olga couldn't make up her mind. She found any little excuse not to buy a bathing suit.

"Olga, I really need to ask you to make a decision and then let's go."

I was getting impatient.

"You don't want me to rush and then dislike the bathing suit later today, do you?"

"No, and I don't want to come back here tomorrow to return it for you," I said sternly.

"You are being unreasonable, Martin."

I took a deep breath, silently prayed and then said, "Okay. I am sorry. I am being impatient. I ask you to forgive me, Olga. I am just so excited to be at Disney World and I want to get out there and enjoy the theme park. Once I have gone on a few rides and showed you some of the attractions of the place, I'm sure I will calm down. Please forgive me!"

She didn't say anything. Rather, she darted to the other side of the store to look at more bathing suits, which all looked the same to me. I was not sure what she was looking for.

Meanwhile, a physically attractive woman in a two-piece, white bathing suit walked into the store. She looked like a model. Olga was beautiful, but this woman looked like she was in top physical condition. I looked at her and acknowledged to myself her attraction, but I noted the difference between loving Olga with my heart and looking at a pretty woman. Very different!

Jesus said that lust of the eyes is a sin. For a moment, I lusted in my heart for this attractive woman with the fine body. However, I silently repented of my sin and asked for God's forgiveness. My sensitivity to love for Olga was so high that I didn't even want a lustful moment to become a burden on me. While my masculinity was naturally drawn to beautiful women, my spirit was attuned to the Lord God and my freedom from sin was through the Lord Jesus Christ. I wanted to keep my priorities straight.

Olga did not choose a bathing suit to purchase, but she finally said, "Let's go!"

"Good."

But we had to wait 45 minutes for the bus to pick us up and take us to the Magic Kingdom. I was not a happy tourist when I entered the "Kingdom" with Olga. Little did I know that the situation would get steadily worse.

"Look at this….Look at that…." I said repeatedly, as we walked around the park.

After an hour, Olga, said, "I am tired of walking. My shoes are hurting me. These are new shoes. They are not good for walking."

I was irritated that she would bring shoes that were not good for walking, when I had told her that we would be doing a great deal of walking. Her line of thinking was baffling to me.

She said, "I am tired of this place. I want to go back to the hotel and sit by the pool."

"We will have other vacations in the future when we will sit by the pool and rest. This vacation is meant to go around the park."

I was fighting a losing battle. We left the park early. I was sorely disappointed. It reminded me of how different my father and my mother are. My mother is the type who would go around the park all day. My father is the type who would want to sit down all day. The fact that Olga and I were turning out to be this different as well was not a good sign to me. But I ignored it because I loved Olga. I was committed to her. We were engaged. I wouldn't question our engagement for such a small matter. It was not like we lived at Disney World, I told myself.

On the next day, we went to Epcot Center, which Olga liked more because there were ample opportunities to sit down. We ate lunch in Japan and dinner in Italy. Only in Epcot!

However, Olga was furious that I made her go to the Christmas jubilee concert. I loved the concert, which was filled with Christmas carols, such as "Hark the Herald Angels Sing" and "O Little Town of Bethlehem." A gigantic choir, supported by a large orchestra, sang powerfully. In addition, each choir member held a candle. When the lights were turned off between songs, the sight of all the candles was marvelous.

This "candlelight concert" was one of my favorite events at Disney, but Olga hated it. She was restless throughout the concert. She asked me continually, "Can we go now?" But I wanted to stay. The songs praised Jesus. Then guest speakers, including an astronaut who had been to the moon, read portions from the Bible. They told the story of Jesus' birth. My attention was riveted. Meanwhile, Olga was preoccupied with her fingernails.

After the concert, Olga was so annoyed with me that she barely talked to me on the bus ride back to the hotel. But I was happy that I attended the concert. It was something that I would remember for a long time with warmth.

It was sad to me that Olga couldn't enjoy it with me. Her heart wasn't open to it. Was it a sign of how closed her heart was to the reason for Christmas? Was her heart only open to me when I did what she wanted? Was this true love for her? These might have been fair questions at the time. But I ignored them, telling myself that, while engaged, I needed to endure the ups and downs. I was in a "down" with Olga and I assumed it was what God wanted for me.

Our communication with each other wasn't improving. An argument was inevitable. It happened the next night.

Chapter Thirty-six

Intense Argument

The next night started out fine. Olga and I rode a small boat on a narrow river from our hotel to Downtown Disney. Sitting in the open boat and looking up at the sparkling stars were special. The boat fit a dozen people on board. The sound of the engine was soothing.

As we came closer to our destination, Olga said, "I'm cold."

I put my arm around her to try to warm her up. Besides, it was romantic and I liked to be closer to Olga. Other couples on the boat were cuddling as well. I felt proud to have my own girlfriend.

I asked her, "How do you like this boat ride?"

"If I wasn't so cold, I would like it more."

"Sorry I didn't bring a sweater. It was hot earlier today. I didn't think it was needed."

"I should have dressed warmer, but I wanted to wear this outfit."

"The material feels pretty light," I said, feeling the material on her back.

She leaned into me and rested her head on my shoulder. Life couldn't get any better than this, I thought. A beautiful woman by my side, awesome-looking stars filling up the night sky, a romantic boat ride at Disney – a dream come true, as far as I was concerned.

But where would it go from there?

I soon found out. The driver of the boat recommended a seafood restaurant in Downtown Disney. I had seen an advertisement for the same restaurant in a tourist guide. Olga agreed with me that we should eat dinner at this restaurant. After the boat dropped us off, we walked a short distance to the place. I was hungry.

As soon as we walked into the restaurant, I smelled a strong, odious odor, but it didn't stop me from going up to the desk and asking for a table for two. Olga tapped me on my shoulder, so I turned around and grasped her hand. Before she had time to speak, I gently pulled her into the restaurant, leading the way to the table.

On the way to the table, she said to me, "I don't want to eat here."

"What's wrong?"

"It smells awful."

"Oh, that's only in the front lobby. It smells like raw fish. I'm sure the food is good," I said, trying to assure her.

"No, I don't want to eat here."

I continued to pull her to the table.

"I have already asked for a table. I don't want to walk out."

"I do," she stated unequivocally.

"We have to eat."

"We'll eat someplace else."

"Please, Olga, don't be unreasonable! Let's try this place. If the food is terrible, then we won't come back."

She raised her voice, saying, "I told you that I don't want to eat here."

A few of the customers at other tables turned to look at us.

I said to her, "Please lower your voice."

We reached the table and I sat down. Begrudgingly, she sat down opposite me.

"You really plan to eat here, don't you, Martin?"

"Yes."

"I don't believe you. You don't want what I want," she said. "You don't care how I feel. You do what you want to do. When I say that we don't eat here, then you should have turned around and walked out with me. I have a good mind to walk out right now."

I had never heard her so angry. I felt that she was making a big issue out of nothing. The smell was subsiding. I couldn't understand why she was adamant, as if it was life or death. But it revealed that she could become extremely angry when I disagreed with her, even something as simple as a restaurant. Before we were engaged, she would have tried any restaurant I recommended. Suddenly, my opinion meant nothing and she made all the decisions.

The waitress walked up to our table and asked if we wanted to order drinks. I ordered a glass of ginger ale, but Olga wanted alcohol. Then Olga refused to talk to me. Just stopped talking! I looked at the menu.

A few minutes later, I asked her, "What are you going to order?"

"Nothing" was all she said.

"I am hungry, Olga, and I am going to enjoy a good meal."

Minutes later, I ordered a plate of fried calms. Olga told the waitress that she wasn't going to order anything. I didn't feel like explaining to the waitress that my fiancée had a problem with the smell in the lobby.

While Olga nursed her alcoholic beverage, I ate in silence. Olga didn't talk to me for an hour. A whole hour! She stared out the window. I couldn't remember a time when she was so moody. She seemed furious. Over a smelly restaurant?

I have to admit that I reacted to her moodiness by becoming introspective myself. I decided that, if she didn't want to talk to me, then I wouldn't force her to talk. I would be quiet, too. Many thoughts passed through my mind. I started to feel as if I didn't really know Olga. She seemed suddenly like a stranger to me. Her moodiness was like a wall between us.

I had not been trying to fight for control with her simply because I wanted to eat at the restaurant we agreed to. Any seafood restaurant would smell a little bit. The only problem I had with the restaurant was the prices. Very expensive!

After I paid the bill, Olga and I walked to the dock to wait for the boat, but we were still like two strangers. We were both extremely intense. She thought that I was being unreasonable and I thought she was being unfair. She acted like a small child who would become moody when she didn't get her way.

And I was marrying this person.

The boat came and took us back to the hotel. We went to our suite and extended our "cold shoulder" session of silence. She went to wash up in the bathroom and I poured myself a drink of cold water in the kitchen. I wanted time to be alone and think.

Minutes later, Olga came out to the kitchen and she had a strange look on her face. She looked angry, but also passionate. Suddenly, she put her hands on my shoulders, pulled me closer to her and kissed me aggressively. I sensed no caring or sensitivity in her kiss. Instead, her kiss seemed methodical and domineering.

In response, I swung my head back and broke loose from her. I didn't know what she was up to, but I was in no mood for any mind games. She strutted toward me and I backed away a few steps. She seemed like a savage in a jungle, trying to tantalize her prey.

Admitting that I was not falling for her trap, she said, "I can't even have my way with you. I don't understand you, Martin. I thought you loved me."

"Love is patient. Otherwise, it is not love. It is lust."

In a huff, she stormed away from me, went into her bedroom and slammed the door. Then she opened the door and slammed it a second time.

"Drama queen," I muttered to myself. I finished my glass of water and went to my bedroom across the hall from her space.

Alone in the room, I thought about the woman I used to "love." She had rejected me years earlier and went to be with another man. I wondered what my life would have been like, if I had married the first woman I cared for. The "what if?" question is not always constructive, but I couldn't help ask myself about it.

Although I was still tense, I fell asleep shortly after ten o'clock. But before I drifted off to sleep, I said aloud, "Help me, Jesus. I don't know what to do."

When I walked out of my bedroom the next morning, Olga walked by me and said in a tense, devil-may-care tone of voice, "I am going to the gym and then to the pool."

Then she slammed the door. She was getting proficient at slamming doors.

I looked up and prayed, "Father, in Jesus name, I need You."

An hour later, I saw Olga at the pool. Before I went up to her, I swam for a while in the pool. She still looked angry and I wasn't exactly happy, but I trusted God to give me the strength and the words to say to Olga. I wanted to show her that a true Christian does not hold grudges. God enabled me to forgive. I decided to apologize to her and ask for her forgiveness. I wanted it to be a powerful Christian witness, not that she could walk all over me, but that I was man enough to say I'm sorry.

I didn't want our relationship to fall apart because of a smelly restaurant and moody feelings. We were having a bad couple of days and I wanted to try to move beyond it.

After I dried off, I walked up to Olga, sat down next to her and said, "I'm sorry, Olga."

She was reading a book and didn't respond at first. She didn't even look up at me. I knew she had heard me, but she was making me wait. I couldn't see her eyes because she was wearing sunglasses. Patiently, I waited.

"You got me angry," she finally said to me.

"I'm sorry. Olga, I want to ask for your forgiveness."

"Why should I give it to you?"

She sounded excruciatingly merciless.

"Because we love each other," I replied.

"You could have left the restaurant with me and eaten somewhere else."

"I know," I said. "I would have saved money, too, if we ate at a less expensive restaurant."

"And I was trying to get romantic with you last night."

"Olga, you are a very desirable woman, but I was upset and intense."

"I can't say that you are moody very often, Martin, but last night you were."

"I guess I was. I'm sorry. I'm really sorry."

I apologized profusely, humbling myself tremendously. But she didn't apologize to me for the way she acted and for what she said. She seemed comfortable with blaming me for wrecking the evening.

On the next day, she was sick and we did nothing but sit by the pool. I was disappointed that I didn't get the opportunity to spend more time in the Disney theme parks, but I felt that I had to be sympathetic toward Olga.

I took comfort in something I said to Olga, "This could be the first year of many years when we come to Florida for a vacation. We'll be back."

"I'd rather go to Miami and to the beach," she said.

"We'll see."

I left Florida without an apology from Olga. She had withheld her forgiveness from me and then gave a counterfeit forgiveness to me begrudgingly. I had taken her to

Florida out of love. In return, she complained.

On the plane, she said, "We did too much walking at Disney. The boat ride was too cold. The restaurant was smelly. I didn't spend as much time at the pool as I would have liked. I didn't practice dancing as much as I would have liked."

Then she stood up and made her way to the bathroom in the back of the plane. She was still feeling sick to her stomach.

I said to myself in a quiet voice, "I didn't praise the Lord Jesus enough while I was in Orlando. I wouldn't have even had the money to go to Florida without the financial blessings from God."

When we arrived home, snow was on the ground. The reality of Disney World was a memory that was quickly fading away, much to my disappointment. But I had fully forgiven Olga. I put our tensions from Florida behind me. I was ready to get back to normal and try to recapture the special romance and nice times with Olga from the past. I didn't feel like I had changed much from the time before the engagement, but Olga was another story.

Chapter Thirty-seven

Swept Under the Rug

Christmas and New Year's Eve were very different for me than they were a year earlier. Olga and I were coming off our tense vacation. I was walking around streets with piles of snow on them. It was appropriate symbolism for returning to stark reality.

When we returned home, Olga and I didn't discuss the issues we had in Florida, as if we swept the issues under a rug. Our communication was getting strange to me. We spoke every day on the phone, discussing superficial things, but we stayed away from important topics. We could discuss the public lives of Jennifer Lopez, Britney Spears, Whitney Houston, Kenny Lattimore and Julia Roberts, but we didn't discuss morality, character, sacrifice, selfishness or religion. For me, these topics were "understood." I assumed that Olga's views would be close to mine – at least when she eventually learned more about them, I told myself.

However, something bothered me during Christmas. My focus was on Jesus, who is the reason for Christmas. I wanted to stay focused on Jesus, praising Him and thinking about how great His love is. I wanted to read the story of His birth in the Bible and listen to Christian Christmas songs. Instead of hearing about Santa Claus coming to town, I wanted to hear about Jesus' mission in coming to earth. Could I do all this? Yes. Was anyone trying to stop me from praying, reading the Bible or listening to Christmas carols? No.

Then what bothered me?

Olga did not participate in any of it with me.

She wouldn't pray with me. She wouldn't listen to Christmas carols with me. She didn't want to hear me talk about Jesus.

And this was the woman I was marrying.

How it made my heart ache!

But I had made a commitment and I was marrying her. I still believed that God would reach her and, consequently, Olga would turn her life over to Jesus. It was just a matter of time. My "faith" held firm. I prayed for her salvation every day during Christmas week. Nothing else mattered to me. Her being nice to me was not enough. She and I were spiritually separated. When I saw her irritated and impatient, I wanted to say to her, "Come to Jesus!" but I remained silent. I didn't want to upset her. How ironic it is that the name of Jesus can get people so upset! Their reaction proves to me that Jesus is God because, if Jesus wasn't God, then people would not get so upset or uncomfortable when I talk about Jesus Christ.

While Christmas passed by without any outward conflict, New Year's Eve capped off the year in dramatic fashion. I took Olga to an expensive dinner and hotel party for New Year's Eve. There was no way that I could outdo the Marc Anthony concert from a year earlier, but I wanted to make it a special evening. Olga and I were dressed up in our best clothes. To the casual observer, we looked like a loving couple out on the town on New Year's Eve.

What happened within the first hour shocked me.

During dinner, music was being played and people were dancing. Of course, Olga wanted to dance.

"I would rather dance later," I said.

"I want to dance now." Her tone was sharp.

"Okay," I replied in my usual way to appease her.

Reluctantly, I followed her to the dance floor and began to dance with her. Since it was a social, casual occasion, I presumed that I could dance comfortably in a free-flowing manner. But Olga had other ideas.

"Do the steps I taught you," she demanded, pointing at the floor.

"Can't I dance like everyone else?"

Her face expressed annoyance.

"Do it, Martin!"

Again trying to appease her, I started to do ballroom dancing steps as best as I could. I had not been practicing much lately, so I wasn't as refined as I had been, but I thought I was doing okay. In contrast, Olga didn't think so.

"You're not doing it right," she yelled out.

I tried again.

She still wasn't happy. Then she stormed off the dance floor and returned to our table. I followed her.

"What's wrong, Olga?"

"You aren't dancing the way I taught you."

"I was doing the best I can."

"No, you don't take me seriously. Tell the truth!"

"What are you talking about? I take you seriously. I am not as good a dancer as you are."

"I've seen you dance better than you are tonight."

"I used to practice more."

"You have gotten lazy, Martin, and you don't practice."

"I find the international style of dancing to be more difficult than the American style, but I know you don't like the American style."

"You could be better if you tried. It is like you want to embarrass me by dancing so bad," she said.

"What? Why would I try to embarrass you? If I could dance better, then I would. Look, I wish I could dance better, but it doesn't come as easily to me as to you, Olga."

"You are just making excuses."

Then she burst out crying. We were sitting at a table in a busy restaurant and she was crying. I couldn't understand why she was getting so emotional all of a sudden because I wasn't dancing as well as she would have liked. She seemed to think that I was purposefully fouling up my dancing. Nothing could have been further from the truth! The truth was that, from her perspective, I was a novice dancer with many flaws. She was much more understanding of my dancing mistakes *before* we were engaged. Her unhappiness with me must have been masking something deeper, but I didn't know what it was.

At a certain point during dinner, Olga and I stopped talking to each other. We were physically near each other, but we were emotionally distant. Party music and people talking were all around us. Balloons were everywhere. New Year's party hats in all different colors were on every table. But Olga and I were no longer in a festive mood. We were acting more like a married couple who had lost the flare in their romance than an engaged couple that seemingly had all the allure of love and romance ahead of them.

Later in the evening, out of boredom, Olga and I went to the dance floor together, but each of us seemed to dance in an individual sphere. The music, the flashing lights and the partygoers couldn't bring Olga and me closer together emotionally. Olga looked angry during every dance, as I'm sure she was disapproving of my flawed dancing.

Spontaneously, during one song, I imitated the dance moves of a couple next to me. They looked at me with annoyance. Not only was Olga annoyed with me, but this couple seemed bothered by me, too. These people weren't helping to inspire me to dance or have a good time. Human nature has a way of ruining a party.

When midnight rolled in like a ship in fog, Olga and I kissed – more out of collective behavior than individual motivation. The kiss seemed mechanical to me. This was a drastic change from the passionate, all-consuming kiss on New Year's Eve a year earlier in New York. I had gone into this New Year's Eve with a relatively positive attitude and I wanted us to have a good time. But Olga took my flawed dancing as a personal insult to her.

We left soon after midnight. I had left the party hats and the noise-makers back on the table. I knew right off that I didn't want "momentos" to remember this New Year's Eve. I wanted to drive Olga home as quickly as possible - without getting a speeding ticket – and then go home and pray to God for wisdom.

For most of the ride to her house, we didn't talk, but as we were a few minutes away from her place, I started to talk.

"Olga, I see our relationship based on friendship and it is something that we have been building on for a long time. We started off as friends and I didn't know back then that we would fall in love and get engaged. For us to have a happy marriage, we need to take things slowly, as they come. I respect you, Olga, and I don't want to use you for instant gratification. Human nature has a way of causing trouble. I have a spiritual view of marriage. That is why I believe that marriage should last a lifetime. I don't believe in divorce. God hates divorce. I take marriage extremely seriously and I believe we need a strong foundation before we get married."

She said nothing. All she did was stare out the window. I felt like a Shakespearean character giving a monologue.

I continued, "I was not dancing badly because I was trying to insult you. I was dancing as best as I could, but it's difficult for me. And another thing is that we live in a society that promotes instant gratification. Patience is considered a flaw in our society."

Olga remained silent.

When I dropped her off at her house, I said, " This week, I will start looking for a place for us to live after we are married. I will look through the real estate pages and talk to real estate people. I will bring information about possible real estate to you and we can decide together where we will live. I also plan to pray for God to lead us to the right place to live. Oh, and one last thing. I would like to talk to you on the phone this week and hear from you what you want in a place to live. What would you like in a house?"

She finally spoke. "Call me!"

She kissed me on my cheek and left my car. I drove home and went to sleep.

Chapter Thirty-eight

Looking for a Place

I was feeling nervous about my real estate search. The uncertainty tested my faith in God. Buying a house or condo seemed like a huge endeavor. I wasn't sure if I was ready for it, but the oncoming marriage jolted me out of my reluctance and I had to start the search for a place to live. But I didn't want just any place. I wanted the place where God wanted me to live. My knowledge of God as personal and interested in every aspect of my life gave me an advantage.

I boldly went to God in prayer like a trusting child going to a father, believing the father can make things right. The gigantic task of finding and buying the right house humbled me and reminded me that I can settle for any house, but it is better to settle for the best place God has in store for me. Yet, I needed to trust Him and, most of all, wait on Him.

I prayed, "Heavenly Father, in Jesus name, I need Your help to find the right place for Olga and me to live after we are married. The real estate market is a complex place, full of fast-talking agents and silly posturing. But with You, Lord, I can cut through the fakes and avoid poor decisions. I need You to guide me in my search and the decision-making. I give You the real estate search to guide in any way You want, Father. I trust You to do what is right and what will glorify You above all others. I praise You and thank You in advance for what You will do to get me settled in the right place. It doesn't have to be fancy or be the envy of others. But it will be home and, when I am under the roof You provide over my head, I will praise You, Heavenly Father. I owe my life to You. How rich I am to be Your servant! I commit my real estate search to You. In Jesus name. Amen."

Then, in a moment of deepening tranquility, I sensed an impression on my spirit encouraging me to "wait" on the Lord for as long as it takes for the real estate. Then I thought about when the wedding was.

I said to myself with confidence, "God will put me in a house before the wedding." My confidence grew from my remembrance of all the past times when God blessed me.

I contacted a real estate agent whose company had been advertising on a Christian radio station. After an hour-long conversation, I was comfortable that this agent, whose name was Rick, was a man of integrity and sincerity. I came to this conclusion, not so much by what he said, but by the way he said it and, moreover, my sense of him as a business person. In addition, I prayed about it and I had a sense of peace about working with Rick on my real estate search.

"Let's go look at properties," said Rick, eager to get started with me on the road to finding a place for me and Olga to live. I had told him about how I was getting married and would be starting a new life with my bride-to-be Olga.

"I don't know yet what I am looking for. I still have to have an in-depth conversation with my fiancée about what would be agreeable to both of us," I said.

"Not a problem at all," he replied. "The reason I would like to take you out to some properties now is to start getting you exposure to what is available these days. Do you have the time? If you have somewhere you have to be, we can reschedule."

"No, I have time to look at some places, but I am far from any decisions."

"Absolutely!" he said. "Makes perfect sense! God will

lead you to the right house at the right time. I have no doubt. I imagine that you will be praying about it and I will pray for you, too."

"Thank you."

"Don't feel pressured!" he asserted. "Take your time! We'll find the right place, no matter how long it takes. Just don't rush into a decision!"

This real estate agent Rick was totally different from the stereotypical real estate agent who is impatiently trying to make a quick sale. In contrast, Rick was advising patience and prayer. He may go down in history as the most unique real estate salesperson ever.

Rick drove me to five properties. The first house was too old. The second house was too small. The third place was a condo that looked dingy and in need of serious work. The fourth place, which was also a condo, was too small and was in a questionable location. The last place we visited was nice but too expensive.

When we returned to the car, I said to Rick, "I feel like I should be saying 'this porridge is too hot' and "this porridge is too cold.' But I haven't found one that is just right yet."

"But you will find the right place to live," said Rick, smiling. "Was it helpful at all to visit these places today?"

"Yes, it was. I have a little better idea of what to look for. You know, location, size of the place, access to transportation, parking and, yeah, a lot of stuff that I may not have thought much of before."

"Good," he said. "I'm glad you found it helpful."

"Now I need to talk to my fiancée Olga about it."

"Great! You do that. Once you both decide together what you want, please e-mail me your criteria and I will do searches every day for you. I have access to sophisticated search tools and I can type in your criteria. I'll set up a profile for you. I'll e-mail you information and we can go see what you are interested in."

"Sounds good, Rick."

Even though the five places I visited were discouraging and made me realize that this search will not be easy, I was encouraged by Rick's professional and positive approach. He seemed to care more about my finding a good place than just making a quick sale.

While I was driving home, I was quietly praying to God about whether Rick was genuine or not. The sense I got was that I should stick with Rick as my primary real estate agent, no matter what happens. I can remember it like it was yesterday. This would sound like nonsense to an unbeliever, but the impression on my mind was "I will use Rick to find you the best place to live," as I believed, by faith, that God was communicating with my spirit.

When I arrived home, I called Olga to tell her the news of establishing contact with a reasonable real estate agent and having visited five properties. Olga's response to me was surprising.

She said, "I can't believe that you are only working with one real estate agent."

"I like him. I think he will help us."

"My mother says that you need to get five or six real estate agents working at the same time for you, Martin," said Olga. "You have never bought a house before. My mother has bought houses and she knows better. You should listen to her."

"I don't doubt that your mother knows a lot about real estate, but I believe this guy Rick is sincere and a hard worker." I was reluctant to tell her that he was a Christian.

"He is going to try to force you to buy a house fast to make himself money," she commented.

"You don't even know him."

"I know the type."

I had a problem. After praying earlier, I had the distinct sense that God wanted me to wait on Him and stay with

Rick as my real estate agent. God would use Rick to help me. God would open doors at the right time. My faith in God was fine. All my nervousness went away.

However, Olga was not on board with my strategy to work with one real estate agent to search for real estate. She seemed dead-set against it. I didn't understand her position and she didn't understand my position. Uncomfortable with sharing my faith position with her, I didn't tell her that I believed strongly how God was leading me in a certain way. As an unbeliever, she wouldn't comprehend it because human nature does not have the capacity to experience God by itself. A person must be spiritually born again through Jesus Christ to experience God. Everything else is emotion, outward appearance or sentiment, no matter how sincere.

Then Olga said, "My mother talked to your mother today, Martin."

"Oh, yeah."

"Your mother wants to give me a bridal shower. I don't want it. I am against it."

"Your mother told you about it?"

"Of course."

"But I thought a bridal shower is supposed to be a surprise."

"We don't have bridal showers in Russia. This is a silly American tradition," said Olga. To me, she didn't seem to understand what a "shower" is, so I didn't understand why she was vehemently against it.

"I think my mother wants to do something nice for you," I said.

"I don't care. I don't like her idea. My mother will call her back and tell her to forget it. I am not interested."

"Okay."

"Your mother also told my mother that your cousin Valerie got engaged."

"That's right. I forgot to tell you about that."

Olga remarked, "I hope my ring is bigger and better than her ring."

"This is not a competition, Olga."

"I want to have a better wedding than she does."

"Come on, Olga, you don't need to be competing. This could ruin the spirit of the wedding."

"Don't tell me how to feel, Martin! I hate it when you do that."

I said, "I'm sorry."

Truly, I was more interested in talking about real estate than comparisons to my cousin's wedding plans. Olga's fierce competitiveness surprised me because I thought love was more important than any competition with another woman.

"Olga, if houses are too expensive, we may need to buy a condo. I just want to tell you that," I said gently.

"No way!" she retorted. "I want to love in a house. No condo! Promise me!"

"I don't think we can afford a house at today's market prices."

"Then go farther out of the city."

"I don't want to live far outside the city. There will be trade-offs."

But she didn't want to understand. Understanding would mean that I was right. She wasn't willing to admit that I may have a point about what we could realistically afford. Since she was still a college student and didn't work, I knew how much money I had. The high prices of houses were a challenge. I didn't think a condo was so bad.

She said, "I want a house near my mother's house. I need to be near her."

"You do?"

It probably wasn't a good idea for me to question her about it.

"Yes, of course," she replied sharply. "I also need access

to public transportation."

"I have already been thinking of that."

"I want big rooms, an eat-in kitchen and central air-conditioning. Nothing too old!"

"I agree," I said. I was bending to Olga's will. I assumed that this would make her happy, but, if anything, it kept her edgy.

"Martin, I want the best."

"So do I," I said.

But I was thinking of God's best. Olga was thinking of a different "best." It is not great for a relationship when the man and woman think of "the best" as very different. I was willing to wait on the Lord God. Olga wasn't. She wanted exactly what she wanted; otherwise, she would be unhappy. I knew it. This created a real problem for me. I was living by faith, leaving all doors of possibility open. I didn't mind if God surprised me. Was Olga ready to be surprised by the Almighty?

Then Olga unloaded some news on me.

"I found a new dance partner," she said. "I am going dancing with him tonight. He is very good at smooth dancing. He is not so good in the Latin style, but he is willing to learn. I am so excited."

"You're going dancing tonight?"

"Yes," she replied. "He and I need to get used to each other dancing. We want to dance in a competition together as soon as possible."

"How much will you be seeing him?"

"I don't know. Three or four times a week."

"What's his name?"

"Luther."

I asked, "When will you and I start practicing our wedding dance? Are you going to come up with some choreography for us to dance?"

She replied without enthusiasm. "Oh, yes, we will start

dancing soon. There's time. I need to think of something that will blow people away."

I could sense that her mind was working hard. If she was imagining certain dance moves, perhaps she was having doubts about teaching the dance moves to me. After all, I wasn't the most agile dancer.

Chapter Thirty-nine

All the Details

Following up on the wedding plans, I made the arrangements for the wedding ceremony to take place at an elegant church and I contacted a Christian minister whom I wanted to perform the ceremony. I also had it in my mind to ask my friend Dean to be the "best man," as well as asking my uncle and my brother to be ushers at the wedding.

Furthermore, Valentine's Day was coming up. Wanting to buy a special gift for Olga, yet not being able to afford anything too expensive, I went on the Internet to search for an affordable, diamond bracelet. I spent hours searching through consumer Web sites for a decent bracelet at a decent price. When I found one, I was slightly reluctant to purchase it online because I couldn't touch the bracelet to examine it before buying it. Yet, due to the low price, I bought the bracelet on faith, believing that Olga would appreciate my sentimental thought more than the product itself.

Before I left to go to Olga's house and help her study for college exams, I went into the kitchen for a drink of water. My mother was sitting at the kitchen table. She pushed her chair back and wanted to talk to me.

"Olga's mother said that Olga doesn't want a shower," my mother said harshly.

"Look, if she doesn't want a bridal shower, then let her go. It will save money."

"It's not about the money," she claimed. "All the women on my side of the family are expecting a shower. They want to give gifts to you and Olga for your wedding."

"They don't have to," I said.

"You are breaking tradition."

"Olga doesn't feel beholden to tradition."

"But it's because she doesn't understand it," my mother asserted. "She is young and doesn't understand these things. How many weddings has she gone to?"

"I don't know. Not many, I would guess."

"So she should listen to people who know better."

"Mom, don't force Olga to do something she doesn't want to do."

"I am upset."

"You shouldn't be upset just because Olga doesn't want a shower."

My mother didn't like that I told her not to be upset. I think she became more upset. I didn't know what to say to appease her.

She said, "Ten years from now, I better not hear from you and Olga that you both wanted a shower. I will scream at you if you complain – ever."

"She won't complain."

"She better not."

"You don't have to say so much about it, Mom."

"I am not saying half of what I could say," she said.

Her comment infuriated me. She was admitting that she had much worse to say to me, but she was holding it back. I considered her just as guilty for thinking the bad things as she would be if she said them.

Raising my voice suddenly, I said, "God knows what is on your mind and you aren't as good as you think, Mom. I don't appreciate your trying to make me feel guilty because my fiancée doesn't want a shower. You care more about my aunts and cousins – and what they will think – than what I think."

"You don't understand anything either," she said to me.

I stormed out of the room as angry as could be. My mother's narrow focus on a bridal shower baffled me. She had made such a big deal about it, as if it was a personal insult to her that Olga didn't want a shower.

Trying to calm down, I drove to Olga's house to keep my promise of helping her study for school. I planned to ask her questions from her notes and the textbooks. I expected her to be prepared. She had told me on the previous day that she would study for hours before I arrive.

When I walked into her house, the first thing I said to Olga was "I had an argument with my mother about how you don't want a shower."

"Oh, don't argue with your mother."

"She is being unreasonable. I don't understand why she thinks the shower is vitally important."

Olga said, "It might make her feel better that I have asked your two sisters to be my bridesmaids."

"I didn't know that. When did you decide that?"

"Last night."

"Okay," I said. "Did my sisters accept?"

"Yes, of course."

When Olga made up her mind, she wasted no time.

As I saw Olga's eyes with a dreamy look in them, I said, "So it's time to prepare for your tests."

"I don't feel like studying."

"But you have to study," I said like a diligent teacher.

"I want to drop my law course. I don't like the professor and I don't understand the textbook."

"You are smart enough to figure it out, Olga."

"I am too lazy to want to figure it out. I want to dance."

"I know you want to dance."

"You can take the test for me," she joked.

"No, I'll help you to study."

She gave me her law textbook. I spent a few minutes

reading the first page. Then Olga yanked the book away from me.

"You don't understand it either," she said to me. "My dance partner said that he would help me to study."

Feeling hurt that she was abandoning the opportunity for me to help her, I said, "But I thought I was going to help you."

"You can help me with history," she said quickly, pulling the history textbook and notebook out of her bag on the sofa.

"Okay."

"My history professor is weird. He talks too low and his hair is always messed up."

"Did you tell your professor that his hair was messed up?" I asked her.

"Of course not!"

After a few minutes of looking through her notes, I started to ask her questions from her history notes. Honestly, she didn't know the answers to any of the questions I asked her. Then she became annoyed with me when I told her the right answer. It was a strange situation.

She said, "I don't like the way you ask me questions."

"Okay," I replied, putting the notebook down on the table.

She changed the subject to dancing. "Luther and I plan to go to New York to take lessons with a professional coach that Luther knows."

"What?" I replied, surprised. "You have school."

"We will go during my spring break."

"Where will you stay?"

"Luther has friends in New York. They will put us up for a couple of nights. It will save me money. Isn't that a good thing?"

"How well do you know this Luther character?" I asked.

"Don't call him 'this Luther character.' He is a good man."

I mumbled to myself, "Famous last words."

"What did you say?"

"Oh, nothing," I replied, raising my head.

"I will go study law on my own."

"Okay. I'll get going. Sorry I couldn't help you study. I thought that you would be ready to answer questions before I got here."

"I didn't have time to study history today."

"What did you do today?"

"I went to the gym and then I danced for two hours."

"You are a sensation when it comes to dancing," I said. "Homework? That's another thing altogether."

"Homework is not interesting." Although she was in her early 20s, she sounded like she was seven years old when she said it.

"You have to make sacrifices and push yourself to get success in the future," I said, sounding like a guidance counselor.

"I hate school. I hate waking up early. I hate my professors," said Olga.

"What do you like about school?"

"Graduating and making money."

I laughed.

"Olga, I want to change the subject."

"Good."

"I want to ask you to be my Valentine," I said, snuggling up close to her. "I love you and I want to take you to a nice restaurant on Valentine's Day."

"What restaurant?"

"It will be a surprise," I said.

"Figures."

Being a romantic person, I left her house thinking about Valentine's Day. I tried not to think about the studying fiasco. However, in privacy, I voiced my concerns to God.

"Father God, I don't know what was bothering Olga so much, but she wasn't committed to studying. Doesn't she want to get good grades? And she got impatient with me when I wasn't understanding the complex law fast enough. Please give me patience and guidance in these situations. I went to Olga's house with every intention to work hard with her to study and I'd encourage her every step of the way. But she gets so negative. She doesn't seem to trust You, Father, and I am getting more concerned that she will make mistakes if she doesn't give her heart to You. I know. Jesus is Lord. I pray for the salvation of Olga's soul. It's nothing I can do, but You can do all things Father. You love us so much. Forgive us for ignoring You."

Then I drove to my friend Dean's house. I didn't want to wait any longer to ask him to be my best man at the wedding. Admittedly, I was a bit nervous to ask him. I didn't know if he would view it as a hassle or not.

But he proved to be enthusiastic.

After I asked him, he said, "Yes, it would be an honor to be best man."

"Thank you."

We shook hands. It put me at ease.

I said, "I want you as my best man because you have integrity and you are one of the few people who understand me as a born-again Christian. I would appreciate your Christian support through the wedding. I appreciate you accepting it. I know it will take up some of your time and you have family responsibilities and all, but-"

"This is important," he said. "I am happy to do it. When do we get fitted for the tuxedos?"

"I have it all planned out," I replied, smiling.

Later, my Uncle John and my brother agreed to be ushers at the wedding. The plan was coming together. It was becoming an emotional thing for me. I liked it when a plan worked out the way I wanted it to.

Yet, I was still seeking God's direction for my relationship with Olga. Strangely, I didn't sense that I had a clear view of it yet. I waited for God to act and touch my life in a more powerful way. This was faith, no matter how feeble.

All that God appeared to be allowing was for me only to take the next step forward by faith. God did not reveal the whole picture of my future to my mind. My understanding was limited, but I could live each day by faith, waiting on the Lord to prompt me to act or remain still.

Getting married to a woman, who was not a Christian, was not changing my faith walk. Getting married did not negate my need for God. Just the opposite! I needed God much more than ever. The impression on my spirit was from God: "Trust Me."

Is God trustworthy? What a question that every human being has to answer for himself or herself. I put my trust in Him and my lifestyle reflected it. When lifestyle matches faith beliefs, then it answers the question.

However, Olga may have had a different answer.

Chapter Forty

The Second Valentine's Day

The diamond bracelet for Olga arrived on the morning of Valentine's Day. It had been held up in the mail. If I didn't receive this bracelet, I would have had to scramble to buy Olga a gift at a store before dinner. I had put my trust in Internet commerce and it almost failed me, but I was relieved to see the bracelet, which was smaller than I expected it to be. Too late to exchange it!

This Valentine's Day was not as exciting as the first Valentine's Day that I shared with Olga. I couldn't explain it. For most of the dinner, Olga talked about the wedding and her dancing. What I realized was that we were not talking about our relationship much anymore. The wedding was replacing the relationship. This concerned me.

But it was Valentine's Day and I tried to stay in a smooth, romantic mood. I waited for what I felt to be the right time for me to give the diamond bracelet to Olga. As usual, I loved to give a gift to her.

"I love you, Olga, and I appreciate that you are with me," I said to her softly. "As an expression of my affection for you, I want to give you this diamond bracelet as my Valentine's Day gift to you."

Her eyes lit up like a Christmas tree.

"Oh, thank you! Thank you!"

She kissed me and then put the bracelet on her right wrist. She stared at it, holding it up to the light. She was smiling.

I commented, "I couldn't get you a very expensive one."

"That's okay."

"But I found a diamond bracelet for an affordable price over the Internet. I searched long and hard for it," I said, nodding my head, as the waiter placed our food in front of us. The food smelled wonderful.

Olga said, "It's the thought that counts."

I liked it when she said that. It made me think that she loved *me*, not the merchandise I gave her. The bracelet wasn't the best, I admit, but it looked nice on her. In the back of my mind, I had the plan to buy her a much more expensive bracelet after we get married, but I didn't say anything to her.

I felt relaxed. We ate dinner and looked at all the well-dressed people out for Valentine's Day. I considered Olga to be a major "people watcher," but I didn't know if it was because she felt competitive with other women or if she liked to see what the latest fashions were. I could understand Olga partially, but not fully. Being in a relationship with Olga required faith. Love requires faith. With no faith, there can be no true love. At this point, I am not even talking about faith in God alone. I am talking about having faith in another person to share a life.

As Olga and I walked out of the restaurant holding hands, I looked at her from head to toe. She looked beautiful.

"You look beautiful."

It must have fed her vanity because she walked more confidently. I had once heard a minister say that he viewed his wife as getting more beautiful all the time. He considered her more beautiful at sixty years of age than he did at twenty. I wondered if this ever-increasing beauty would mark how I view Olga for the next fifty years. I sure hoped so. Outer beauty can change and is a matter of opinion, but inner beauty could shine brightly.

I wanted to know more about Olga's inner beauty, for all women have inner beauty. It's too bad that many cloud up their inner beauty because they focus so much on their outer beauty. A woman would be quick to notice a blemish on her face, but a blemish on her soul is much easier to hide.

Then Olga said to me, "Talk."

"What do you mean?"

"You are so quiet," she said to me.

"I just had a nice meal and I am relaxed."

"I don't know what is going on in your mind."

"What do you want me to say?"

"How is work?"

"Good."

She said, "You see, you only give a short answer. I know there is more going on at work. You spend 10 hours there every day."

"But I don't want to bore you, Olga."

"Tell me something you talked about today or heard from your co-workers."

"Let me think."

She giggled and asked, "Is it that hard?"

I smiled and replied, "When I leave work, I leave work behind. I only want to be focused on you and our relationship tonight. I'll think about work tomorrow."

We continued to walk down the street toward the parking garage.

Then, flinching, I said, "Wait, I can tell you something I heard at work earlier today. The guy who sits next to me told us that his girlfriend got laid off from her job. She worked for our company for the last year. She got laid off and is now nervous about finding another job. She has to pay her rent and her bills."

Olga replied, "Well, the guy should invite her to move in

with him. They can live together. It's cheaper for them."

"What?" I shouted, losing my relaxed veneer. "They aren't married."

"So what? If they care for each other, the guy would ask her to move in with him."

I nearly jumped into the air.

I said forcefully, "I disagree."

Then I let go of her hand and started to walk faster than her. She became annoyed.

"Why are you walking so fast?"

"I can't believe you said that you think the girl should move in with the guy. Did you ever hear of morals?"

"We live in the twenty-first century."

"That has nothing to do with it," I said. "People with their sinful human natures have been trying to run away from God since the beginning. If anything, it proves that the Bible is correct when it says we are living in the last days."

"The Bible! The Bible!" she screeched with mockery.

Undaunted, I continued, "The Bible says that society will become more sexually immoral and this would be a sign that we are near the Second Coming of Jesus Christ."

"I already told you that I don't believe in Jesus Christ," she stated fiercely.

"Whether you believe in Him doesn't matter. Jesus is who He is."

"If I don't believe in Jesus, then Jesus doesn't exist."

"Don't be silly!" I replied.

Then Olga and I stopped talking for the next forty minutes. We were angry with each other. I couldn't believe that Olga could be so shameless as to say that the best answer to getting laid-off was to have my co-worker's girlfriend move in with the guy. Olga ignored what God would think or what the girl's parents would think about it. Do parents really want their daughters to have sex with lustful men before marriage?

I knew my co-worker fairly well and I knew he had no intention of settling down and marrying this girl. What would the girl's future husband think of her moving into another guy's apartment?

After our long silence while I was driving Olga home, I said to her, "Moving in with a boyfriend or girlfriend because of financial stress would be a temporary fix. Long-time, it is a recipe for disaster."

Olga asked, "Do you really believe in God? Do you *really* believe in the Bible?"

Her tone was full of skepticism. She sounded like the serpent in the Garden of Eden asking Eve, "Did God really say you couldn't eat from the tree?"

My response to Olga was "Yes!"

"So you don't believe in evolution?"

"No. Scientific evidence even contradicts the theory of evolution. It takes greater faith to believe in evolution than it does to believe in Jesus. There is more proof about Jesus than there is about evolution."

"Not so."

"People believe what they want to believe. People find what they want to find."

"You'll do whatever it takes to protect your Christian faith," she accused me. "You are more moral than you need to be."

I wanted to laugh at her comment, but I knew she was serious. How deceived an unbeliever can be! I still loved Olga, but the truth was clearly that she was deceived. She was deceived into thinking that sex does not have a spiritual component that affects a person's soul when misused. She was deceived into thinking that sin was harmless. She was deceived into thinking that pre-marital sex had no consequences.

"God created sex for marriage. Period," I said. "If evolution was true, then we would all be asexual beings. Sex is inefficient from an evolutionary standpoint. Only a loving God, interested in us personally as people, would create sex. God is love. And there is a whole book in the Bible about romance and sex. The world has hijacked sex and turned it into something misused. Then people wonder why their relationships fall apart or they get diseases or unwanted pregnancies. Come on! People have to wise up!"

I was shouting into the air at this point, as if I was addressing the whole world.

"I don't understand you, Martin."

Silence reigned again.

However, my feelings of love started to re-emerge inside me. I may have been too harsh in my response to Olga, I thought. I should have given her more slack because she didn't understand spiritual things. I knew she was upset and I wasn't comfortable letting her stay upset.

I finally said to her, "This is not what I had planned for us to discuss on Valentine's Day."

"I just made a comment, Martin, and you got so serious. What is with you?"

"Moral integrity is important to me, Olga," I replied, lowering my voice. "But I love you and I don't want to upset you."

"Well, you did," she said.

"I'm sorry."

"There's nothing wrong with a man and woman living together."

"I respect your opinion, Olga," I said, calmly. "But I don't agree."

"You are old-fashioned."

I was feeling emotional.

"I want to make love to you, Olga."

"Right here in the car?" she remarked, looking shocked.

"No, that is what our wedding night is for. We will make great love together." I touched her arm. "We will consummate the marriage. Why else would we have a wedding night? As a Christian, I value marriage as a God-given institution and I will do it His way."

Olga didn't comment.

I continued, "If I had sex with you, Olga, before we are married, then I would be self-centered and settling for the poisonous consequences of instant gratification. I would be cheating us of a beautiful, long-term relationship, built on trust and faith."

Silence seemed to allow my point to sink into Olga's mind.

Chapter Forty-one

PATTERN OF PROBLEMS

In the days and weeks following Valentine's Day, Olga and I did not talk about our "morality" argument. This avoidance might sound good to someone who is afraid of confrontation, but, looking back on it, I wonder if we should have talked about the moral issue further.

A pattern was developing. Olga and I would have an argument. We wouldn't talk to each for a short time. Then, wanting to preserve our relationship, I would apologize and affectionately try to make up with Olga. This pattern was evident in Florida and then it unfolded again on Valentine's Day. It would be fine, except that I was starting to apologize for taking a moral stance.

Something was eroding, but I wasn't sure what.

Preoccupied, I spent the next few weeks extremely busy with the real estate search. I evaluated hundreds of houses and condos, looking for what would satisfy Olga. Throughout the real estate search, I had Olga's interests in my mind, but I still had faith in God.

The real estate agent Rick and I visited dozens of properties and systematically eliminated most of them from my list. Some were too expensive. The condo fees surprised me, in particular. Some places were in rough shape and in desperate need for fixing. In one case, I liked the townhouse, but another buyer bid on it before I had the opportunity to do anything. At a typical "open house" for a new piece of property, forty people would show up. Competition for good places at good values was stiff.

I wanted Olga to come with me to see real estate, but she was often busy. Rick had alerted me to a very interesting townhouse and he arranged for me to go to the "open house" on a Sunday. I invited Olga, but she had to go to my cousin's bridal shower, she said. So I told her that I would evaluate the townhouse alone and update her later.

On Sunday morning, I prayed to God.

"Father, in Jesus name, I ask You to lead me in the right direction. I don't know if the place I will be visiting this afternoon is the right place You want me in, but I ask You to show me whether it is or not. If it isn't the right place, then I keep my faith in You to lead me to other real estate in the future. Even though the wedding is coming up soon, I believe You will pull through for me and Olga. Even though competition for real estate is high these days and someone may take a house away before I can bid on it, I trust that You will get us to the right place. I will wait. I am not in a hurry. Keep me focused. In Jesus name. Amen."

An hour later, Rick picked me up and drove me to see a townhouse on sale. As soon as I walked into the place, I was very impressed. It looked unique. The floor on the first floor was wooden. Wall-to-wall carpeting was upstairs. The townhouse had a built-in garage. When I walked onto the deck in the back, I looked up and saw huge rocks, as big as boulders, lining the backyard.

"I like the rocks," I said to Rick. "Very unique! And it reminds me of how Jesus is the rock. He is the firm foundation on which to build my life."

Rick nodded and smiled knowingly.

When the seller's agent answered her cell phone, I whispered to Rick, "This is the place. I sense it in my spirit. God wants me here. He has opened a door. Now I need to take a step in faith forward. I have waited a long time and I trust that God will make a way."

"It's great that you are interested in this townhouse, but I suggest that you refrain from expressing your enthusiasm too openly to the seller's agent. We need to negotiate and it's in your interest not to get caught up in first impression emotions. I think this is a nice place and we can make a deal with the seller."

"Good."

While Rick worked out the financial details with the mortgage representative in the afternoon, I took a walk alone. I was extremely happy and I couldn't wait to give the good news to Olga. Grateful, I thanked God profusely. My heart was pouring out gratitude. A tremendously warm feeling overwhelmed me as I felt God was saying to me "You see, I am faithful."

I praised Him. "You are faithful, Father. Thank You, Lord Jesus, for all that You have done for me. I appreciate You answering my prayers. I know You will work out a deal for me. I praise You. Thank You, Jesus. Thank You, Lord. I cannot do this without You."

Soon afterward, I wrote a check for $1,000 to hold the townhouse for me. I also signed papers indicating my intent to purchase the townhouse. I was thrilled. When Olga arrived to her home after seven o'clock, I called her and could barely hold back my enthusiasm. I felt like God had done something wonderful for us and I was incredibly grateful.

"I have great news, Olga," I started. "I found a great townhouse. It fits 95 percent of our criteria and we can afford it, although it is at the maximum we can pay."

"When can I see it?"

"As soon as possible."

"Before I go see this place that has you hopping, I need to tell you something."

"What?"

Olga said, "I didn't like the way your sisters treated me at your cousin's shower today, so I just sent them both e-mails saying that I don't want them to be my bridesmaids anymore. I don't want them to be in the wedding."

"What did they do to you?"

"They had attitude."

"Attitude?"

"They weren't friendly to me. They barely talked to me. They don't seem very interested in the wedding preparations. I tried to talk to them, but they don't see me as a priority, even after I have asked them to be part of my special day. It's my wedding day."

She stressed the word "my" when she said "It's my wedding day." I would have thought she'd say "our wedding," but she didn't.

I asked, "Have my sisters responded to you yet?"

"No, and I don't care what they have to say." She seemed very angry.

"My mother won't like this," I remarked.

"I don't care," replied Olga.

I didn't say anything else about it.

"Martin, I have something else to tell you."

"Not more bad news?"

"No," she said. "I want a shower for me."

"I thought you were against a bridal shower because it is not part of your Russian tradition."

"But now I like the idea. Today's shower was the first shower I have ever been to. I want to have a fun shower, which means your mother cannot plan it, Martin."

"Who is going to put it all together?"

"You are, Martin," said Olga.

"I am?"

"Can't you?"

"I guess so."

I was bending to her will again.

She said, "I want to invite my friends from the dance studio and then a few people from your side."

"My mother will want to invite many women from my side."

"Don't let her!"

I knew that another argument with my mother was looming in the not-to-distant future. I did not like the idea of being in the middle of what I was calling the "shower controversy."

"Olga, can you come look at the townhouse right away?"

"Yes, and I will bring my mother."

Then I alerted the real estate agents that my fiancée and her mother were coming to look at the townhouse. I was confident that Olga would like the place, which was nicer than I thought possible for us to buy.

A half-hour later, Olga and her mother drove up to the driveway of the townhouse. Her mother was eager to show me pictures of Olga, but all I wanted to do was show the inside of the townhouse to my fiancée.

"Follow me," I said.

Olga walked around the inside of the townhouse, looking at the different rooms. I was waiting for her to shout out "I love this place." At that point, I would lift her in the air and kiss her.

But the situation turned sour when Olga and her mother walked onto the deck in the back and saw the rocks – the exact rocks that I liked.

Her mother said, "No, no, the rocks are no good." Then she spoke to Olga in Russian for more than a minute.

Olga said to me, "My mother says that we will get big floods when the rain comes off the rocks and when the ice melts in the winter."

I was dumbfounded. Floods?

I said to Olga, "I like this place. The rocks won't be a problem."

Then her mother walked up to me and commanded, "Do not buy this condo! It's no good. Let's leave now." Even though she spoke with a thick Russian accent, I understood every word. Worse, her tone was domineering. She fully expected me to bend to her will.

I may have bent to Olga's will many times in the past, but I was not going to bend to the uninformed will of her mother, who was not God. I perceived the command of Olga's mother as trying to get me to disobey God and follow her ways.

Not going to happen!

I said to Olga, "I am not giving up on this townhouse."

She was surprised that I took a strong stand.

"How dare you insult my mother by ignoring her advice!" said Olga. "She knows more about real estate than you do, Martin."

To Olga, it was okay to insult my mother, but it was not okay to disagree with her mother at all. An hour earlier, I had been full of gratitude for God's grace, love and faithfulness. After the argument about the rocks in the back, I was full of irritation. I couldn't even speak to Olga about it. I would have shouted. Her mother was trying to dictate how we should live.

"Olga, I need to go. I'll talk to you later," I said. Then I told Rick that I would call him in the morning.

"Will you be getting out of buying the townhouse?" Rick asked me after the others went outside.

"Her mother does not dictate to me what to do," I replied. "Keep the process moving to purchase this place. I have such strong assurance in my heart that God has led me to this townhouse. I am interested in pleasing God, not people. I appreciate what God is doing to open the opportunity for me to be a homeowner."

Rick nodded and then walked out. He knew I was serious.

I needed to be alone to think. Later, when I was at home,

I checked my e-mail account and I saw that Olga had e-mailed me.

In her e-mail, she wrote, "You need to get out of the real estate deal for the bad townhouse. I don't like it. My mother is right that we would have flooding problems because of the big, stupid rocks in the back. I don't want a condo or townhouse. I want a house and I saw nice houses for sale on the way to see the townhouse you seem to adore. I think you need to take a few days and change your mind before it is too late."

Olga was trying to dictate to me that I should change my mind. About what else would she try to change my mind in the future?

I didn't respond to her. I waited on the Lord.

Chapter Forty-two

THE SHOWER

People who are constantly looking to complain are bound to be unhappy most of the time. I felt that Olga and her mother were seeking something – anything – to complain about when it came to the townhouse I presented to them. They ignored the good of the place and focused on a far-out, marginal possibility of flooding because big rocks were in the backyard. A bigger problem existed, but I couldn't quite figure it out.

Olga and I were not communicating effectively about how we felt or what we thought. We were going through the motions of preparing for the shower and the wedding, but we were growing more distant from each other. I still tried to please her. I did everything she wanted for the shower.

I even supported Olga when she told my mother that my sisters were not invited to the shower. This infuriated my mother beyond belief. My mother almost didn't go to the shower, but she eventually relented and accepted the invitation. God knew that my mother would not let me forget about all this tension.

On the evening before the shower, Olga invited me to her house for dinner. She seemed to want emotional support because she was feeling down. I eagerly went to her house and gave her a big hug as soon as I walked over the threshold. Yet, as the evening went on, our conversation remained superficial, reinforcing my sense that we were not as emotionally close as we had been. I noted this concern to myself because I wanted to make it better.

I was not giving up on Olga. I still prayed for her in private as well.

While we ate at her house, we talked about the weather, music and celebrities.

She said, "Britney Spears seems like she is changing a lot."

"I think she is a Christian, but she doesn't seem to take the Bible seriously. Some of her songs and videos lately have been very sensual."

"You sound like a professor or something else."

"What?"

"Nothing."

I let it go.

I said, "Britney's ex-boyfriend Justin Timberlake seems more like an artist who is true to himself. I read that he is a Christian and he is spiritual. I guess the difference between him and Britney Spears is that Justin is sincerely spiritual, which means he is different from most everyone else. He doesn't have to sell himself out like some people do. That means something."

"Yeah," muttered Olga, looking intently at her fingernails. She was bored with the conversation.

Seconds later, she looked up hastily and said to me, "You know, it's expensive to be beautiful."

I looked at Olga in bewilderment. Her tone was strange. I looked at her closely. She was dressed in a jogging outfit. Her hair was tied back. The clothes and hair meant nothing to me. What grabbed my attention was the expression on her face. She looked, not just unhappy, but downright bitter and mean-spirited.

At that moment, I realized that she didn't have the joy of the Lord Jesus to keep her going in life. She seemed trapped in her moodiness. Without Jesus, life can be depressing. Without hope, life is drudgery.

Then Olga made a statement that was very disturbing.

"I am not as nice as you think I am and I sometimes don't like it when you expect me to be so nice. I am a little devil," she said. "Are you okay with that?"

"I think I should get going," I said. "You are clearly not in a good mood."

I chalked up her wild statement to her moodiness.

On the next day, I received an e-mail from her, blasting me for wanting to buy the townhouse. She wrote, "If you don't cancel buying the townhouse, you will be living there alone. I can't believe that you want to buy the place. What's more, I cannot stand that I have lost control of the process to buy a house. I am not used to it. I am very upset about this townhouse and I think you should get out of the deal immediately. We will find a better house someplace else. I know what I want. Love, Olga."

There was the truth – the real issue! It was about "control." That is what was eluding me. That was what was fueling the tension. She wanted control. How foolish was I to miss it? She may have thought I was in control, but I wasn't. God was in control. I gave God control of my life, but Olga wanted control of her life. This was a conflict when the two of us were trying to buy a house together.

Control.

How simple, yet profound. How human nature-ish! How foolish!

It can be a losing battle when one mate serves another master!

Later in the day, at the bridal shower, I was ready to call off the wedding. When Olga's father said to me, "Olga and my wife are very angry about you buying the townhouse," I nearly told him that the wedding would be cancelled. When her mother told me to sit at a different table, I nearly walked out. I stared at her mother with a fierce look that could scare the wool off sheep. I was in a foul mood from the start of the shower.

Olga walked into the shower with her dancing coach, a woman who had won ballroom dancing championships from the past. Olga looked completely different than she did on the previous night. Her hair was done up. She wore sexy, tight clothes. She was wearing loads of make-up. And she was smiling. The moody, mean-spirited expression from the previous night was gone from her face. She was carefully managing her outward appearance, especially since her dancing coach was present.

While she enjoyed the food, gifts and conversation, I sat at a different table across the room, having followed her mother's instruction. I sat with her father and my uncle. While my uncle talked to her father, I stared out the window. Normally, I would enjoy a chicken dinner with a side of linguine, but I lost my appetite.

Later, when Olga's father went to the men's room, my uncle asked me, "You seem angry."

"I am."

"What's wrong?"

"Earlier today, Olga sent me an e-mail demanding that I break off my real estate deal and she told me that it is because she wants control. She doesn't like it that I have been proactive or that I have an opinion. She wants to call the shots. And then when her mother told me to sit at a different table than my own fiancée at the shower, I realized that I am frustrated."

"All along, I have been concerned that Olga has been using you," my uncle said.

"You didn't say much about it."

"I figured that you wouldn't listen to me. You seemed so in love."

"You're probably right," I said.

"What are you going to do?"

"I don't know yet. I need to have a heart-to-heart talk with Olga. We need to get some things out on the table to discuss. Communication has been awful between us lately. We only talk about superficial things."

Toward the end of the night, Olga walked up to me after her coach went to the ladies' room. I knew that Olga was planning to go to a nightclub with her coach after the shower.

"You seem upset, Martin," she said to me in a soft, sweet tone. "What's wrong?"

"I need to talk to you when you get home from the nightclub tonight. I don't care what time you get home. Call me at three in the morning if you have to," I said intensely.

"Let's talk now. I don't want to wait."

She tried to pull me up from my chair. I stood up and we faced each other. My uncle was watching us from the side. I didn't want to deal with the serious issues in the restaurant, but I couldn't hold back my feelings any longer.

"Olga, I didn't appreciate your e-mail earlier today at all. We have a serious problem. I believe we should buy and move into the townhouse. You are dead-set against it."

Then Olga wrapped her arms around me, smiled and kissed me. She said, "Oh, don't take it so seriously. My e-mail may have come across more harsh than I meant it."

"Really?"

"Yes."

She rubbed her body against me and enticed me with her sensuality.

"Martin, tell me that you love me," she said, smiling. Then she kissed my neck. I thought that she was going to take her clothes off and ask me to have sex with her in the middle of the restaurant. My emotions responded to her sensuality and I started to focus on her as a lover. Just a few weeks away to the wedding, I told myself. Everything would work out after we are married, I thought. Olga and I would be lovers and we would be so passionate that other problems would take care of themselves. I was thinking superficially because I was looking superficially upon Olga, while still trying to maintain my moral integrity. The temptations in the world are very enticing.

When her coach returned, Olga said, "I need to go to the club with my coach, but I'll talk to you tomorrow. Okay?"

"Okay," I uttered, feeling strongly attracted to her. My anger seemed to have dissolved in the cauldron of Olga's sensuality.

After she left, I realized within seconds that Olga had *manipulated* me.

My uncle asked me, "How do you feel?"

"Manipulated," I replied, looking out the window.

"I am shocked that Olga would go to a nightclub right after the wedding shower. What is that girl thinking about?"

"Herself," I said. "Totally herself! I will pray for her. I am not giving up on her. I made a commitment to her and I love her. She is young, confused and full of the pride of life. Only Jesus can save her from herself. I am going to go home tonight and pray for her."

"While your fiancée goes to a nightclub, you go home and pray. What a contrast!" remarked my uncle.

"We are different," I said. "God knows how different. But God put love into my heart for her. It is this love that keeps me committed and true to her. God is giving her another chance. She better get right with God before she does herself great harm."

"Or does you great harm," he said.

Chapter Forty-three

One-sided Wedding Rehearsal

Olga wanted a Jewish rabbi at the wedding and she found one who would do a joint ceremony with a Christian minister. We arranged a meeting at the church with the rabbi and the minister. I wasn't apprehensive about the rabbi's involvement because, first of all, the Jewish people are God's chosen people and, secondly, I had a hope that the rabbi would see Christ Jesus in me. I was open to God being glorified in any way.

Before I went to the church for the meeting with the minister and the rabbi, my father said something that stuck with me.

"I am praying for you," he said to me. "I have also asked the pastor of the church to pray for you." My father went to a church I had not visited. I didn't know the pastor of his church. But having my father and this pastor pray for me made an impression on me.

"Thanks."

"I told the pastor about your situation of marrying a Jewish girl."

"Olga told me that her mother is Jewish and her father is Christian."

"The pastor asked me if Olga had given her life to Jesus

Christ and whether you and her were in complete understanding of each other."

I bowed my head and replied, "Olga is in God's hands."

"Son, if marrying Olga is what God wants you to do, then I pray that He pours His blessings out on you," said my father with a sincere tone. "But if marrying her is outside of God's will for your life, then the pastor and I pray that God stops it in its tracks. I know that you are abiding in Christ, so I will support whatever decision the Lord leads you to make."

"What do you think of me marrying Olga?"

"I don't know," replied my father. "Honestly, there is a conflict in me. I like Olga and she is a very nice girl, but something doesn't quite seem right."

"You can say that again," I commented, but I didn't elaborate for my father.

"The truth will come out," he said.

I nodded and then left to go to the meeting. I was the first to arrive at the church. Minutes later, the rabbi walked up to me.

"Are you Olga's fiancé?"

"Yes. How did you know?"

"It's not like a young man like you sits in front of a church at exactly seven o'clock every day," replied the rabbi with a humorous tone. "So Olga is going to be late?"

"I don't know."

"When I talked to her on the phone, she seemed easily distracted. I asked her many questions about her relationship with you, but she was evasive."

"I am a Christian."

"I know that much."

"How do you think the wedding should go with both Christian and Jewish elements?"

"I just did a wedding like this two weeks ago. I speak and sing a little. The minister does his thing and then we break glass and party."

I laughed. I wasn't expecting a rabbi with a sense of humor.

Olga arrived twenty minutes late and the rabbi poked fun at her about it.

"Hey, Olga, you're not going to be this late for the ceremony on the wedding day, are you?" The rabbi was bold with her. Olga smirked.

As we walked into the church, Olga whispered to me, "I do plan to be at least fifteen minutes late to the wedding."

"You're kidding."

"No."

"You need to be on time for the wedding."

"I disagree," she said.

This was a strange, yet brief, disagreement. Her staunch stance on a position like being purposefully late for the wedding seemed odd to me. It seemed useless and only a seed of discord.

"Olga, since when did you get religious?" I asked her. "You weren't religious when I first met you."

Olga didn't like the question.

"What a stupid question! I can be religious when I want to be."

The rabbi, who was extroverted, began to give a tour of the church, not to me and Olga, but to another couple. The church's coordinator ran by me, saying, "He doesn't work for the church." The coordinator broke up the rabbi talking to the couple. It was funny.

Minutes later, standing near the altar, the rabbi explained how the ceremony would unfold. As he spoke, I was slowly swinging a bag by my side.

"Put the bag down!" he finally said to me. "Your swinging it is distracting me."

I laughed and put the bag down.

The rabbi continued with his explanation. I thought that he was very reasonable. He was not making an issue of Christian elements of the wedding. He was open-minded.

The best thing he said was about a famous description of love in the Bible.

The rabbi said, "The best thing ever written about love is in the New Testament. 'Love is patient, love is kind. It does not envy, it does not boast, it is not proud. It is not rude, it is not self-seeking, it is not easily angered, it keeps no record of wrongs. Love does not delight in evil but rejoices with the truth. It always protects, always trusts, always hopes, always perseveres. Love never fails. But where there are prophecies, they will cease; where there are tongues, they will be stilled; where there is knowledge, it will pass away. For we know in part and we prophesy in part, but when perfection comes, the imperfect disappears.'"

I turned to Olga and said, "It's ironic that this Jewish rabbi knows the Bible better than I do. I couldn't have recited all those verses like he did."

I liked the rabbi.

Then, when he brought up that he would be wearing a Jewish cap on his head during the wedding, he was surprised that Olga started an argument with me.

"I want Martin to wear a Jewish Kippah on his head," she said, even though she had not discussed it with me.

I said, "No, wait! I didn't say I would wear it. I am not Jewish."

She said, "It's my wedding and I want you to wear a Kippah. We will have a choopa and-"

"I am fine with the choopa, but I would prefer not to wear a cap. To me, a Kippah represents the Jewishness of a man. I have some Jewish friends and I respect them very much. I would feel that I am disrespecting them if I wear a Jewish cap that they deem personal. It is a symbol of something important. I don't want to treat it flippantly."

The rabbi interrupted, "By the way, where is the minister who was supposed to be here tonight?"

"I don't know," I replied.

"I hope he shows up for the wedding," said the rabbi.

"Me, too."

After the rabbi finished the meeting and left, I told Olga that I was fine with having the rabbi be part of the wedding.

"I like the rabbi. He is open-minded and he knows the Bible," I said.

"And you will wear what I want you to wear at my wedding."

"Olga!"

"I think it is insulting that your minister didn't show up. I think you should fire him."

"Something may have come up," I said. "You were late."

"I had to get gas for my car. The guys at the station gave me a free cup of coffee."

"Why?"

"They like me," she replied, smiling.

"Do you like that they like you?"

"I like to have men's attention," she admitted.

"Isn't my attention enough?"

"Of course, Martin! I just mean that I believe when a woman has it, she should flaunt it."

"I disagree."

"Sometimes, Martin, you are naïve."

The truth was that she had a tendency to wear low-cut, tight blouses. Her self-consciousness made her less attractive to me. Her attitude was stuffy.

I asked her, "Do you want to go out to eat?"

"I can't. I have to meet Luther to discuss our trip to New York. Call me tonight after eleven."

"Okay."

I wondered if Olga would be late to the wedding if she had to practice dancing. I was also bothered that Olga insisted on saying "my wedding." It may have been a small point, but it made me feel somewhat distant from the wedding.

"Before I leave, I want to ask you something, Martin."

She rubbed her body against my body. "I want to ask you if I can have four hundred dollars for me to go to Miami to dance in a national ballroom dancing competition after the wedding."

"We have to go on our honeymoon after the wedding," I shot back.

"It's two months after the wedding. How about it?"

She caressed me and kissed me, trying to entice me.

"It's just money," I said. "God has blessed me with money."

"Does that mean you will give me the money?"

"Yes."

She was thrilled. She hugged me tightly and whispered into my ear, "I love you, Martin."

"I love you, too, Olga."

Then she went to meet Luther. I went home and heard a voice mail from my best man Dean. He said that he had the "bachelor party" all set up. He knew that I wanted something very tame – meaning, no strippers. He got tickets to a baseball game and then made reservations at a restaurant near the park. The plan sounded good to me.

I didn't want strippers because, if I wanted to see other women naked, then I wouldn't be getting married. Frankly, I wanted to see Olga naked after we get married. That was the exciting thing. Strippers would be a disappointment. No love there! Love magnifies everything!

Only seven people were going to come to the bachelor party. Dean, my uncle, my father, my brother and two friends - in addition to myself – were coming. Dean was taking care of contacting everyone. I appreciated Dean's efforts very much.

I went to bed early and didn't talk to Olga.

Chapter Forty-four

BACHELOR PARTY

"For your bachelor party, you are going to go see strippers," Olga accused me with laughter in her voice.

"No, I am not," I said in a serious tone.

"You might as well go see strippers," she said. "This is your last chance to see other women naked."

I didn't like what Olga was conveying to me. The idea of going to ogle at strippers a few weeks before getting married made no sense to me because I was focused on my bride-to-be and the forthcoming intimacy on our wedding night. I also wondered whether Olga was planning to go see male strippers. If I went to see female strippers, then she would feel less guilty, I wondered. She didn't tell me anything. I didn't tell her that I felt sorry for strippers because those are women who are demeaning themselves to strip naked for the disgusting, lustful desires of men.

I could not look upon a woman as a piece of meat. Every woman is someone's daughter. Moreover, God did not intend women to parade naked in front of men. At some point, the will of God needs to be considered by everyone.

Troubled by Olga's insistence that I go look at strippers for my last hurrah, I met the small group for my bachelor party. Dean drove us to the baseball game and distributed the tickets to all of us. My uncle, my brother, two friends and Olga's father were with me. We had good seats. Prior to the game starting, we bought food and beverages. Having grown up playing baseball, this was the best bachelor party atmosphere I could ask for. *It was just the guys!*

Olga's father was the only person who didn't understand baseball because he didn't see American baseball in Russia. My uncle spent time trying to explain the game to him, but baseball is a complicated game to the beginner.

During the fourth inning, everyone suddenly needed to go to the bathroom or needed to get a refill of a beverage, except for me and Olga's father. I continued to watch the game intently, but Olga's father leaned toward me from two seats down the row. I wondered what he wanted, so I turned to look at him.

He said to me, "You have made a big mistake."

"Really?" I replied, thinking that he was referring to how much Olga disliked the townhouse I was buying. I was going to give her father the respect to listen to what he had to say about the townhouse.

However, the next thing he said had nothing to do with the townhouse.

"You have made a big mistake," he said again. "You did not have sex with my daughter."

His statement shocked me beyond belief.

"What?" I blurted out, knocking over my drink on the ground.

He shook his head in grave disapproval of me. I didn't know how to respond to such a disturbing statement. Here was a father telling me that I made a "mistake" by not sleeping with his daughter *before* we get married. This was one of the strangest moments of my life. Honestly, a grown man was criticizing me for having morals. He would have been more proud of me if I had had pre-marital sex with his daughter. What's wrong with this picture?

I said, "But we are getting married in three weeks." I didn't know what else to say. A righteous anger became immense in me. Moral outrage was screaming in my mind. My heart was aching for the godlessness that had been conveyed to me. In my heart – with silent prayers – I was crying out to God to handle this situation.

I was hurt because I knew that Olga had told her father something about being unhappy with my abstaining from sexual intercourse until marriage. Her father was reflecting to me what she must have been discussing in the privacy of her home. She had not shared with me her complaints directly about sex, but an element of truth had landed on me at the baseball game.

When the others returned to their seats, I said nothing to them. With my mind racing and my emotions numb, I sat through the rest of the game. I wanted to leave, but I didn't want to alert the others to my problem. I loved Olga and I was willing to do virtually anything for her, but I was deeply troubled.

The hometown team lost the game, making everyone else look somber. This was good for me because I looked somber for another reason. After the game, we all went to a restaurant to eat dinner. I talked very little. I let the others do most of the talking. Furthermore, I did not look at Olga's father at all during dinner. I refused to look in his direction across the table. I was disgusted by his godless, unhealthy, backwards attitude about sex for his own daughter. If I was a father, I couldn't have his attitude about sex. No way!

Later in the evening, I was glad to be alone. Desperately, I needed to pray.

"Heavenly Father, in Jesus name, Olga's father revealed to me the immorality that rules in people's hearts. As You know, I am greatly disturbed by this revelation that Olga dislikes the fact that we have been waiting to have sex on our wedding night. Her attitude goes against Your instruction in the Bible and is also unromantic to me. I will obey You, Father. I pray for Olga. Please show her the truth about You.

She is being carried away by her lusts. I don't condemn her. I will still marry her, but she needs You to change her. She needs to be redeemed by the blood of Your Son Jesus. She has no other way to escape from the bondage of her lusts and foolishness."

Then the Holy Spirit must have been convicting me of my own sin.

"Oh, Father, I am guilty of lustful thoughts. I ask for Your forgiveness and Your mercy, based on the shed blood of Jesus. I have not guarded my thought life. Forgive me, Lord. I receive Your forgiveness by faith. I also confess to You that I have tried to control situations with Olga and make her believe what I believe, but I can't do it. I need to turn everything over to Your hands. If we are going to have a happy marriage, then I need You to step in. Show me the truth! Show me the way! Cleanse me of all unrighteousness, as only You can. Please give me the strength to do what is right. In Jesus name. Amen."

I spent the next two days thinking about what Olga's father had said. I didn't call Olga at all. I needed time and space to think clearly. Hungry for God, I read the Bible and waited on Him. I was silent before Him, yearning to receive wisdom from Him in a spiritual sense. The reality of God was powerful on me. I knew that I could not lean on my own understanding. All I could do was acknowledge the Lord Jesus Christ and let Him direct my paths.

I had tried to direct my paths earlier in my relationship with Olga because I wanted to fulfill my daydreams and get what I wanted, when I wanted it. I had waited on the Lord, but I had not waited long enough. I had compromised and was trying to help God out. But now I had come to a crossroads.

If God wanted me to marry Olga, I was ready to marry Olga. I was going to be obedient to Him, no matter what.

On Tuesday morning, I checked my voice mail at work and I had a voice from Olga. She had said in the message,

"Martin, I need to talk to you." She sounded extremely serious. "I cannot wait any longer to discuss something with you. Please call me and we need to talk tonight."

I didn't know exactly what she wanted to discuss, but I was going to mention to her what her father said. I needed to find out her true feelings. Because I didn't want her to manipulate me with her sensual charms, I wanted to have this conversation over the telephone. I called her back and set a time to talk to her at 10 p.m.

It felt like a long day, leading up to this call. When I called her at the appointed time, I was focused in my heart on Jesus.

"Olga, it's Martin," I said into the phone, as I sat in my room.

"Martin, I have a problem," she began. "We need to talk about it."

"Oh, yeah. What's that?" I replied calmly.

"We have not had sex yet," said Olga with an edge on her voice as sharp as the tip of an arrow.

"We are getting married in three weeks. We will become intimate sexually on our wedding night. I don't understand why you are bringing this up now. I have been working hard to find us a place to live and to help you with college work. We'll be married soon."

"I want to have sex before we get married," she announced.

"You know I am a Christian."

"That has nothing to do with it," she retorted. "My father is a Christian, too."

Her statement that my Christian faith had "nothing to do with it" punctured something in my soul.

"The Bible says that God created sex for-"

She interrupted, "Don 't give me that nonsense! All religions say not to have sex before marriage. It doesn't matter. I know what I want."

Trying to salvage our relationship, I gave Olga the opportunity to calm down and stop her rampage about pre-marital sex. I was still going to marry her, even though she had wounded me emotionally with her verbal attack.

I said, "I think you need to see it from my perspective and I will make love to you when we are married. I will try hard to be a good husband to you and-"

She wouldn't let me finish.

She screamed, "You should look at it from my perspective. We haven't had sex yet. Everyone has sex before marriage."

"That's not true. As a Christian, I have a commitment to Jesus Christ and I follow His ways."

Still shouting, she said, "I need to find out what I am getting into."

"What?"

"I need to find out if I will like you in bed, Martin. If you love me, then you will have sex with me before we are married. I need to find out if we are sexually compatible. Maybe I won't like you in bed."

I felt like someone had banged on a giant bell right next to my head. My ears were ringing from what Olga said. Maybe she wouldn't like me in bed? She was going to judge my sexual performance with her as criteria on whether she marries me.

Reeling from my many emotions, I remained silent.

Then Olga, who seemed to be full of confidence in herself, said, "If we don't have sex before the wedding, then I don't see what I will do with you on the wedding night. After all the guests leave at the end of the reception, what are we going to do? Probably not have sex! You'll probably want to sleep in a separate bed, too."

Her sarcasm was like a wolf biting me in the leg. Olga was showing me that she was like a wolf in sheep's clothing. All her human "goodness' meant nothing. She was dominated by her lusts and she had no clue of the righteousness of Jesus Christ that cleanses a person of sin and guilt.

On the verge of tears, I said, "Olga, I think we need to break up. You don't respect me as a Christian. You don't accept my Christian values or my Christian faith. A true Christian follows Jesus, who said, 'Do not commit sexual immorality' in no uncertain terms."

She shot back with a fierce rebuttal. "You won't make me a Christian." A demon couldn't have said it more arrogantly or sinisterly as Olga did.

All my trust in her left me. To satisfy her own desires, she ruptured our relationship. She lifted up sex on the altar of her life and demanded her way. She demanded that I bend to her will and have sexual intercourse with her before the wedding so that she could evaluate my sexual performance in bed. Her words -"Maybe I won't like you in bed" – rang in my mind.

I said, "We should cancel the wedding. We should not get married. I don't know you anymore, Olga."

"I am insulted," said Olga. "So you want to cancel the wedding? Fine!"

"It's the right thing to do."

I knew with clarity in my heart that the Lord Jesus was leading me to cancel the wedding. I was giving up my marriage for Jesus and I knew it was the right thing to do. The truth about Olga came out three weeks before our wedding. I concluded that she and I were spiritually incompatible.

"Whatever you want, Martin," she said sarcastically.

"I still respect you, Olga, and someday I hope you come to realize what my moral integrity means. I will not turn my back on Jesus, who is my Lord and Savior. Having sex with you before marriage would be impulsive, Olga. It is time that I live with purpose. Jesus is Lord. Goodbye."

I hung up the phone. As tears streamed down my face, I dropped to my knees and cried out to God.

"Heavenly Father, in Jesus name, thank You! Praise Your

holy name! Thank You for showing me the truth and putting a stop to something that would end in greater hurt in the future. You see much deeper than I do and You have revealed what is in Olga's heart. I cannot make her happy. She will fight my Christianity in our marriage. I cannot stop being a Christian. My inner nature has already been redeemed and transformed by Your Son Jesus. Olga can go off and be a world champion ballroom dancer. I pray for Olga and I ask You to continue to watch over her, but it is right for me not to marry her."

I paused, closing my eyes. I was shaking. I felt warmth and chills simultaneously. I wiped the tears from my eyes.

Then I continued to pray: "I am thinking about my future children. If I had children with Olga and our children would have to see Olga and me fighting about Jesus or religion all the time, it would hurt the children to see a mother and father divided against each other. I won't do that to my future children. I have to protect them. I will wait on You, Father, for the right woman – a Christian woman – to marry. When I get married, I will invite Christ to join the marriage. I love You, Jesus. I love You, Lord. You know that marriage is the one thing I wanted most in life, but I give it up for You. Use me for Your purpose to reach out to other people, introducing them to You and Your love. Only because of Your love, Jesus, have I lived a moral life. I owe everything to You."

My heart's desire was to stay in moral agreement with God.

Chapter Forty-five

Reaction

My mother's reaction to my decision was different from my father's reaction. My mother accused me of making a "hasty decision" and predicted that I would go back to Olga within hours because I would miss her. She didn't understand me. I was of the mind that marriage needs to be more than just an emotional, impulsive decision.

In contrast to my mother, my father said that God had answered prayer to stop the wedding if it was not something He wanted for me in my life. My father said that he supported my decision. He recognized that I was giving up my heart's desire – to get married – but his faith in God to take care of me was greater than anything else. I appreciated his encouraging support. He was more interested in whether I was doing what God wanted me to do. He said he had a sense of peace about what I was doing. He knew why I had made the change. I told him everything.

My parents were split on their view of my action to cancel the wedding and permanently break off the relationship with Olga. The most painful comment came from my mother. After I tried to convince her that, no matter how difficult it was, I had to stand firm, she said to me in a scathing tone, "You will never meet the dream Christian girl you think exists. You'll end up marrying an ex-drug addict who has found religion and you'll try to tell me how great she is, now that she has found Jesus. Nonsense!"

Injuring me more, my mother's comment went straight to the core of my insecurity. Would I ever meet the right woman? Had I just messed up the only opportunity in my life to get married?

Miraculously, I found courage in myself to stay true to my decision to stop the wedding. Without my mother's awareness, God was making me extremely strong from within. My spirit was on fire for Jesus and doing the right thing. It was as if my soul had suddenly been bulked up with spiritual muscle. I was balanced and holding tightly on a firm foundation. I had gone to the rock of my faith and He was delivering with powerful strength to sustain me through this difficult time in my life.

I called my "best man" Dean and told him the news.

"Dean, the wedding with Olga is off. We are fundamentally different from each other. We are not compatible."

"Oh, no."

"This is a very difficult decision, but it will be better in the long term. I realize now that the communication with Olga has been poor, especially over the last few months. We talked about superficial things regularly, but we didn't talk about the important issues that we should have discussed before taking the giant step into marriage. If Olga and I get married, I am convinced that we would get divorced within five years."

"If you feel that strongly about it, then you are probably doing the right thing," said Dean. "Most people would go ahead and get married; then they would discover all their problems after they get married and have to deal with them. Half of marriages fail."

"When I get married, it is for life," I said. "I love Olga, but I don't trust her anymore. She has shown me that she is very demanding and controlling. She jeopardized trust by things she said."

I started to shake as I ventured into telling Dean the statements that Olga made to me. Tears were on the verge of bursting from my eyes.

"Dean, she said to me that, if I really loved her, I would

have sex with her before we get married. Do you want to know why? So she can evaluate whether she likes my sexual performance in bed. It's like she wants to put me to a sex test and then she would decide if she really wants to marry me."

"It sounds like she wasn't as committed to you as you have been to her."

My voice was quivering. I had trouble speaking.

"She said, 'maybe I won't like you in bed, Martin.' I would have to live up to an expectation. She is not accepting me with unconditional love. She is adding a condition to it. She is being impatient and she is demanding her own way."

"But you both would be getting married in just a few weeks. It's a wonder why this comes out now."

"She claims that she wouldn't know what to do with me on our wedding night after all the guests have gone home. This is her justification for us to have sex before marriage."

"That is ridiculous," asserted Dean. "She is ignoring what God wants."

"Exactly," I said. "And I realize now that I had underestimated so many things in our relationship. I also ignored God's warnings. I am saved by the blood of Jesus, but I had acted impulsively when I rushed into marriage plans for the wrong reasons. I failed to wait on God. I was doing it because I was tired of waiting after years of failure with women. But God is making me strong from inside myself to stand strong for my convictions. I will not compromise God's morality for the whims of a moody person. She wants to base our relationship on the vicissitudes of emotions. I can envision her one day becoming unhappy with our marriage and walking out on me. I can envision her fighting me on how to raise children. I will teach any children about Jesus. They need to know it because Jesus is the light of the world and no one can escape the power of sin in this world without Jesus Christ. I would love children enough to want to tell them the truth and encourage them to walk with the

Lord for a better life."

"I think you are right that these are fundamental differences between you and Olga. It is courageous for you to do what you are doing."

"I gave everything I had to give to Olga. I was as generous as I could be and I supported her in what she wanted many times. I bent to her will on a regular basis, but she was constantly unhappy anyway. Her happiness was always temporary and then she would become unhappy with everything. She was almost like a child who knew no discipline and no principles. But, driven by her unhappiness, she asked me to give up my faith in Jesus and my love for God by violating my own moral principle to satisfy her unsettled, untamed desire. No! Absolutely not! I had to come to the point of 'enough is enough.' I am not bending on this one. She has pitted God versus herself, forcing my hand to choose. How foolish she is! I choose Jesus, just as He chose me. I cannot allow her faithlessness to poison my growing faith."

"I understand," said Dean. "I will pray for you."

"Thank you," I said. "I'm sorry that there will be no wedding. I hate to disappoint everyone. I know many people were looking forward to it."

"Hey, don't worry about that! People will understand," he said.

Invited guests may have understood that sometimes a wedding is cancelled, but Olga didn't understand. She had her mother call my mother and criticize me up and down, making false accusations about me. Olga also demanded that I give her all the bridal shower gifts. She was more concerned about possessions.

I heard later that she told people I had insulted her. My aunt said that she didn't seem hurt by the breakup. She was angry and, of course, insulted, but she told my aunt that she accepted my decision. Feeling insulted in this situation seems to be a reflection of deep-rooted pride. As I was humbling myself before God, Olga was going in the opposite direction, stirring up her pride.

She kept the diamond engagement ring, but she sent me back the bracelet I had given her on Valentine's Day. Her note, which accompanied the bracelet, stated: "I had the bracelet you gave me appraised. The bracelet has fake diamonds. You told me that the bracelet was very expensive. Our engagement was as cheap as this bracelet."

I had never told her that the bracelet was "very expensive." I had bought it over the Internet and I thought that the diamonds were real, albeit small. Olga seemed to remember what she wanted to remember, like a true revisionist trying to change the past. *It's the thought that counts, she often said.*

Regardless of her cruel intentions toward me as a reaction to the cancelled wedding, I wished her well. I believed that she would become a world champion ballroom dancer someday. In fact, she may fall in love with her partner and marry him. In that case, Olga would thank me years down the road for giving her the freedom to pursue the sexual adventure she viewed as the basis for marriage. I did not wish any harm to come to her. I still prayed for her, asking God to open up her heart to His love, which is infinitely greater than my love.

Asking Jesus to come into her heart as Lord and Savior would be a defining moment of triumph in her life. She didn't have to live a life of unhappiness, greed, selfishness jealousy or bondage to sexual lust. To this day, I am praying for her salvation in Jesus Christ – simply confessing to God that she is a sinner and recognizing Jesus as God's Son who died on the cross and was resurrected from the dead – because I want the best for her.

She needed more focus in life than "maybe," just as I needed a relationship more focused on Christ than on a "maybe." Some people saw me as acting with courage to make a life-changing decision after having considered the consequences, but Olga didn't see my decision to cancel the wedding as any act of courage. I'm sure Olga and her mother saw it as a sign of weakness.

In the end, I had to make a decision to please God, not people. I had to hold true to my principles.

Chapter Forty-six

WHAT I LEARNED

Just as Eve offered the apple in her control to Adam, Olga offered the fruit of her sexuality in her control to me. I am a fallen man like Adam, but Jesus restored me.

The Bible says, "Do not let anyone lead you astray." Even though Olga had many good qualities and she is still within reach of God's grace, she made a life-changing error to underestimate and deny the validity of the Lord Jesus Christ. She seemed to think that Jesus was just a "good" person, but Jesus is the way, the truth and the life.

Instead of thinking of Jesus as on the throne, she put herself on the throne of "self" and made herself the ultimate decision-maker for her life. Her pride denied her the realization that Jesus stands alive today in the universe with unspeakable power and glory. When He was on earth, He predicted that the people of the world would reject Him or not recognize Him. He predicted correctly. He also predicted the consequences of people's failure to have faith in Him and obey His commands. Olga was in the dark about what Jesus had meant.

The most important lesson I learned was that God is faithful to me personally, even when I fail Him through impulsiveness, impatience and doubt. I am an imperfect man following the lead of the perfect God. I do not understand all the ways of God, but I know that God knows best.

My experiences in my relationship with Olga tested my character. The critical question was, "Was I going to obey Jesus at the peak of sexual temptation?" Since sexual temptation is the biggest weakness in my life, the dark spiritual forces of hell knew to attack me, not in blatant ways, but in subtle ways to entice me and soften me. I couldn't have predicted exactly how I would have acted in the moment of temptation. I had rational reasons to have unfettered, ego-boosting sex with Olga, who was willing. Like a man who wonders how he will react in a fight on a battlefield, I wondered how I would react when I faced a moral choice. I learned that I can do all things through Christ who strengthens me.

Olga's viewpoint was to use sex to gain control. This was actually a misuse of sex. She also believed that selfishness is justified in a romantic relationship. I don't think she purposefully tried to hurt me, but her self-centeredness got the best of her. Ultimately, she has responsibility for her selfishness. Helpless to her self-centeredness, she needs Jesus as Lord and Savior all the more.

She needs to recognize herself as a daughter of Eve, the first woman. Olga has a fallen nature and can only rise up and soar on the wings of God. The issue is not her conduct or her good intentions, but the real issue is her nature. I want her to soar. I want her to be truly happy and satisfied. I want her to have power in faith and know that God loves her unconditionally.

Even if Olga continues to rebel against God and His right to her life, I will continue to pray for Olga for the rest of my life. Even if she sleeps with other men in immoral relationships, I will ask God to bless her. Jesus promised that a believer, abiding in Him, can ask for anything in His name and He will do it. Moral love has the character of Jesus reflected in it, but Jesus is so much bigger than morality. Jesus is life to the empty, spiritually deadened human being.

I do not condemn Olga. She was acting according to her

natural desires and influenced by the way other people live their lives in society. But I was the wrong man for her. I thought that she understood my Christian identity, but she didn't. She thought that it was just a "religion." She didn't realize that Jesus changed me when He entered my heart at the point of salvation. The emptiness in my soul had been filled by God. I was a completed person, even without a wife.

I did not mean to make Olga's life difficult or discouraging. Ending the marriage plans was the right thing to do. She and I needed time apart to think about our lives. We would be divorced if we continued on in our superficial relationship. Because of my own weaknesses and idiosyncrasies, I was bound to disappoint Olga on different matters.

I also learned that communication is extremely important in a romantic relationship. It needs to go beyond the superficial. The growth of love is hindered by secrets, untold feelings and selfish thoughts. Confession is a means toward cleansing. Unsaved people, unaware of Jesus' power in their lives, would be shocked by such confession. They cannot overcome their pride and love for false appearances.

I confess my mistakes and I ask God to change me, in the name of Jesus.

As I listened to Pastor David Moore (www.mooreonlife.com) explain on a tape that a Christian needs to understand what he is getting into when he marries, I realized that I didn't understand what I would have been getting into. I made the mistake of ignoring the Bible's instruction to marry another Christian, but I was impatient and I wanted to be married for the sake of marriage. I also failed to understand Olga's history. She would have brought emotional baggage into our marriage and I would have been knocked over. I would have frustrated Olga with my interest in Jesus. We needed a change.

"God is in control" is a statement that I often heard Dr. Charles Stanley (www.intouch.org) say on his radio and television broadcasts. During my difficult time in the aftermath of breaking up with Olga, I depended on this truth about God and it helped to carry me. I had to let go of all control, which is difficult to do for a planner like me. I also remembered something else Dr. Stanley often said: "Jesus is sufficient to meet all your needs." I love the Lord and I was willing to sacrifice my life for His love, which is more precious than diamonds.

I want to praise Jesus more!

A Christian man like me is dangerous in the sense that I will follow the will of God, no matter what the consequences are. No doubt, a woman like Olga is surprised that I act with courage because I have earthly things to lose. With a natural bent away from God, "natural man "wants to maximize opportunities for himself and refuse to let go of domesticated life that is under his control. But while natural man's adventure is contrived and logically controlled, the Christian man's adventure is more challenging, more dangerous and more thrilling.

God has me on an adventure that appeals to the deepest longings of my heart. I've had to make a tough decision and, by the grace of God, act with courage. I've had to let go of the contrived to be set free to explore the frontiers of radical, moral love, born in my heart and yearning for growth and expression.

In an immoral society, the passionate expression of moral love – its power unleashed in marriage – is seen as a threat. Morality insinuates the existence of God, which means people living immoral lifestyles and compromising their integrity for cheap thrills will be held accountable after death. Olga may have considered herself as "beautiful and dangerous" like Moscow, but, in the end, uplifted by the power of Jesus, I proved to be the most dangerous, defying popular thinking and behavior.

The fact that the Bible bothers people so much and

exposes the sins of the heart is one piece of proof that the Bible is correct. The Bible needs to be studied in its entirety. People need to *know* God.

If people believe that I am simply a "nice guy," then they don't know me. In my heart, I am a warrior, fighting to preserve moral integrity and moral love.

My spiritual journey – life on earth as an ambassador of Christ – is an unparalleled adventure because Jesus, the living God, marks my course. He leads me to beauty. Whatever my future holds, I know it is good because God is good. Moral love flourishes in the love of God for people to experience.

Greater hope I have today for the Lord to lead me to the right Christian woman to be my mate. She will appreciate that I waited for her, while God used difficult circumstances to test me and mold me. If I had given up on Jesus and indulged in sexual gratification, not only would I have virtually slapped God in the face, but I would have been giving up my own heart.

Moral love preserves.

No matter how immoral society gets, my faith in Christ is as solid as a rock. The Lord has rescued me more than once from dangerous situations that would have hurt me badly. The Lord has been my friend since childhood, comforting me in my inner being at times of loneliness and insecurity. The Lord has been faithful to me and has kept His promises. He has inspired, motivated protected and sustained me, from the top of my life's experiences to the valleys in my life.

God has never asked me to do anything sinful. I have come to experience a greater outpouring of the Holy Spirit as I have let go of my natural inclinations and turned my life fully over to Jesus – God with us.

My sense of connection to the Lord Jesus is constant all day, every day. I had to do what God wanted me to do. I had to obey the Bible and *not* marry an unbeliever. Olga demanded her own way, but love does not demand its own way unless it is a counterfeit love based on selfishness. As soon as I stopped making her happy, Olga would have divorced me and moved on to another man. She already proved to me that she can't stay happy, so I was destined to make her unhappy. I could have avoided causing both of us pain if I had obeyed God in the beginning, but I had been fooled by my own emotions, lust and selfishness.

How amazing to have a moral God come into a personal relationship with a man like me, who has an immoral nature. The love of Jesus goes beyond what I can comprehend. He changed me and taught me about moral love. I am blessed with the knowledge of Him.

After experiencing the love of Christ in my heart, I cannot accept selfish love as a basis for marriage. I put all my trust in the Lord Jesus Christ. I don't know everything, but what I know is that Jesus Christ's death and resurrection are the ultimate expression of the heart of God.

My heart's desire is to marry a woman and enjoy with her what is sexual in morality, by the grace of God. Being a real man! Courage to be pure! Sexual in *morality*! An old concept and a lifestyle to change the world in a new way!

When I chose moral love, I was walking in the light of the Lord Jesus Christ, who is the light of the world. I was living in moral agreement with God. The truth about my heart, as well as Olga's heart, was exposed. Truth has consequences.

Love set me apart by truth.